Chasing Redemption

Farley Dunn

THREE SKILLET

CHASING REDEMPTION, Dunn, Farley L

First Edition

●◆● THREE SKILLET

www.ThreeSkilletPublishing.com

ISBN 978-1-943189-15-1

Chapter 1

"YOU TOO can feel your heart cradled in God's love."

The words murmured from the sound system, and their truth was real. No one dared look away. The Most Reverend Trooper "Two Points" Kincaid paused in his impassioned delivery, his eyes wrapped in moist tears of sincerity.

On the first row sat his wife Sharon, one year his junior, and at fifty-three, still strikingly beautiful. Jeffrey "Jack" Kincaid, twenty-eight, sat on the platform at the Reverend Kincaid's back. He took after his mother, and he was being groomed to take over the ministry. Somewhere in the balcony of the enormous building, seventeen-year-old twins Cody and Casey, high school basketball stars as their father had been, were surely surrounded by adoring school-age girls just hoping for a bit of their attention.

As on every Sunday morning, Trooper expected to

have his family with him. He was well aware of the two enormous video screens at his back that made him into a man larger than life, and he made sure every nuance of his expression wrung empathy from his congregation. His family played a part also, and yet his eyes still searched for his daughter Lindsay. Like her brother, she also carried her mother's stunning features, and when the family gathered on the platform at the end of each Sunday's live broadcast, her beauty smoothed out the tall, angular frames of her father and younger brothers. Now twenty-one, her presence made the family sparkle, and her attendance each week was worth many a donation in the day's offerings.

This week she was nowhere to be seen.

Behind him, members of the choir hummed softly as hydraulics underneath stepped risers lifted them aloft for the end of the morning service. Great plaster columns ringed the platform, and burgundy carpet extended for acres. Anchoring the platform, an enormous white Bösendorfer stretched along for over ten feet, costing well over a grand for each of its hundred-twenty-plus inches. It gleamed under lights that seemed to twinkle from between the exposed superstructure of the old sports arena. Along the platform's perimeter, a garden of tropical flowers softened the ten foot drop from stage to concourse.

Trooper glanced down at his custom-built pulpit for a moment, and then he looked across the vast space enclosed by the coliseum's free-span roof. In spite of his missing daughter, as he spoke, he made sure his voice was warm and convincing.

"God is faithful, my people. My life is evidence of that."

His words echoed across the auditorium, and pausing to give them time to infiltrate his listeners' hearts, he soaked in the choir's soft melody. The barest of a smile hovered at the corners of his mouth, and he let his eyes look up for dramatic effect. As the smile spread across his face, he glanced to his wife. He watched her roll her eyes, and a sour knot twisted in his stomach. He hoped he could trust her to be on her best behavior when he called the family to the platform to show their unity under the Divine Hand of God's presence.

He looked out into the spotlights rimming the balcony in the distance. He motioned with one hand across the broad swath of people.

"As I invite my family to come and stand by my side on the platform, I would like to encourage those of you with a need, whether personal, physical, or financial, to gather with the pastors and their wives standing near you and allow them to offer your need to God."

A muted rustle told that the people were already moving.

He continued, "Also, please keep in mind those outside our walls who need the help of the Father. I recently learned that just last week a couple in our fair city lost their lives when their home burned to the ground. It was by the grace of God that their only child was spending the night elsewhere. The Word says Jesus loves the little children. As you lift your own needs before the Father, remember this young man who needs our prayers. His family is gone, but God will be there for him." He had no doubt the Hand of God would provide for the child's needs, for God rained mercy and love upon the just and the unjust. However, He especially loved little children.

He went on to encourage his congregation, the timbre of his voice growing deeper, "The Word says that where two or three are gathered in His name, there He will be also. Please gather for prayer as my family draws to my side."

The music swelled in volume, and the white Bösendorfer rang with fortitude. All around the great arena that was home to Trooper Kincaid Christian Ministries, in the shifting colors of people's clothing, and in the murmuring of distant voices, it was clear his people were doing just as he had asked. Still, the Reverend's heart beat uncomfortably fast in his chest. He hadn't located Lindsay, and the lights and cameras were readying to carry the image of the Kincaid family around the globe. Trooper Kincaid Christian Ministries depended on that image, and it would not do to have it tarnished.

"Get here, Lindsay," he muttered, even as he held a smile on his lips. He loved Lindsay, God knew that. He loved the beautiful young woman with all his heart. It was just that he never seemed to understand her, and it was beyond him why she couldn't see the importance of this final moment in front of the cameras each Sunday morning.

Catching movement in the video monitor built into the top of the enormous pulpit, he glanced down. The monitor was telling him his family was gathering at the Family

Altar, and the cameras were ready.

Turning, he smiled at the sight of his beautiful Sharon. She wore a blue and purple sequined dress this morning, probably Vera Wang, if he knew his designers. Her shoes shimmered from black to purple, and he knew they had set the ministry's accounts back more than whatever she had spent on the dress. She looked beautiful, though, and that was what counted. Jeffrey reached to his mother's elbow to pull her close and whisper something in her ear. She smiled and gave her son a kiss on the cheek, completing the picture.

A commotion at one of the sets of steps leading from the concourse caused Trooper to turn, and he closed his eyes for a moment. The twins were tall and lanky like he had been at seventeen, and while they danced a ballet of magic on the basketball court, in tan chinos and coordinating polos, they were oversized, rambunctious puppies that constantly tripped on too-big feet. Casey had stumbled on the steps, and his brother yanked him upright, doubling the disorder that was sure to be picked up by at least one camera now that the sermon was over.

Stepping forward to catch up to his teenage boys, he placed his hand on one son's neck. "Have you seen your sister?" He thought this was Cody, although he wasn't entirely sure. When he caught sight of a camera and noticed a red light flicker on, he smiled and waved his free hand, aware that a good image of a father and son together on the platform would go a long way.

"Lindsay?" The boy glanced at his father and grinned impishly.

That was when Trooper was certain which son he held in his hand. He threw his arm over the boy's shoulder and pulled him close as he spoke through his smile, "Tell me she's here, Cody."

"Sure, Dad." With a characteristic lack of pretense, he reached and grabbed his father's jaw in his big, athlete's hand, and he kissed him full on the cheek. "She's here, if you want me to say so, but I haven't seen her. Ask Casey. Besides, she's been off her feed the past few weeks." He kissed his father's face again and laughed before letting him go. "Better yet, ask Jack." He pointed to his older brother. "He'll know." Then, he was gone, crashing into his brother, creating yet another disruption.

"Two Points, I've just come from outside."

A voice at Trooper's side made him breathe easier, and he was relieved to feel a familiar hand on his shoulder. It was John Winston, the only person who ever called him by his old high school moniker. His voice had a layer of warmth no other person ever offered the central figure of Trooper Kincaid Christian Ministries, one that spoke of true love and not words that were just another way of staying in the boss's good graces.

"It's Lindsay, John. Have you seen her?" He reached for John's free hand and grasped it in his own, pulling it to his waist as if warmly shaking the hand of one of his most devoted ministerial staff.

"That's what I've come to tell you." John leaned in close to his ear, pulling in his proffered hand until the two men stood chest to chest, one in a pale suit, the other wearing dark, literally touching. His lips brushed the

10

minister's ear, privacy being paramount. "She's just arrived, but she's rather disheveled. Talk to the cameras and say something. Anything. It'll take me a moment to get her into something presentable, and I'm sorry, Two Points, but she'll have to wear a hat. I think knit with all her hair gathered underneath."

Trooper looked down at the burgundy-carpeted floor for a moment. Hats were not Sunday morning attire, not for his family, not on television for broadcast to the entire world. Sundays were for hairdressers, highlights, and hairspray. Sundays were for glittering with all the magnificence God had given His creation. The Word clearly stated that a woman's hair was her glory, and to cover it with a hat was to demean what God had meant to be shown in praise of the Creator.

"Knit, John?" He glanced away to see his eldest son flash a grin, one that matched his mother's, as he motioned with his head for his father to join the family. The boy was good, he had to admit that. The cameras were rolling, and even though they weren't broadcasting yet, Jeffrey had signaled in a way that no one would catch, even keeping a smile for the viewers. However, Trooper knew that particular tilt of his head, the one that said his father needed to drop everything and get to the Family Altar. The twins would never have that subtlety about them, not even at twenty-eight.

"I don't think Lindsay wants to be here today, Two Points." John glanced at Sharon. "Your wife looks good this morning. Is that a new dress?"

Trooper cleared his throat. "When isn't it a new

dress?" He smiled as he said it, and to the cameras it was just a warm cordiality for an old friend.

"Dad!" Jeffrey's impatience showed as he waved to his father, but his tone was still bright and cheerful. "Check on Lindsay." He smiled, but his words were a signal that he hadn't been able to find her either, and he was concerned.

"John says she's on the way," He gave John's hand a final shake before separating from him. "Thanks, John," he said more quietly. "You're the friend every man should have, and I love you for it." As John's face flushed with pleasure, Trooper slapped him appreciatively on the shoulder and moved toward his family, the lights shimmering in his hair.

He was aware of the shimmer, even though he couldn't see it himself. It was the hairspray he used, one designed for televised sports. It had real gold in it, and with the pump of a finger, the highlights became real. Of course, those same highlights washed out when the televangelist stepped back into the workaday world of family, friends, and a business that had become just that—a business, but they sure looked good under the lights. Those gold highlights made the man seem, well, a little closer to the One he tried to emulate, a bit nearer to God than those around him, and for that, people came when the doors to the old sports arena opened, and when the call for finances filtered out over the airways, people responded, and generously, too.

It was the ointment in the alabaster box, washed across Trooper's life to show God's love to His most favored

12

servant, and Trooper appreciated it as his due from the Master above.

There was a fly in the ointment, though. Bucky Simms with the *Chronicle* had become interested, and for the last week, he had been very interested indeed. No one would talk to him, though. No one at all wanted to talk to Bucky Simms of the *Chronicle*, not last week, not next week, and if they could help it, not ever. Bucky Simms was known for finding flaws, even where there were none.

No, Bucky Simms was not welcome at all.

Chapter 2

SHE HAD been good once, Lindsay knew. She had been twelve, and when she was twelve, she knew she could find God, that He would show up if she did something just for others, something magnificent enough to get His attention. She hadn't accepted then that God was just what He appeared to be, a sham. She knew it now, had become convinced that God was something invented by her father, by all the fathers of the world, by all the fathers of *history*, for the sole purpose of manipulating others. The cash they garnered didn't hurt, either. God knew, her father had certainly come out on top in that phase of the game.

She had truly been good then, back when she was twelve, or she had at least believed she was. She had wanted to be, and she had wanted God to be real. She hadn't known how to get His attention, though, not until she'd seen the frantic reporter on the television unable to control her normally staid emotions, as yet another mobile home washed away from the town's last refuge for those who did the real work of the world: the housekeepers, the janitors, and the laborers who worked at jobs that paid them just enough to survive.

Creekside Mobile Home Park had its picturesque qualities when the sun was bright and Rockaway Creek burbled along, neatly bound within its rocky banks. There had even been a bridge once, a small footbridge that led over the shimmering water's surface to a small grassy area just on the other side. When Creekside Park was new, there had been picnic tables sitting around the green space, and families had enjoyed the amenities that the secluded area offered. The tops of the trees had rustled in the breezes from earliest spring to the first touch of winter, and there were birds, glorious birds that built nests in the tallest branches. After great windstorms, it had been a favorite pastime of the local bird watching society to scramble through the green space looking for small birds that had been blown out of their nests, gathering them up in the hopes, sometimes successful, that the small creatures could be reared to adulthood and released back into the wild.

However, no one had visited that area in decades. The bridge and the tables had all washed away in one of the creek's many flash floods several years after Creekside Park was built. By the time Lindsay was twelve, the floods happened with every heavy rainfall. Many of the homes carried an odd odor of mustiness that never seemed to dissipate even on the brightest of summer days. Plug-in air fresheners and scented oil sticks barely took off the sour smell that permeated even the clothing the occupants wore—and they were just that, occupants, people there for the duration. No one *owned* the trailers in Creekside anymore, no one, at least, who lived there. Creekside Mobile Home Park was a place a person moved to when options were limited to none at all, and those who could get out, got out as quickly as possible.

Those who were forced to live in Creekside Park soon learned an important lesson. The first hammering of raindrops on tin roofs was the signal for residents of the park to gather essential belongings into one location, ready to grasp and run if they had to sprint for the safety of higher ground. On that night when Lindsay was twelve, one family new to the park was caught unawares. Had the flood been a normal one, they would have quickly learned from the drenched shoes underneath their beds and the precious memories stored in boxes at the bottoms of closets that had to be thrown out when the waters receded, but this flood was anything but normal.

The week before, in a minor downpour, garbage in the creek, accumulated over the decades, and catching on rocks and filling the pools that could have long ago absorbed much of the sudden influx of water, had finally filled to the bursting point. Shifting once again, it had blocked what little drainage was left. The flooding water had not quite reached the floors of the mobile homes along the creek's bank, but it had been very slow to drain.

A number of the park's residents had commented on the fact, but each of them considered themselves transitory, even if the moving on they regularly talked of had been postponed many times for some of them, finances defeating them at every turn. Under other circumstances, they might have been able to guess just how bad it was, but no one remembered the way the creek had been many years before when the park was built, back when Rockaway Creek was a beautiful place one would actually want to visit.

Now it was just a junk-filled wasteland that was ignored when possible, and at other times put out of mind as soon as could be done so, the residents grateful their musty carpets hadn't been soaked once again, and they could all sleep in their beds that night, despite the old smell of water that never seemed to go away.

That new family had been asleep in their beds that fateful night. New to the city, just in from the country and desperate for a fresh start, the young family had been forced to take the cheapest home Creekside had been able to offer. It had seemed livable, if a bit mustier than the other homes in the park. It was small, but then all the homes in Creekside were small. However, running water could be heard just outside the windows, and that had appealed to the young mother.

With the central air conditioning system broken many years before, and only one small window unit to purr along in the larger of the two small bedrooms, the family slept together under the coolness of the murmuring compressor, with the baby in the crib, and their kindergarten son on a soft pallet on the floor. The water that night swelled so fast, the small air conditioner didn't even have time to quiet its soothing murmurs before the tin walls containing the struggling family and all their possessions were yanked from their cinderblock stanchions and thrust into the roiling flood.

That was the reason for the reporter's tears. Other residents, ones who had taken the time to talk to the young couple and gotten to know them, pleaded on air for someone, anyone, to do something, telling what they knew of the people whose home was now just an empty expanse of black water. The reporter's normally expressionless face broke at the realization that this family had come to Creekside looking for a fresh start in life, and now their lives had been taken from them, and all because this particular mobile home park happened to be located just over the edge of the city's boundaries, making no one responsible for the upkeep of Rockaway Creek. That lack of responsibility had just caused four people to be swept away, four people who in all likelihood were already dead.

It was when the reporter's camera aimed into the night lying heavily across the black waters, and the floodlights picked up debris carried along by the flooded stream, that the budding teen watching knew what she must do. This was her opportunity to accomplish something big enough to get God's notice, something that would cause Him to pay attention to her, to Lindsay, and to prove He was real. She had been galvanized. Surely God cared that these people had just lost their lives and that more people living in Creekside Park might soon follow.

She had done what she had planned that night. She got her teachers and classmates involved, put up flyers in local businesses, and elicited the participation of anyone who wanted to help clean the creek. Parents of her classmates began to offer backhoes and trucks, and from there, the responses reverberated as a cause extraordinaire throughout the city. Trooper and Sharon saw the notices in the paper, as well as reporters on television telling of the upcoming Clean Up Rockaway Creek Day that had been initiated by Lindsay's school. They had no idea it was Lindsay's proposal, though, and their own involvement in their ministry efforts—as well as decorating a new home in the city's most affluent subdivision—conspired to keep them so busy that the Clean Up Day was acknowledged as just one more good thing on God's agenda, something that He was doing through the good people who lived alongside them in their fair city.

Jeffrey, a freshman in college at the time, learned of his sister's project when he happened to be home the weekend of the Clean Up Day, and Lindsay made her bid to drag him along.

"Jack, you must come with me!" With a brightly colored bandanna tied around her head, she flew into his room early that Saturday morning. She was dressed for working, and her clothes were the most rugged she owned. "You have to drive me down to the creek. You must! We'll be late, if you don't hurry."

He rolled over and groaned, pulling his pillow over his head. This was his first night to sleep in the new house, and his bedroom had been low on his mother's priority list for blinds. The multilevel flat roof was raised in every possible room to allow clerestory windows to wrap the ceilings, flooding the interior spaces with light. In addition, his bedroom had a solid wall of sliders that opened to a balcony that hung over Stone Creek.

"Jack!" Lindsay jumped onto his bed. "You have to know about this. Get up and go with me."

"Get up?" His words groaned from underneath his pillow.

"Yes, Jack! Get up!" She reached and rumpled his hair. Her big brother was her favorite person in the whole world, and with him home, how could the weekend be any less than perfect?

JEFFREY had come in from college a day early to catch the final meeting of the Youth International Rally held at the church just the evening before. He had attended the rallies since entering the youth department at thirteen, and he had been unwilling to miss this year.

Now he wished he had. *She* had been there, and in that unexpected meeting, the life he had known was changed forever.

Chapter 3

IT WAS YOUTH camp, and Jeffrey was fifteen. The camp was large, and churches came from hundreds of miles away. With his mother's good looks and his sideways grin, he attracted the girls like flies to a pot of golden honey.

All week one fourteen-year-old girl doted on him. It wasn't love. Even Jeffrey understood that. He didn't even know what love was, just that when he was with her, he felt good, and by the end of the week, he wanted to be with her as much as possible.

On the last night of the camp, several of the counselors planned a series of events to exhaust the campers, one of which was an extended hike through the woods. As the group passed the stockade-fenced pool enclosure, he impulsively grabbed the girl's hand and pulled her aside, laughing as he held his hand over her mouth. As he giggled and put his arm around her to hold her still, in the darkness, with the sounds of the other campers growing fainter in the woods, he held her far longer than he should. However, she didn't seem to mind, and once the sounds of the others were gone entirely, he removed his hand from her mouth and whispered to her quietly.

"May I kiss you?"

He could barely get the words out. It wasn't that he had planned to ask her to kiss when he pulled her aside. He had only felt he needed to be as close to her as he could, and kissing seemed the one thing he knew.

"If you want."

As his lips touched hers, his arm brushed the catch on the gate, and it suddenly swung in, causing them to stumble and almost fall to the ground. He laughed, catching her. He blamed the pounding in his chest on the near fall, not realizing there were other things happening just at that moment that could be equally responsible, things like having a girl alone with him in the darkness, a girl with a too thin tee and a willingness to offer him a suddenly desired first kiss.

"I've never swum alone in the pool. I'm going to get in." The fact that Jeffrey had gone forward three times during the week to offer his heart to God was washed away in the intensity of this one moment in the darkness. All that was now important to him was spending time with this beautiful girl. To make matters even more enticing, the pool fence offered them total privacy.

"We don't have suits, silly. Besides, there's no lifeguard." Her words were whispered with intensity, but in the warm darkness of the evening, they didn't say no at all, not the way Jeffrey heard her speak. "The lights aren't even on. We can't see."

"And no one can see us. We won't get in trouble." With clammy hands that could barely grab the damp fabric of his shirt, he pulled it quickly over his head.

"You're really doing this?"

"I've swum in my boxers before. They're no different than a swimsuit. This'll be fun." He kicked his sandals aside and stepped out of his shorts, hanging them on the fence. His boxers hung limply from his fifteen-year-old waist, and in the darkness, they did seem much like trunks. "Go in with me, please? The water's warm."

Somewhere in the darkness, a frog started up its throaty call. It was as if the two campers had the night to themselves. The girl laughed, and she rubbed her arms as if suddenly chilled.

"You go. I don't have anything I can wear. I'll sit on the side and watch you swim." She pushed him on the chest with her hand, letting it rest against his skin a little longer than she might if she hadn't felt much the same as he did. However, after a moment, she pulled it away and removed her shoes, sitting on the side of the pool and dropping her feet into the warmth of the water. "Go, now. Just don't make waves. I have to stay dry."

He leaned in and kissed her cheek, then before she could respond, he slipped into the water, sinking to the bottom, and leaving her alone.

JEFFREY had met that girl again the previous evening,

and he hadn't even known who she was. She had walked straight up to him after the meeting and shaken his hand cordially. There had been something familiar in her manner, but he hadn't known just what.

"You never called, but then I realized I never gave you my phone number. He looks just like you." Her voice was bright and friendly. "I saw him just once before his new parents took him. I couldn't name him, of course, but when they came for him, I called him Jack, for you. They had no other family, they said, and he would be special to them." Conversations of people from many different youth groups entwined around them. "I wasn't supposed to meet the parents, but I refused to turn loose of him, forcing them to come to me."

In that moment, Jeffrey felt his stomach turn inside out.

HE SURFACED at the opposite side of the pool and shook the water from his head. Just a touch of the moon could be seen rising over the trees, and he could barely make out the girl sitting on the far side.

"Come over here, Jeffrey. Swim back to me."

He put his arms in front of him and pushed the water aside in a smooth breaststroke. Coming to rest in front of the girl, he placed his hands on the concrete coping on either side of her and looked into her face. He could see the outline of her head with the enlarging moon just behind her.

"Kiss me again. You never kissed me properly after the gate fell open. On the lips, like you started to do. Then we have to go before someone finds us." She teased him, touching his hand where it rested beside her.

With a surge of motion, he thrust himself out of the water. As he broke free, his mouth found hers, his heart pounding with the brazenness of what he'd done. This time he rested both of his arms on her legs, pulling her feet around him and leaning back in the water.

"Don't. You'll pull me in," she whispered, but there was laughter there, and she didn't really sound as if she meant for him to stop. "I can't get any wetter, or my counselor will know I've been down here at the pool. I'll get in so much trouble."

"Get in," he pleaded. "What does it matter now?"

"One more kiss, and we have to go. The hike will be over before long, and we can't be found in here."

Her words were soft and short, and to Jeffrey, in the sultry night air, they were the taste of chilled water sliding down a parched throat. A cricket nearby chirped loudly, almost breaking the spell. For a moment, he tried to focus. He really did. Just for an instant he knew he should climb out of the water and gather his clothes, then the two of them should rush to join the other campers as quickly as possible. He certainly shouldn't be planning to pull this girl into the water with him.

Then, those rational thoughts slipped away.

"I REALLY loved you that night, you know." The beautiful young woman, certainly no longer a mere girl, turned, distracted as laughter rang from one set of seats nearby. Her eyes had begun to turn red.

Jeffrey suddenly saw her as she had been in that pool that night, the moonlight shining on her face as he held her. His heart slowed to a standstill, the world around him fading. Someone else whispered his words for him.

"I didn't know."

He glanced the direction of the laughter, suddenly cold, not really seeing what had caused him to look that way, and then back to the girl, wanting to speak, and not knowing what to say. What could he say? He was in shock, and his vocal cords were as frozen as his thoughts in his head.

A child? He was only nineteen.

HE PULLED on her legs, pulled hard so she would fly into his arms, sinking with her into the pool. His feet quickly pushed them both to the surface of the water, and he laughed as they broke through to the mugginess of the night air.

"Jeffrey! Look at me—" In spite of her admonition, she couldn't finish her words, because he pressed his lips to hers, stopping her in mid-sentence, only releasing her after several long, silent moments.

"Call me Jack." His words escaped with an intensity that surprised even him.

"Jack?" She giggled, caught off guard by his words.

"Besides, you told me to kiss you, and I did." He was delirious with the audacity of his actions.

"Sure, Jack." She giggled again, her arms resting across his shoulders.

"I like it when you say my name. Say it again. Call me

Jack." He pulled her closer.

"Jack. The name fits you." She leaned forward and kissed the end of his nose.

AS HE HEARD music start up, canned, the background noise that told the ministry staff to start shutting the building down section by section so the crowds would slowly empty, he simply looked at her. His mind had gone numb. In the balcony far above, he was distantly aware of the top tiers of seats going dark as the first set of lights was turned off.

"I wasn't ready for the responsibility, and we really should have gone on that hike. Did you truly love me, Jeffrey?" Then, quickly, she caught his hand and held it for a moment, shaking her head. "No, don't answer that. It's been four years, and it's the ancient past by now. I hoped you would be here; that's the reason I came when my youth group decided to attend. I did love you, though, Jeffrey. I just want you to know that." She dropped his hand and sighed, brushing her hand down her skirt, fingering the material nervously. It was her eyes that told the truth of the matter. They shimmered with moisture, and she spoke her words quickly.

"He's three, now. His birthday was last week."

FINALLY, with a sudden, all-consuming realization of what his body had been attempting to tell him all along, intent sprang full-blown into Jeffrey's mind. Before, if they had been interrupted, even accused of impropriety by the camp staff, he wouldn't have understood the charges, because there had been no intent in his mind. However, now, in the pool next to this girl, with his body pressed against hers, he was no longer innocent of the possibilities that were open to him. With an immediate clarity of purpose, he *knew* what this moment was all about, what had to happen, and the situation changed for him.

It would have been better if it had been love. Not right, but better. It was not, though. This girl had doted on him all week, and he had only pulled her away from the group because she had been at his side when the opportunity had provided itself.

"Jack, no," her words whispered, when he pulled her tight.

"I love you. I thought you loved me, too." His lie was whispered and urgent.

"I do love you, but—"

"Then you love me, and I love you." They were the first passionate words he had ever whispered, although he didn't think of them that way. He thought of them as convincing, and they were. "And that means we should do this."

With those words, her resistance melted, and events raced down a path no fifteen-year-old should follow. Neither should a fourteen-year-old, if the matter be told. However, that road was soon traveled, even if the full realization of their actions didn't hit them until the moment was done.

After rescuing cast-off clothing and exiting the pool, the two children couldn't find the courage to look in each other's eyes. The other campers returned, their laughter driving the frogs and crickets back into the decaying leaf litter along the trail. Their friends called to Jeffrey and the girl, surprised to find them already back at camp. Had they taken a short cut? Their hair was wet; they must have had a water fight. Could anyone join? And before too many minutes passed, water fountains were filling cups and plastic bags, balloons were scrounged, and eager hands were sending watery projectiles flying through the air.

Jeffrey loved water fights, but he didn't love that one. He sat on a bench, looking for signs of the girl, wondering if she'd tell. Even when a water balloon hit him on the head, he didn't cry foul, or that he would be getting even for such a dastardly deed. It was when one of his friends tackled him, taking him to the ground, the mud filling his mouth, that he began to retch. Everyone thought it was because of what he had swallowed. Only Jeffrey knew it was because of what he'd done. Well, one other person knew, but she wasn't anywhere around, not anyplace Jeffrey had been able to find, anyway.

It was a small favor, he'd thought at the time. He couldn't have faced her. It was the worst thing he'd ever done.

WHEN JEFFREY looked up, she was gone. Later, he knew she couldn't have just disappeared. The massive auditorium was too large, too open for that. He must have been in shock. After camp, he'd destroyed everything from that week, telling himself he'd never show an interest in girls again. He'd spent weeks reading his Bible for hours, praying for forgiveness.

At nineteen, he knew better. God had specifically built each man to be attracted to women in just that way. It was up to the man to control those drives and use them properly. Eventually, he had learned how to accept what he and the girl had done, to understand that it had been no more than one brief moment in his past. It was regrettable, but it was also something he could not undo.

Now, nearly four years later, waves of ratcheting guilt held him tightly bound in a straitjacket. His teenaged indiscretion was not simply an awkward memory.

It had taken solid form. He had a son.

Chapter 4

JEFFREY reached a hand up, pushing Lindsay away. He couldn't face the day, much less with her harassing him. Get up and go with her? Sure, Lindsay, and he had a three-year-old son he'd never met. He really did not want to face this day.

He felt her yank the pillow from his head, and before he could hide once again, she grabbed his face in both her hands. She leaned to touch her forehead to his, and her nose pressed against his nose. She spoke in the most charming voice she knew.

"You are my sweetest big brother, perfect in every way. You know you are, Jack, and I love you very much. Get up, please. For me."

He refused to open his eyes, and he groaned. "We live on the creek, little sister. Walk out to the balcony and jump off. You'll land in it. Why do I need to take you there?"

She pulled at his eyelids with her fingers, but he simply squeezed them tighter.

"Look at me, big brother. Jack, please look," she pleaded. Then, she threw herself down beside him. "You came home all this way just to go to that meeting at church, didn't you?" When he pulled his arms up and wrapped them over his face, she poked him in the side before reaching up to squeeze the muscle in his arm.

"It's real, Lindsay." He laughed. His sister's teasing was bringing back memories of better times, back when he hadn't known he was a father.

"Are you working out?" She giggled. "I'm one of your college sweethearts. Tighten your arm for me. I want to know what your muscle feels like." She squealed as he did so. "Dad tells Mom that he's lucky to have such a perfect son—"

One of his arms interrupted her torrent of words, as he clamped a hand over her mouth.

"Stop it with the perfect stuff, Lindsay. I'm not perfect, and you know it." The girl from the night before. A three-year-old. Even when he did something outstandingly stupid, his family saw him as perfect. It was an impossible standard to have paraded before him year after year. This morning, it was crushing.

"How are you not perfect, big brother?" Lindsay grabbed his arm and played with his fingers. "Even I think you're handsome, and that's saying something, because I have really high expectations. You're not even mean to me, and I pick on you all the time. Now," and she jumped up onto her knees, pulling the comforter off him, "you have to get up. I need to go to Rockaway Creek."

"Rockaway?" He tried to remember what it was he'd heard about Rockaway Creek. A clean-up effort, perhaps? He sat up, squinting as a ray of sunlight through one of the clerestory windows hit his face. "Say one of Dad's prayers for me. Ask God to turn off the sun until after I get up."

She knelt across him, one knee on each side of his torso, blocking the sun, and once again she grabbed his face in her hands. "That's why you've got to do this for me, Jack. This is so important, even God's got to notice." She leaned down and kissed him on the cheek. "And yes, Rockaway Creek."

"Why Rockaway? That's just a trailer slum down there." Impulsively, with a suddenness intended to catch her off guard, he grabbed her around the waist with both arms and rolled her over onto the bed next to him. "Why Rockaway Creek? Tell me, little sister, or I'll tickle you until you wet your pants." He held one finger up as if he might do exactly that, and it caught the strip of light streaming in from overhead. It glowed. He glanced at it and grinned.

"What, Jack? That's sunlight, you know." She giggled.

"No, it's not," he said ominously, although he couldn't keep a grin off his face.

"Yes, you bully. I know sunlight. Now, let me up." She was her grownup self now, or as grown up as a girl of twelve could be. "You've got someplace to take me." She struggled but not seriously.

"No," he repeated. "This is the Holy Hand of God. The

33

light is the presence of God that shined on Moses's face when he descended from Mt. Sinai, and it's about to speak directly to one twelve-year-old girl's ribcage, if she isn't forthcoming with news about Rockaway Creek."

She squirmed from underneath his hand, dragging the comforter with her as she scrambled off the bed, holding it over her head and chanting loudly into the room, "Jeffrey's got to get up. Jeffrey's got to get up."

On her third pass, the bedroom door flew open, and in ran their eight-year-old twin brothers, Cody and Casey. Even at eight, the boys already had their father's lanky build, and they were dressed identically.

"No! Not the twin tornadoes!" Jeffrey laughed to see Speed Racer plastered across their chests.

"Jack!" Their voices chimed out as one as they ran to the bed. One tow-headed boy scrambled up to jump on him, and Jeffrey knew it was Cody, because he was the live wire of the two. He was always first, and he sprawled on the bed and curled into a ball, Jeffrey's hands tickling him.

"Cody, you're dead meat, you know that? No one attacks me on Saturday morning without paying a very steep price. No one."

"Jack, I'll pay." The second twin climbed on the foot of the bed, and he stood with his arms extended. It seemed that Casey wanted what his brother had, and right then, his brother had Jeffrey. The second twin leaped into the fray, pleading for his big brother to tickle him, too.

"You, too, little Casey? You can't offer to pay. I just take what I want, and right now I want a piece of you.

Take that!" He reached and grabbed his brother's ear, yanking on it until the eight-year-old squealed in delight. "Can't take it, huh? I'll get the other one, then. You'll pay. I don't get revenge; I get even. How many times have you heard me say that?"

"A million," Casey squealed in a high-pitched voice.

"How many?" Jeffrey turned, grabbing at Cody as he leaped off the bed and out the door. "Help, Lindsay. One's getting away."

"A million," Casey called out once again, his laughter taking his breath away.

"Louder, little twin. Tell me again." He pulled the boy close, wrapping him in his arms.

"A million," he yelled at the top of his voice. "More than a million!"

Right then was when Cody bounded back into the room with a can in his hand. Knocking the top off, he jumped on the foot of the bed, aimed it at his siblings, and pushed the nozzle hard. Silly String pumped from the can, shooting across the bed. Jeffrey reached to grab his leg, missing his ankle, but snagging the pajama bottoms, causing the boy to stumble off the bed and to the floor. When he stood to run, Jeffrey called to him to freeze.

"No, you don't, you little shrimp. No one gets away with spraying Silly String in my room." Jeffrey leaped from the bed. He scrambled to his feet just in time to scoop the boy in his arms. Tickling him to make him drop the can, it clattered to the hardwood floor, just as a pair of sock-clad feet stepped inside the door. Jeffrey sat hard on the floor and looked up with a grin.

35

It was his father, tall and lanky, looking barely older than his pictures from high school. His hair stood straight up, and he yawned.

"Just get up, Dad?"

"You did make it home, Jack. How was the Youth International Rally last night? Last big meeting of the week, I heard. There's a girl been looking for you all week, I understand. Someone from summer camp several years ago. Really nice and exceptionally pretty, or so your Uncle John says." His father winked. "Don't let the pretty ones get away. Find some way to snag 'em, because those are the ones that always go quick. Did she find you last night?"

At his father's words, the straitjacket was back. He held his brother, because he didn't know what else to do.

"Sorry, Dad. We didn't mean to wake you." He put his face next to his brother's and breathed in the little boy smell that was his. He wondered if she'd told Uncle John what she'd told him.

"Did you, Jack?" His father walked over and rumpled Cody's hair. "John said she was there every night asking for you."

"Did you get to meet her, Dad?" He reached and pulled Casey to his side, now holding one brother under each arm. His question was nothing more than a distraction to keep from answering his father's question. He hoped he wouldn't call him on it. He did not want to talk about this girl.

"Nah." Trooper yawned again. "John just told me about her. I thought if you saw her, maybe you might invite her over for the day. After church tomorrow, of course, possibly for lunch, if you want."

"Did John say if she said anything else?" Jeffrey blew a raspberry on Casey's neck, grabbing a shock of the boy's hair, as he searched for ways to keep from looking at his father.

Trooper turned to walk out the door, and then he paused and frowned, looking back at his son. "She met you at summer camp when you were fifteen or sixteen, or so she told John. That was the age you were the last time you went. You know, even back then I never could decide what made you quit attending. You always seemed to enjoy it. Anyway, she said you two swam together once that week. That was odd, I thought, because I don't remember the camp ever having coed swim times." He paused, pulling at an ear, and then he ran a big hand through his hair and laughed. "Oh, well. I'll tell John she missed you again. It's good to have you home, Son." He walked out the door and then reappeared, rubbing his chin with a frown. "Yes, and your sister has a job for you today. I told her you might have other plans, but she seems to think what she needs is more important. You know how to handle her, though, so I'll leave it in your hands." He waved and was gone for good.

"The creek? Will you go with me, Jack?" From behind, Lindsay threw her arms around his neck and leaned her head onto his shoulder to whisper in his ear. "Please?"

Jeffrey knew one thing. He didn't want to stay around the house. What would his family do if that girl actually told someone he'd fathered a baby when he was only fifteen? He couldn't lie about it. He wouldn't. If anyone found out, it would be a disaster worse than anything he'd ever known. Today, he needed to be gone, somewhere no one would ask him about his old summer camp days.

"Sure, Lindsay." He drew in a deep breath. She would be his ticket for the day. "What are you planning to do there?" Something that could include him, he hoped, anything that would keep him out of the house.

"I'm going to help clear the creek. Lots of people are planning to be there, and we're making it safe for the people who live there."

"Safe? What's wrong with the creek, and why are you helping?"

"Silly! So their houses don't flood anymore."

"Go play, boys." Jeffrey pushed his two brothers away, calling after Cody, "Don't forget your can of Silly String. You'll want that." He turned to Lindsay. "They're just trailers, you know. There are no real houses on Rockaway Creek."

"They're real to the people who live there. Just because the people who live there aren't rich doesn't mean their houses should flood. God cares about them, too."

"That's my little sister." He reached an arm and hugged her tight. "I love you, Lindsay."

She laughed. "You should. Now get dressed, because everyone else is already there."

Once she was gone, he stood and walked to the sliders, pushing them back to open the room up to the balcony. He felt the sun on his bare skin, and as it warmed him, he leaned onto the waist-high stainless steel railing, resting his elbows. Craning his neck, he looked down into the creek far below, hearing the sound of the water as it tripped over the stones that cluttered their way through the ravine. The trees that his parents had paid someone to trim to within an inch of their woody lives cast dappled shadows onto the surface of the water far below, and on the opposite side, hundreds of yards away, flowering shrubs had been planted, just perfect for viewing from his family's home.

He shivered as a cloud dimmed the sun for a moment. He had a son out there. He couldn't have imagined that a day ago. This place could have been that boy's home, too. Yet, he didn't even remember the girl's name. He could still see the tears that had filled her eyes the evening before. She missed the baby, even now, three years after giving it up. Would he have felt the same, if he had known?

The sun came back out, and Jeffrey felt his skin warm. He turned when he heard Lindsay burst through his door.

"Jack, you haven't gotten ready at all. We've got to go!"

Her voice was the epitome of exasperation, but he just smiled. "Coming, Mother, dearest. Your growl is my command. That bandanna on your head becomes you, Sis."

"Just hurry, Jack." She dug through several of his drawers, pulling out a pair of jeans and one of socks, and throwing them on the bed. "There. Put those on. I need you, Jack. God needs you. If you're there, He'll surely notice what I'm doing. Please." She put her hands together in a pantomime of a prayer, and she made a face that was a desperate plea for his cooperation.

He placed his hand on her head and yanked the bandanna off. "This is what's been slowing me down. I need one of these for me." He laughed and put it on his own head. "I'm ready, now. Let's go."

"Jack!" She grabbed at it, as he held her at arm's length. "Give it back. Beside, you can't go without a shirt. Get dressed, first."

"I can't go without a shirt?" He raised one eyebrow. "I'm that horrible looking, then, that you refuse to be seen with me?"

She jumped and snagged the bandanna. "No. The newspaper will be there. They'll be taking pictures, and you know how Mom and Dad feel about you and shirts in public. You get your picture in the paper without a shirt, and they'll roll over. Me?" She giggled. "I'd show it to all my friends and tell them it's my favorite brother in the paper."

He laughed, pointing his arm to the door. "Go, Sis! I'll pull a shirt on, and if you're really good, I may find a place where the newspapermen can't find me, and I'll pull my shirt off just to cool down. If your friends are watching, I can hardly stop them, can I?"

Giggling, she ran from the room, calling back, "There's bacon in the kitchen. I fixed it especially for you."

He did get dressed, tossing his flannels on the bed and slipping on the things his sister had dug out for him. He also pulled out an old shirt from the bottom of a drawer, one that wouldn't suffer too much extra damage from a day in the creek. Then, the smell of Lindsay's bacon pulled him from his room.

Chapter 5

"THIS IS cutting it close, Lindsay." John Winston studied the beautiful young woman in front of him, and as he shook his head in dismay, he reached a hand to massage the back of his neck. What a time for the jackhammers to kick in, and just when he needed to get Lindsay to the platform. She certainly couldn't go in the torn jeans she wore.

"John, don't make me do this. I shouldn't be on that stage, and you know it." She was curled up in a chair, her eyes dark with lack of sleep. "Just tell Dad and Mom that I feel bad and have to sit this one out. I do feel bad, you know."

She laughed at that.

John grinned. "You hate this, don't you, Lindsay. Why do you have so much trouble giving your folks ten minutes just once a week?" He said it lightly, but without her on the platform, the donations for the week would suffer, and God help them, that was a thought no one wanted to contemplate. The ministry was at a crux in its finances, and he knew those finances inside and out. It was a year's salary for some men just to run the lights in the auditorium, and that was just a fraction of the cost to heat and cool the facilities.

He pulled a pale yellow dress from a wardrobe, one with a summery feel to it, and he held it out to her. "You're the one finishing up a degree in fashion. What have you learned in that school? Tell me, is this the latest in runway design or not?" It had a gauzy overlay on the outside with a nubby texture across its surface, and he felt it would flatter the casual look of the knit cap he intended for her to wear.

She sighed very dramatically, and he understood as if she had bared her soul. It wasn't the dress he held. It was the cameras, the fake smiles, the knowing she didn't mean any of it. More importantly, she was convinced that God wasn't really there. She had made that clear to him more than once.

"It's all a sham, John. You know that." She caught the dress as he tossed it at her, laughing. "Summer? You want me to wear summer this final time, John?"

"It goes with the hat you'll wear to cover your hair. You are beautiful, Lindsay. You do remember that?" He dug in another wardrobe and pulled out the knit cap, tossing it her direction. "Lipstick is the only makeup we have time for, so get dressed, Lindsay, for me, if not for your parents."

43

"You love them, don't you, John?" She looked up from the chair, still holding the dress and cap. "Whom do you love the most? Mom or Dad?" Then, she laughed. "Don't answer that, at least not in public. It would paint you in a bad light. Has Dad ever found out?" When he frowned at her, she laughed again, and it was pointed. "He's a smart man, John. Forgiving, too. Don't you trust him?"

"Do you hate him that much, Lindsay?" Her words cut deep, and he felt his jaw tense. The jackhammers pounded. "Me, too? Do you hate me that much? Your secrets have always been safe with me. I hope mine are safe with you."

She laughed, standing, as she threw the dress and cap onto the chair. Crossing the room, she pressed one hand to his face and closed her eyes for a moment. Then, she reached and kissed his cheek.

"I think you're the only one I love, John. I used to worship my father, but he's never understood me, and I certainly don't understand him. Mom? She's just Mom, and I have to take her as she is." She patted his face. "You didn't ask about Mom, did you? I do love the twins. Dear God, I love them, and Jack most of all."

"God? You mentioned God, Lindsay. Have you ever found room for Him?" He knew they needed to hurry, but Lindsay rarely talked to him, really talked anymore, and he missed their chats, as oddly misinformative as they could be.

"I was twelve, John." She pulled off her shirt and threw it aside, then reached to unfasten her pants.

He turned away. She had dressed in front of him,

probably hundreds of times. He thought nothing of it, anymore, but while in the church, the appearance of propriety was important.

"I invited God to my party when I set up that mission to clean Rockaway Creek. Jack came, and even you. You were there. We performed a miracle for those people, and God never showed. Did you catch what I said, John? *We* performed a miracle, and I got my picture in the newspaper and everything, thanks to that brother of mine. I didn't want that, you know, the recognition. I wanted God. However, God didn't come to my party, John, and I don't intend to go to His, not without complaining, anyway." She had the dress on by then, and she grabbed the cap to pull it over her hair. "You do have the lipstick? I have none with me." She grinned at him impishly.

As he opened the tube, he offered it to her. "Did it ever occur to you that you were the hand of God to those people, that a little girl of twelve saw the need and brought God's miracle to them?"

She grabbed the lipstick and slashed it across her lips. "Don't you dare suggest that to me, John. *I* saw that news report where that poor family was washed away, and *I* worked to get others involved in cleaning that creek. *I* gave God the chance to show up, and He never did. Don't you tell me that I brought *God's* miracle to those people. I brought *my* miracle to them. There is no God. I thought I must be wrong when I was a child, and at twelve, I thought I'd been given the perfect opportunity to prove it." She thrust the lid on the lipstick and slammed it into John's waiting hand.

"You'll smile for the cameras, Lindsay?" He hoped so, but he wasn't entirely sure this morning. "You do look beautiful." She needed to believe in herself, and besides, it was certainly true.

She snorted and then grabbed his jaw with her hand. "Marry me, John. You and I would be perfect together. Marry me."

He kissed her on the cheek. "That's the Lindsay I love so much. Just smile, girl, and the world will love you for it."

"I will smile, John." She sighed heavily. "Just promise me you'll be in front of the television monitors, and that you'll watch. Then, someone will know my lie, because when I smile out there, it's only because you asked. I want someone to look at my smile and think, 'My God, that girl can lie like a rug, and no one can tell. Damn, she's good.'"

"No profanity, please, not in the church." He smiled to soften his words as he reached to a shelf and held out a pair of shoes. "Thank you, Lindsay. We must hurry."

"When must we not?" Her tone was very cryptic, but still, she slipped the shoes on in record time, and the two of them were soon at the back entrance to the Family Altar. Through the door, it was clear her father was covering her absence very handily. There was even laughter from those still out on the auditorium floor, as he finished what was obviously a very amusing story.

LINDSAY watched John walk away, wondering for the hundredth time why he hadn't been her father. John understood her. She always felt bad, and John knew all of it. Uncle John, she'd always called him as a child. Jeffrey never had, but the twins still did. He *was* an uncle to them, and John seemed to love them as much as he was devoted to her father. Strangely devoted, she had thought when she was a teenager, but now she accepted John as John, having come to know people at the university who were so much stranger. Besides, she had grown fond of him, and he was able to listen and not divulge anything she told him, no matter how horrible it might be. She knew, because she had made up some whoppers over the years, just to see if they ever got back to her parents. Not one ever had.

She turned back to the Altar, just for a moment practicing her smile for John. Oh, God, it felt fake! How could she go out there and pretend it was real? It made her as bad as her father.

She knew there was more, though. The pain was all of her life wrapped in a nutshell, and it hurt to crack it open in public with a smile no one believed. It was no more than window dressing, and she was certain it must carry over the broadcast to the viewers. It must, or they were as deluded as her parents.

Another round of laughter filtered in around her. She wouldn't be surprised if the jaunty stories were about her, either. She had always seemed to amuse her father. Inspire him? Never. He always seemed to find new and inventive ways to refuse to show his love to her, and that was what made her want him to feel her pain as deeply as she had felt it for years.

Chapter 6

SHARON felt good this morning, and she laughed at Trooper's stories, joining in with those still in the congregation, those faithful souls who would stay in their seats until the last Kincaid was off the platform and had left the building. They were the core of the ministry, the "old-timers," some would say. In her darker moments, those times when the world seemed pitiless and hostile, Sharon might use the same derogatory phrase, but today was not one of her darker moments. Something in her brain chemistry was working correctly on this bright and enjoyable Sunday morning. Her endorphins were bleeding crazily into her system, and her neurons were flashing their messages on steroids. Today, Sharon *wanted* to be alive, and she felt generous to those still in their seats.

"Jack." She leaned to her son's side and whispered for his attention, even as she smiled for the cameras. She would play Trooper's game today, the one that said they were a perfect family, united under the Holy Hand of God, the game that held the Kincaids up as a bastion of excellence the rest of the world could emulate, all because God had sanctified this family over and above other less deserving ones. Besides, she was beautiful, and this morning, she knew it. At fifty-three, it helped to have a designer dress covered in sequins to keep the focus off the fine lines around her eyes, but even so, she had no doubt about the splendid figure she cut in front of the television crews. She even did her own hair and makeup, and on this morning, she was proud of how good she looked.

"Mother?" Jeffrey kissed her on the top of her cheekbone, just below her eye.

"Your father must be frantic." She laced laughter into her words. However, she could see Jeffrey was equally anxious, and she knew he would feel her words were aimed at him, too. She patted one side of his face to soften her comment.

"How so, Mother?"

"Your sweet sister. She seems so far away on this beautiful Sunday morning . . . so far away, I cannot seem to make her out at all. Do you think she has been raptured?"

"Be sweet, Mother." Jeffrey grasped his mother's hand, and he squeezed it gently. "She's here already, and John's bringing her along."

Sharon laughed gaily and lightly, knowing her eyes sparkled in her well-applied mascara and tasteful eye shadow, and she kissed his hand, gently, of course, so that her lipstick remained unscarred. "I should not worry, then. Did you notice the pearls?" She patted one ear. "I wore them just for you."

"I love you, too, Mother. However, I also know pearls and rubies are all you wear. They do suit you, but then you know that." He touched the ring she wore. "See?"

Just then, the crowd began to chuckle at something Trooper said, and Sharon whispered, "I know this story. This one's about you, Jack. Remember? You took your sister across the country on your father's motorcycle. I was so frightened the whole time you were gone."

But she smiled. Other, darker things frightened her now, and for this one morning, she didn't intend to let any of them through to mar this perfect morning.

JEFFREY remembered. Lindsay had been fifteen, and he had already been away at college for four years, sleeping in his new bedroom in the Stone Creek mansion only a couple dozen times in all those years. He thought he had lost his little sister forever by that time. After the day he'd gone with her to clean up Rockaway Creek, she'd seemed to change, to distance herself from her family, her parents most of all. The church, too. It seemed she lost interest in Trooper Kincaid Christian Ministries after that, and being away so much, Jeffrey had seen it more clearly than the others. He caught the changes in flashes that were often months apart. Each time the difference was palpable, and he had felt his sister as more withdrawn than the time before.

The spring break before his graduation, he had come

home for two nights to finalize plans for his upcoming trip to Europe, his parent's graduation gift to him. He had been in the garage toying with his father's motorcycle, polishing the gleaming monstrosity. All four of the garage doors had been open, and the sunshine streaming inside had felt good.

Lindsay had stepped into the garage, a younger version of her mother. She had been wearing ragged jeans and a too-low tank top, and she had taken his breath away. She wasn't the little girl who used to jump on his bed any longer. When she tucked a strand of hair behind one ear, he saw what his mother must have been at the same age, and suddenly he knew he must do something to hold on to this sister he loved so very much.

"Come try it out, Lindsay." His voice was bright, as he swung a leg over the seat of the bike. It was low-slung and black, the essence of power. "Has Dad ever let you take this out?"

She laughed. "I'm fifteen, Jack. When has Dad ever let me do anything?" Her expression sparkled, even though there was something tortured behind her words.

"Get on, Lindsay." He jerked his head to emphasize his words. "See how it feels. Remember that old commercial we used to watch years ago? Try it; you might like it."

"Sure." She put her hands in her back pockets, and she moistened her bottom lip. However, she didn't move toward the motorcycle. Instead, she leaned back against her mother's car, also big, the largest model they made. Pushing her thick blonde hair back over one shoulder, she spoke to the floor. "I waited for Him that day.

Remember?"

"Waited?" He picked up the helmet hanging on the handlebars, and he began to polish it with his sleeve. It had been a long time since his sister had talked, really talked with him. He wanted it to happen today.

"At the creek. You remember; you were there." She raised her head and grinned. "You never did take your shirt off. All my friends wanted you to. They followed you like little ducklings. You can't have forgotten that. You were a madman that day, working like God wouldn't show up if you didn't make it all happen yourself."

He smiled into the helmet at her words, and he could see his resemblance to his sister in his reflection. No, he had not forgotten, but there had been other pressures crowding his mind during that cleanup. Only by keeping his hands very busy had he been able to get through that day, those intolerable minutes strung together along the banks of that creek. The thought of holding a small boy who looked like him had flooded through his thoughts continually.

He turned and glanced at Lindsay. "Get on. You can, you know. I don't bite." They had been very close once, and he was used to the feel of her arms across his shoulders. He missed that.

"Why?"

He knew he was being taken to task. Her tone was that of the old Lindsay. "Escape. That's what a motorcycle is, you know. It's not just two wheels and a motor. Those are simply the mechanics of the machine. What a motorcycle really is, is freedom. Get on. I think you need a bit of freedom."

She laughed, and tears began to flow down her cheeks. "Oh, big brother, you have no idea. For freedom, for *escape,* I'll do as you ask. Where's my helmet?" She sauntered to him, and slapping her hands on his shoulders, she swung one leg over to nestle at his back.

"Welcome, little sister. I've missed you the past few years." With the massive new church building the ministry had just bought, he knew he would be expected to show up each Sunday; and while he might see his sister more, seeing her was not what he wanted. He wanted to have her back, to enjoy the sister who had teased pitilessly with him, who had pushed him mercilessly just to get a response from him. He missed that Lindsay, and today, just for this moment, she was with him again.

"Where's my helmet, Jack?" Her voice was insistent this time. When he handed her the one he was holding, she slipped it on and clipped it under her chin. Then, with both arms around his torso, she leaned her head against him. "Anywhere, big brother. I'm willing. Take me anywhere; just don't leave me here."

"That bad, huh, Sis?" He paused, and then on a whim, he hit the starter. The big bike rumbled into life.

"Thanks, Jack. I've always loved you best, you know. I've missed you, and I've wanted to tell you that so many times. You're just so perfect, so untouchable, and I'm not perfect at all. God doesn't even like me, anymore. I thought maybe you didn't like me, either."

Jeffrey revved the motor, unsure how to respond. He was the imperfect one, the Kincaid who had made such a gross mistake at fifteen that sometimes he woke at night in heart-pounding fear, certain that his world was crashing down upon him. At those times, he felt just one day away from a DNA test that would prove he had betrayed his family's honor all those years ago.

"I'm not perfect, Lindsay." He whispered his words, though, and when Lindsay asked him what he'd said, he called out something entirely different.

"Hold on, little sister," and with a screech of tires, they were a black arrow shooting down a quarter mile driveway that looped through the trees, finally reaching the wrought iron and wooden gate that kept all intruders at bay. Then, as it dutifully swung aside, Jeffrey hit the gas, and the big bike surged onto the road, tearing the air as it took them where they needed to go, away, far away.

They did have to return, though. The bike was not Jeffrey's, and they had made no plans. It was exciting, however, and there was a new look of life on Lindsay's face as she sat behind her brother when he backed the bike into the garage. Taking her helmet off and handing it to him to hang on the handlebars, she leaned over and rested her head on his back once again.

"Thank you, Jack. It wasn't true freedom, but it was enough of a taste that I know it could be real. I needed to know that, to know that escape might be possible some-day. I might never make it out, but just to know it's there is important."

He felt wetness on his shirt that told of the tears that were leaking from her eyes.

"Go with me, Lindsay." His words were impulsive,

and he wasn't sure at that exact moment just what he meant. He did know he wanted to reconnect with his sister, and not just for a crazy half hour on his father's motorcycle.

"Go with you?" She chuckled, rubbing her hand across his back. "Where? Church? School? I'm only fifteen, Jack. Where would you take me? You're leaving for Europe this summer. Like Mom and Dad would let me do that."

That was exactly what he wanted, though. How great would it be to spend two months with her traveling to places they'd only heard of! Plus, he would be far away from little boys that were just now turning six. He wanted to know that boy sometimes, and at other times, he wanted to run far away. Even so, he knew his sister was right. His mother and father would not send her to Europe with him. And so, he shifted his plans to what was within his grasp.

"On this bike, Lindsay. Go with me on this bike." He said the words firmly and with conviction. He could do this, just take the bike, even if his father said no. He could. He knew it. For Lindsay, he would. This moment with his sister was that important.

"Now, Jack?" She laughed, and he could feel her hand as she reached to her face to wipe her eyes. "That sounds so good to me, even if we both know we can't. Thank you for the offer, though."

"This summer, Lindsay. All summer. We can do that." He looked out of the garage past the shadowy outline of the doorway, and he saw a redbird land on the asphalt. It hopped around for a moment, ignoring the two people in the garage, and after a bit, it snatched something from the ground. In a flicker of wings, it was gone as if it had never been there at all.

"Your trip, big brother. Europe." She whispered her words into his shirt. "You smell good, the same big brother I remember from so long ago. I miss your smell, just as I miss so many other things when you're not home."

Her words steeled his determination.

"I want you, Lindsay, not Europe. Can you understand that?" His words were suddenly tight and fast. "I'm not going to Europe. I'm taking Dad's bike to California, then to Oregon and Maine. Anywhere, and I'm not making any plans at all, just to go." He turned to look over his shoulder at his sister, grinning when she looked up to catch his eye. "Want to take a ride?"

She laughed and pulled her arms tighter around his waist, her expression quickly fading to misty eyes. "Don't tease me like that, Jack. I would want that too much to tease about it. Please start the bike again. I want to imagine you would really do that for me."

He did start the bike again, but later he also told his parents his change of plans. Now, on this Sunday morning, his father was regaling his audience with excerpts from that bike trip. The crowd was eating it up.

"Mother." Jeffrey touched her elbow with a smile, noticing the door at the back of the Family Altar. Someone emerged, and there stood his mother's beautiful mirror image, Lindsay, his sister. "It seems the rapture has left our loved one here for another day. Lindsay is just behind you, and in a cap, nonetheless."

Trust his sister to stir things up in the most original way possible.

SHARON turned and reached for her daughter's hand. She pulled her forward, extending one hand gently to touch the knit cap covering her hair.

"How charming, Lindsay." Her words were sweetly spoken, though. After all, Lindsay did look charming. She could look no other way, because she had her mother's beauty, and even in her most ragged moments, there was a charisma about her that no one could deny.

"It was John's idea. I ran late this morning."

"Yes, John takes good care of us." Sharon impulsively kissed Lindsay's cheek. She would have done so anyway, but at that moment, she noticed a camera pointed right at them, and the red light on the front had suddenly flickered on. "Camera," she whispered. "Smile."

She was pleased to see Lindsay do so. It lit up her face. At that moment, she saw Trooper turn to his glowing daughter to blow her a fatherly kiss. Stepping to join them, he gathered his two basketball players to his side, standing at the back of the group of six. In front, Sharon pulled Jeffrey to stand between her and Lindsay. What a picture she knew they made, three lanky basketball players in back, and three beautiful blondes in front. Even without looking, she could see Trooper crinkle his eyes as he began his family speech to the whole world.

"Welcome to the end of this Sunday's service at International Faith Center. I would like to introduce each member of my family to you and have them say a few words. First, I would like to present my charming daughter, Lindsay. Lindsay?"

Sharon watched the camera shift to the young woman in the knit cap. When she spoke, her eyes were clear and honest, and her words touched people's hearts. Trooper had said it before, and he was right. Lindsay was the one that rounded out his family, and without her, nothing would ever be right again.

IN THE SOUND booth, John arrived out of breath, just in time to see the camera shift to a full-screen shot of the beautiful young woman he had just delivered to the Family Altar. When her smile broke across her face, it was real, and no one could have said otherwise. For a moment, even he was convinced. Then, he leaned in to the monitor and chuckled, remembering Lindsay's request. "Damn, she's good." When the technician working the controls glanced at him with a puzzled look, John just winked. "It's a direct quote. My apologies. You have to know the whole story to understand."

He stood, his hand automatically reaching to his neck to ease the throbbing that no longer seemed to go away. It eased for a moment, and he let his hand fall away before it got there. He smiled. Lindsay was good for him. He felt like his old self, the one who used to play tennis and go camping in the woods. There was little doubt in his mind that once she excised the demons that haunted her, she would go far in life, and he would support her all the way

However, his stomach had begun to rumble, and until lunch was over, he would let himself think of nothing other than steak, not Lindsay, not tomorrow, and especially not the devil, himself, in the form of Mr. Bucky Simms, once again knocking at the ministry's door.

Chapter 7

SHARON stepped out of her shoes and tossed them into a corner of the log structure she had called home for the past three months. Private Drive No. 27 was on the Green Fork of Little Elbow Lake, only a short twenty minutes from the city. Reaching to the alarm controls at her side, she punched in her own personal code, knowing it would disengage the alarm sensors in the house as well as make sure the driveway gate was fully secured. She could also open the gate from this location in order to let people through, but right then, the afternoon belonged to Sharon and her beautiful, if oddly dressed, daughter. She wanted the gate closed.

With one hand, she removed her red Gucci sunglasses from her face, laying them on a side table. Then, with a practiced arm over her shoulder, a clasp was released, and the sequined dress fell at her feet, leaving the beautiful

Mrs. Kincaid standing in a vibrant, plum silk slip, one that was every bit as stunning as the designer dress she left lying on the floor. Stepping aside, she picked up the dress and shook it, tossing it over the arm of a chair.

Seeing Lindsay walk in, she chuckled, reaching to pull the knit cap from her head. "My heavens, Daughter. Where did you find this? It's so bohemian. I could use one just like it. Slip it on, and I would never have to do my hair at all. How magnificent!"

"Thank you, Mother."

Sharon gave her daughter a sharp look. Lindsay only called her "Mother" when she was irritated. Then, she frowned at Lindsay's hair. The cap had left it out of sorts and frumpy. "My word, does your hair really look that bad? I think you're turning into me." She laughed, and the sound was bright and quick, a jab that could be the pinnacle of praise or the knife blade of condemnation. It was a good day, though, so there was no meanness in it. That would come later when her week mired her in depression and self-pity, alone and without her family at her side. For now, she had her daughter with her, and this Sunday would be a good one.

"Would that be so bad, Mother?" Lindsay poked at her hair, mussing it more than anything else. She closed her eyes and dropped her hands to rub her shoulders.

"Not today, dear Lindsay. You can be me today. Just don't be me during the week. You wouldn't like yourself very much if you did." Sharon laughed and stepped to her daughter, reaching a finger to the edge of the girl's lips. "You were careless. Your lipstick isn't on straight."

"I didn't have a mirror. I did this blind." She pushed her mother's hand away. "I guess I should take it off. I'll borrow your cold cream . . . oh, I'm sorry." She smirked. "You only have cleansing cream, don't you? Only the best for the Kincaids. I'm headed to your bathroom to steal some. Then we'll have a wonderful mother-daughter afternoon, just you and me." She blew her mother a kiss, and her face was bright.

"Are your brothers joining us?" Wonderful mother-daughter afternoon? Sharon saw the transparent lie, but then she understood her daughter better than her husband did. She wrestled Lindsay's angry demons herself, or if not exactly the same ones, at least equally irate ones. She suddenly hoped the twins would come out. Jeffrey, too. Today she was up emotionally, proof that she no longer needed her medication. Her children would see, and word would get back to Trooper that God had performed one of His oh-so-holy miracles. He wouldn't call her deplorable any longer.

The click of the bathroom door latch was her answer.

"Your brothers?" Sharon repeated her question, knocking on the door. "Lindsay? Did they say if they planned to come out today?" She could hear water running on the other side.

"It's not locked, Mother."

Sharon twisted the knob and pushed the door back. "Fajitas, Lindsay. Will the boys want fajitas?" She leaned her head in to see just how the lipstick removal was progressing. "You, too? I have all the makings for fajitas."

"Fajitas?" Lindsay looked up from the sink to make an

awful face. "For a vegetarian? You must be teasing." She lifted a thick towel to pat her face dry. Refolding it to lay it beside the sink, she rubbed her hand across the embossed logo in the thick, terry fabric. "KCM. Why just KCM, Mother? Shouldn't you have put the ministry's full acronym onto the towels?"

"Space." She picked the towel up, squeezing the dampness that was still fresh from her daughter's face. "I tried for all four letters, and the manufacturer could only fit three. Three, barely. The space is very small." Her face brightened. "So, my towels just say Kincaid Christian Ministries. What's so bad about that? After all, your father's at the mansion all the time, and it's just your poor mother here. I guess it's rather appropriate, don't you think? KCM, just for me."

"Why not put just your initials on them, then?"

"Now, Lindsay," she chuckled. "That would be going too far, wouldn't it? Now, are you planning to wear that dress all day? It's so unlike my beautiful daughter to be in anything except jeans and a tank. You surprise me."

"I left my things in your car, Mother. Would you get them for me? If you don't mind, I might take time to shower after all, just a quick one."

"Take something from my closet, sweetie. It all fits you. Wear anything you want. It's all old stuff, anyway. You should choose quickly if you like anything. I'm donating everything I haven't worn in the past six months."

"Go, Mother. I'll pick your plainest jeans and the simplest top you have. Thank you, thank you. Call Cody.

He'll be here in a heartbeat if you promise him eggs with catsup on the side. If Cody comes, you can be sure his brother will be right here with him. You know you really had conjoined twins. It's just that no one can tell."

Sharon smiled at the picture of her seventeen-year-olds as conjoined, and her eyes grew damp with anticipation at seeing them again. "I will call, dear. Then, we can all go downstairs after we eat and have a swim. Do you think the boys will like that? I have suits for all of them. I want Jack here, though. Help me get him here, Lindsay."

"You want everyone?"

Sharon could only nod. She already sensed the signs that her good day had started to fade, and she didn't want it to. She had enjoyed being on the top of the world for the past few hours, and she didn't want to sink into the blackness that often consumed her for weeks at a time. She felt the signs, though, and she intended to fight to keep them at bay.

"Do you have any sushi?" Lindsay teased.

Sharon grimaced, knowing her daughter was quite well aware she didn't. Sushi repulsed her.

"Then you're out of luck, Mother. I guess Jack will spend the day with that debutante of his. What's her name? Celebration?" She put her hands on the counter, and she pressed her eyes tightly shut. It was a moment before she relaxed. "Oh, I don't mean that. I just feel jealous, sometimes. However, it certainly won't matter much longer." She smiled as she pushed at the corner of the enormous mirror that spanned the wall over the sink. Soundlessly, a large section of it swung aside to reveal an equally large medicine cabinet lined with bottles.

"Pshaw! You know better. You'll always be jealous of your brother." Sharon had seen Lindsay's "moment," but her daughter's barbed remark had lifted her mood once again. Her voice was bright, and her words rang with laughter. "It's Celadon, and you can call her Cookie, just as your brother does. Just think of her as a tasty treat. Now, into the shower, and I have phone calls to make. Good heavens, your father might even come!"

Lindsay wrinkled her nose, and with a deep sigh, she shook her head. "Round steak and onions. I can't believe you ever married a man who enjoys that." She barked out a rough laugh as she ran her eyes over the exposed bottles, pulling out one that was small and white. A smile grew on her face.

Sharon patted her daughter on the arm with a chuckle. "Maybe we shouldn't invite him after all. The smell of round steak and onions kills my appetite."

"And fajitas don't?"

"Shush! Perhaps it's your father that kills my appetite." Sharon could afford to tease for now. Tomorrow was when she would mean it. "Let's just enjoy the afternoon. I'll put your father to the test another time." She tapped manicured nails against the wood, nails that matched the sequins on the dress still draped over a chair in the living room.

"New polish?" Lindsay reached to touch one of her mother's nails. "Pretty color."

"New dress. They came together." She took a deep breath, and with a sudden, conscious determination, she smiled with anticipation. "Now, I'm leaving you, and your brothers will be here soon, even if I have to serve eggs and catsup with pizza flavored chips on the side. Go!" She stepped outside, pulling the door shut after her.

"YOU STILL don't understand, Two Points." John sat back in his chair and shook his head, reaching a hand to absently rub the base of his neck, right where it connected to his spine. However, the throbbing pressure was gone for now. His action was simply that of habit for an unwelcome friend.

He looked at the food on Trooper's plate and rolled his eyes. They were in the city's finest steak house. Overhead was a carved, wooden ceiling, coffered, nonetheless, with full, leaded crystal on the table. The chairs were top-grade leather with rolled arms and high, winged backs. The tables had white linen coverings. Even the dinnerware was solid silver, and still, the man had to order round smothered in onion.

"I do understand, John." Trooper held his fork in one hand and his knife in the other. With a swift, sure motion, followed quickly by a second, he carved a bite-sized section of meat from that on his plate, and he lifted it to his mouth. His expression was one of bliss as he placed it onto his tongue.

"How can you eat that? It makes me ill just to watch."

"You don't have to eat it. You just have to sit there. I eat it because it's good. Very flavor filled. Would you like to try it?" He held out his second bite to his friend, carefully balancing the strands of cooked onion on the morsel of meat. "It's yours if you want it."

When John made a face, Trooper laughed, placing the steak in his own mouth and chewing in delight.

"Nasty." John sliced into his own more expensive cut, carving away a sliver at a time, eating in small, manageable mouthfuls. "This is real food."

"It's a matter of taste. By the way, I do, too, understand. I just disagree that money's tight. God has no limits on the funds he provides. Do you ever pray, John?"

"That's a ridiculous question. Of course I pray."

"What for?"

John glanced away. He heard the amusement in Trooper's voice. Trooper had this knack of keeping his public persona very up and out for view anytime he was in the public eye. Even with his closest friends, he maintained it, and it was very convincing. It was only behind closed doors that he felt safe in letting it slip, and not always then. Now, it was as if they were giving a televised talk show, and Trooper was the host.

He took a deep breath and answered his friend's question. "For you, Two Points. I pray for you every day." He sliced into his steak once more, and spearing the wafer-thin morsel, he held it on his fork without placing it in his mouth. Just then, an aproned waiter, one he did not recognize, stepped up and bowed slightly.

"Would you like to see the wine list, sirs? We have a very good house cabernet sauvignon. May I bring you something?"

Trooper stifled a laugh as John glared at the man standing at their side. Then, he motioned with his hand, telling the waiter they were good, and no, they would not like to see the wine list.

"Doesn't that offend you, Trooper? He should recognize you. He must be a new hire. Would you like me to speak to the maître d'?"

"John, relax." Trooper reached and placed his hand on his friend's. "His was an honest mistake. Did the Good Lord curse the prostitute or the tax collector? No, because those were the very people he wanted to reach. Be kind. Now, back to our conversation. I appreciate your prayers. However, those I know about. Anything else?"

John glanced down at the hand lying on his own. He felt his pulse quicken, and his neck warmed. As the heat moved towards his face, he so wanted to pull his hand free. This was Trooper, though, and he couldn't.

"I'm sorry, John. I seem to have embarrassed you. My apologies?" Trooper lifted his hand, and he chuckled.

"No, Two Points." The words were rough coming out, and he cleared his throat before continuing. "What you did was fine. You were reassuring me, and I appreciate your thoughtfulness. It's just that it's suddenly warm in here, and I need to catch my breath."

"Warm, John?" Trooper laughed, and his eyes crinkled as he watched his friend wipe his hands on his napkin. "Are your hands sweaty, too? Those are all the classic signs of a man in the presence of a beautiful woman. Who is she?" He glanced around the room conspiratorially. Any number of attractive women were in the room, and several were alone. Whispering, he leaned forward, "Is it finally time to give love another chance? You're what, fifty-three, fifty-four—"

"The same as you," John interjected. He pressed his lips together. This was not a subject he wanted to discuss.

"—which is still quite young. There's many a woman who would jump at the chance for your hand. Don't let that bimbo from twenty years ago spoil you on marriage forever." He winked at him. "Marriage has its finer points."

"Not for me, Two Points. Trust me." He took a deep breath, looking directly at Trooper. He smiled, belying the sudden pressure he felt at his temples. He hoped it stayed away from his neck. Dear God, he hoped that.

"Are you sure, John? After all, there's no more glorious place for a man than to be between a woman's breasts. You're missing out. You've been married. You know what I'm talking about."

He did, too. However, his marriage had been his attempt to reconnect with his best friend after Trooper's marriage. Once Trooper and Sharon were married, Trooper's focus had changed. It had been couples this and couples that. His own attempt at marriage had worked, too, at least at first, throughout the bachelor parties and the wedding rehearsals. Then had come the marriage bed, and he hadn't been quite so successful at that. The first few nights, he had been able to chalk up his ineffectiveness to bashfulness and inexperience. Eventually, the vows had been consummated, but the actual act had been lackluster on his part. His new wife realized that, but what had really blown the marriage apart eight months later was when he had been at the height of his passions and cried Trooper's name out in the dark.

Trooper had never even questioned him on why his marriage had fallen apart after just eight months. John worshipped Trooper for that, but he loved him, always. Yes, he knew what Trooper was talking about, but that held no interest for him.

"Back to prayer, Two Points. Why were you asking?" He needed to shift the conversation to safer ground.

"I love my family, John. I hold them up in prayer every day. Do you think I do that because I believe, or because I think all this is a sham?"

"A sham?" Lindsay's words floated through his mind, haunting him. "You believe, Two Points. You must, or you couldn't do what you do."

"That's my boy." He laughed. "I appreciate your confidence."

"Why did you use the word sham, Two Points?" His interest in his steak was gone. It had been far too much to eat, anyway, but now he didn't care about the meal or about the fancy room they were in. Trooper had his attention; he was doing to him what he always did to anyone who listened to him speak, what he did at the pulpit each Sunday morning. He was winning him over.

"Oh, forget sham, John. My point is that we pray for what's important to us, and God provides." Trooper smiled, and it was filled with confidence.

"What do you mean by that, Two Points?" He knew Trooper's words weren't exactly true. A scene flashed through his mind of two teenaged boys in a tent, one regaling the other with stories far into the night, exhausting his friend until he crashed into a deep, dreamless sleep. He'd prayed earnestly over a time span of forty years for something more, and it had never happened.

"What does the Word say, John? Do you remember? Let me paraphrase it this way. If the funds are not here, then they're on the way. God provides. You know that's Biblical. So, the ministry's a little short right now. We borrow. So, my wife spends a bit much on clothes. My point is, God provides, and it all works out in the end." Casually, Trooper reached out and covered John's hand again. "You're my best friend, one I've had for a lifetime. Do you trust me?"

He could only nod. With that touch of Trooper's skin on his own, his blood churned through his veins, and his vision clouded until that hand was all he could see. Finally, he had to pull back. They were no longer kids, and he didn't have Trooper alone in a backwoods tent. All he had was a friend who trusted him, and he couldn't allow his own wants and desires to take even that from him.

"Good." Trooper seemed satisfied with his friend's response. "Now, let's get back to our steaks. We still have tonight, and while my family might be able to skip out on the evening services, I must be forefront and dead center. I can't do my job on an empty stomach. Eat, John."

John did, but he no longer enjoyed it. The ministry's finances were falling apart faster than a dandelion in a summer breeze, and no one was curbing the spending. That frightened him. It frightened him a lot. After all, if Trooper were thrown to the wolves, what would happen to those close to him? John didn't need his life dissected and inspected through a microscope. He had things in his past he didn't want exposed, some of which had happened a long time ago in an old tent in the woods shared with a teenaged friend, and this threatened to do exactly that.

CODY KINCAID snatched the ball from his brother's hand and twirled 360 degrees. Three bounces later, he jumped and slammed it into the basket at the side of the driveway. They'd arrived home, only to find they were locked out of the house with a dead garage door opener. Waiting on someone to let them in, they'd pulled an old basketball from the bed of the black F250 their parents forced them to share.

"Time out!" Casey Kincaid's breathing was labored, and he stopped to catch his breath. "Traveling this time, and you can't deny it. I counted your steps."

"Hey, I resemble that, wimp!" Cody grabbed the ball and jumped once again to violently slam it into the basket a second time. "I'm just better than you." Panting, he darted beside his brother and patted the side of his face, then he laughed, and with quick feet, he pounded the ball all around him, daring him to take it.

"Yeah, when you're cheating." Casey dropped onto the asphalt and leaned against the stainless steel clad garage door. "Take a break, Bro."

Casey was the better player of the two. That was a given. He'd proven it when he shot the final basket for the winning points at the state championship the previous year. His failing? He found it difficult to press his advantage too hard against a favorite brother, and for that reason, his coaches often labeled his performances as brilliant but erratic.

Cody had no such compunctions. His real goal was to be in the pros, and if he had to romp on his brother's game to build his skills, then romp he would do.

"Can't you play in the heat, Casey?" Cody slapped a big hand against his brother's knee. "Too weak for a real game?"

"Not a fair one. Besides, I'm hungry. Text Dad and see where he is. I bet he went to lunch with Uncle John, and they won't be home for hours."

"You text him. I'm busy with my game." Cody laughed, slamming the ball onto the driveway and standing back as it flew upwards through the hoop.

"I left my phone on the counter this morning. I can't." Casey reached up and ran a hand through his hair. "C'mon, Cody."

"Mine's in the truck, if you want it. If he's with Uncle John, they won't come home at all. Bet on it. We're here alone. Get it? Home alone? Want to grease a staircase?"

"Grow up. That was a movie. No one does that in real life. Here, you call." He jumped up, reaching inside the truck and grabbing the phone from the dash, and he tossed it at his brother. "Catch!"

In midair, the phone began to ring, and Cody grabbed it with one hand just as easily as he would have palmed a basketball in play. With a singular, smooth motion, he flipped the phone over and pressed the talk icon.

"Howdy. Future pro-baller Cody Kincaid, here. Do

you have my contract ready to sign?" He shot his brother a thumbs-up sign, smirking all the while.

"Cody, this is your mother. Is Casey there with you?"

"Hey, Mom. You want to talk to him? Here he is," and without waiting on her reply, he tossed the phone back. "Mom wants you. I bet Lindsay's there. See what's for lunch." Cody tossed the ball into the air, caught it, and shot it directly into the basket, cheering with an arm punched into the sky.

Casey was already back in the truck. "Yeah, Mom?" He looked through the windshield at his brother and grinned. "Eggs for Cody and pizza chips for me? Yeah, we'll be there." He paused a moment, listening, and then he laughed into the phone. "The opener's dead, and we don't know where Dad's at. We're starving. We'll be right there."

"Hey, let me have the phone." Cody reached through the window, grabbing it, and putting it to his ear. "Mom? Is the pool warm?" He glanced up at his brother and shot him another thumbs-up, with a grin. "It will be? Good. Don't forget to start the heater before you begin the food. Thanks. Bye, Mom." He tossed the phone in the air as if he were shooting a basket, catching it as it came down.

"And? We're swimming, too?"

"Yeah, Bro. You, me, and everyone else we can fit in this truck. I'm not going out there by myself. Mom and Lindsay are there together. If Mom's not crazy depressed, Lindsay will be. I want moral support."

"Whatever you say, big brother. If you like 'em, I'll swim with 'em. Mom didn't invite Dad, then?" He glanced away, looking down the drive.

Cody slapped him upside the shoulder. "Hey, Case. Cheer up. We have food waiting on us, and Mom's heating the pool. Besides, you know Dad loves Uncle John and his church more than us. He's not coming home just because our opener is dead."

"Don't say that. Dad loves us, Cody." He blinked rapidly, wipe at one eye with a lifted shoulder. "You know it, too."

"Yeah, right. Move over, Case. Food's on. Besides, we still have to pick up whoever we're taking along." Then, he threw open the truck door and leaped inside, shoving his brother on the shoulder. "Case! Move! I'm hungry!"

"I'm moving," he called. As his brother slipped on his black Oakleys, he grimaced. "All I have with me are my Ray Bans."

His brother pulled off his sunglasses and handed them to his brother. "I resemble those glasses. Trade for the day?"

He grinned. Then his brother reached in the glove box and pulled out a second pair of Oakleys.

"I came prepared. I always watch out for you, Case. You know that."

Then, the truck roared to life, and with spinning tires, the two were off to gather their friends. They had a swim party to attend, and food would be there, too. At seventeen, that made it about as good as it could get.

Chapter 8

CELADON "Cookie" Hamilton sat at her family's dining table next to her fiancé and across from her parents. She brushed one half of an old-fashioned pageboy from her temple, hooking the hair over one ear. The cut was stunning, suiting her perfectly, although she never thought of it that way. It was just a good look for her face. On her exposed earlobe, a substantial diamond glittered. Another one, larger, sparkled around her neck. Her eyes caught the stones' clarity, sparkling, and to set it all off, her skin glowed. Of course, Esteé Lauder, direct from Neiman-Marcus, helped. Quality makes one look like quality, Mrs. Hamilton always told her daughter, even when it comes to the makeup one buys.

Through the expanse of floor-length windows that covered one wall, and past the great sweep of lawn that stretched down to the street, a long limousine floated past, its brake lights flashing as it pulled into the drive opposite the Hamilton's sumptuous home. The bright midday sun glinted off the car's rear window, just for an instant catching in Cookie's eyes. After a moment, the taillights dimmed, and the big car pulled past a large set of stone pillars. A gate slowly closed after it.

"Mrs. Burke is home, I see." Cookie smiled, and she lifted her napkin to dab one corner of her mouth.

"Mrs. Burke?" Jeffrey looked out the window, as the taillights disappeared into the trees.

Mr. Hamilton leaned toward him. "She's been at her son's in Anaheim, and she always hires a car for the trip in from the airport. I think she's bringing her grandson home with her for the week."

"Little Bennie is so cute." Cookie laughed, remembering him from a previous visit. She placed her hand on Jeffrey's arm. She was reminded of Memphis, and her aunt and uncle. "I met the cutest little boy at Uncle Jim's this week."

"I'd forgotten, dear. You stopped in on the way back from Paris. You must tell us everything." Mrs. Hamilton smiled warmly. Her eyes glowed, also, for she was her daughter's mother. It helped that their makeup was the same brand. Her dessert plate still rested in front of her, and she gently set it aside. "Are you listening, Father?"

"Yes, Mother." Mr. Hamilton nodded his head toward his wife, but he winked at Jeffrey. "I'm listening."

Jeffrey could only watch Cookie and grin.

"You will not believe me when I tell you about Uncle Jim's and Aunt Bonnie's. It's all about you, Jeffrey." She squeezed his arm before pulling her hand away.

"About me?" He sat up a little straighter. "I've not met your Uncle Jim or your Aunt Bonnie."

"Cookie, shall we retire to the living room before you begin your story? It sounds as if we could use softer cushions. Six courses! I think I'll need to let out my belt, or I may not be able to concentrate at all. How about you, my boy?" Mr. Hamilton patted his stomach to make his point, looking directly at Jeffrey.

"I told Betts you wouldn't be able to resist dessert. I saw you take a double helping." Mrs. Hamilton chided her husband. Unspoken was the fact that Betts Fitzgerald had been with them since before Cookie could walk, and she knew every nuance of the Hamilton's preferences.

"Three helpings." He winked at Jeffrey.

"Cookie, dear." Mrs. Hamilton chuckled, placing her hand on her husband's, looking from his face to her daughter's. "You must tell us your story, and quickly. Your father will soon have us in front of the television, and he'll snore us to death."

Mr. Hamilton shook his head. "I'm not going anywhere I don't have permission to go. Now, Cookie. What is this unbelievable story you wish to tell?"

"Go on, Cookie," a voice filtered in from the kitchen. "You've got me on pins and needles. Tell it loud enough for the help to hear."

Mr. Hamilton called out, "Betts, you might as well come on in here. This girl is too enamored of her new fiancé to get to her story. I don't want you to wear out your knees before you get the kitchen clean."

The kitchen door swung open, and a middle-aged woman wearing a white apron stepped into the dining room. "I believe I will, Mr. Hamilton, that is if Mrs. Hamilton don't mind. I can take this empty chair right here." Betts paused for a moment with a prim expression on her face, and at Mrs. Hamilton's nod, she pulled out the chair and sat. Looking at Cookie, she nodded curtly. "Get to it, girl. Like your daddy says, I got a kitchen to clean."

"The floor's all yours, Cookie," Jeffrey grinned with anticipation written all over his face.

"Well, you know how Uncle Jim has midweek church services in his living room. I've told you, Jeffrey. Remember?" She put one hand under her chin, smiling, as she absently reached to move her napkin to her plate, and when she set them aside, the plate bumped her water goblet. For a moment, it seemed it might fall.

"Careful, girl." Without a blink, Betts reached and moved it back a safer distance.

"I'm just jittery with excitement." Cookie used both hands to push her hair from her face. Her earrings glittered for a moment before her hair fell back into place, gracefully draped in the exact same position as before.

"Go on." Jeffrey reached and took her hand in his.

"Well, there was this couple there, older, you know, and they had this boy with them. He was adorable." Her words died off, and she felt her face warm. It had all seemed so magical in Memphis. Now, she felt silly with what she intended to say. She looked at Jeffrey and then to her parents. They were so *expectant*, and for a moment she was unsure of herself.

Betts interrupted the silence with a laugh. "I see where this is going, girl. You know you can't bring him home. You and Jeffrey got to have your own. Remember that when you see other people's children. Parents don't give up their kids to just no one."

"Oh, Betts, they weren't even his parents." She looked out the window for a moment, watching but not really seeing a big black Mercedes drive by. "The saddest thing happened. The boy's parents were killed just under a week ago, in a house fire right here in the city, only the little boy was spending the night at a friend's. Uncle Jim let the four of us sit at the kitchen table and visit after everyone else was gone, and I found out the little boy was adopted when he was a tiny baby. Poor thing. Even his parents weren't his real parents. The people he lives with now aren't even his legal guardians. They were just the only people he could go to. It was so sad."

"Cookie, honey." Betts patted her hand. "Why are you telling your parents this? Does the boy need their help?"

"I'm not sure. Anyway, that's not really what I wanted to tell you—"

"My father requested prayer for a family just this morning at the end of the service," Jeffrey interrupted. "This might even be the same boy. If so, I'm sure people in the church will help in any way they can."

"Oh, no," Cookie began, smiling in renewed excitement. She could just see the boy's face, and her earlier doubts were gone. "I don't know that they need money." She touched her ring, fingering the massive diamond Jeffrey had given her. "It's possible, but I don't think so."

"What, dear?" Her mother pursed her lips, reaching a hand to her daughter, although not quite touching her.

"The couple are retired and live in a one bedroom apartment, so he sleeps on the sofa, but I suppose a boy might like that." She brightened again. "Oh, I wanted to bring him home to meet you, Jeffrey."

"Now, Cookie," her mother laughed, pulling her hand back. "Remember, this boy is not yours, and he is not Jeffrey's. You leave him in Memphis."

"She knows that, Mother." Mr. Hamilton smiled and put his hand on his wife's.

"Tell us, Cookie." Jeffrey grasped her hand in his. He grinned, his eyes locked on hers. "What was so special about this boy?"

"He was you, Jeffrey. Really, in every way."

JEFFREY'S face went numb as his heart raced at Cookie's words, a long-ago statement by a much younger woman springing unbidden into his thoughts. *He looks just like you.* It had been nine years, but almost every day he was haunted by those words.

"How do you mean?" His words twisted sourly from his throat, but his expression was frozen, his smile carefully held in place. He still hoped this story might be just that, an odd tale about an unusual coincidence. Then, his brain pieced together exactly what Cookie had said. Not *looked* like him. Cookie had said the boy *was* him. His stomach churned, and his temples began to pound.

"How interesting," Mrs. Hamilton remarked. "What do

81

they call that? A doppelganger? I read spy novels, you see, and that's an old spy term for someone who looks just like another person. I love this story. Tell us more, Cookie. How old was the boy? Four? Five?" She turned to Jeffrey and touched his arm. "If this elderly couple has no room for him, perhaps your family could take him until they find him a proper home, Jeffrey. He would fit right in. How would that be? Now, how old was he, Cookie?"

"Twelve, Mother. A small twelve, but he had Jeffrey's eyes, and his hair, and even that cute little grin of Jeffrey's that I love so much." She pulled one hand free and stroked his frozen expression. "I seem to remember you saying you were small at twelve, Jeffrey."

She turned and looked at her mother. "I even talked to the boy. His name is, um, Jackie or Jack, I think. Don't your siblings call you that, Jeffrey?" She winked at Betts, grinning. "When I first saw him, I actually wondered whether Jeffrey might have a younger brother I hadn't met. I know that was a silly thought, but he looked enough like Jeffrey that he could be, or I don't know my Jeffrey's face at all."

"Now, Dear, I think we would have heard about that." Mrs. Hamilton's lips fought a smile.

Jeffrey hardly heard the discussion. His thoughts were a whirlwind, interspersed with the name Jack, being twelve, and adoptions that matched too closely to one he was familiar with. No, Mrs. Hamilton, he managed to piece together in his thoughts. I don't think you would have heard about that. Not a younger brother, anyway.

Finally, Cookie seemed to notice the frozen look on

82

his face, and at that point, her voice began to falter. "I mean . . . I . . . some people find brothers they never knew they had . . . I mean, just, he was so much like you, Jeffrey."

She looked at her parents, and her eyes were red. "I've said the wrong thing, haven't I? Jeffrey's parents . . . they're important pastors of a big church . . . they wouldn't do that to one of their own children, would they? I shouldn't have ever suggested that of them." Tears suddenly flooded down her face. "Jeffrey?"

Her voice had become a quavering whisper, and now, with a wail, she leaped from the table and ran from the room.

"Cookie," Mrs. Hamilton called. She jumped up to follow her, her voice fading into the hall after her. "Cookie, it was just a coincidence, and you were mistaken. Jeffrey understands."

Jeffrey's mind was calculating, though. He had graduated from college six years earlier. He'd been a freshman when he was told he had a son. The boy had been three at that time. Even in the groggy haze his mind was plowing through, he knew those numbers added up to twelve. His fiancée had found his son. It had to be him. He was in Memphis, and Jeffrey could find the boy, see him, know him, this child who looked exactly like him.

Yet, he knew there was another side to this news. His son could also find him. People could demand a DNA test, and they would *know*. The news roiled inside his gut, and suddenly he did not feel well at all.

"Jeffrey?" Mr. Hamilton reached to gently pat the

young man's wrist. "Cookie was mistaken, that's all. She didn't mean anything against your family. We know they're good, upstanding people. We've visited at your father's church numerous times. This is all a misunderstanding." He squeezed Jeffrey's arm in reassurance.

Jeffrey knew better, though. This boy was his, this boy who lived in Memphis, and his fiancée had spoken to him. He suddenly wanted to see this boy, and yet at the same time, he wanted him to go away forever. He wanted this son he had helped create, and yet he knew that to acknowledge the boy as his own was also to wreck his life forever. Wracked with indecision and overwhelmed with the massive debt of responsibility that had been surreptitiously dumped upon him, Jeffrey's body could take no more. With a great thrust of upheaval, everything he had eaten during the meal disgorged itself onto the dining room table.

"You poor baby!" Betts jumped up immediately and pulled her apron from her waist. With a practiced hand, she surrounded the offending offal, gathering it into a mound, and covering it to get it out of sight.

Jeffrey sat there, his shirt splattered with his own vomit. Mr. Hamilton expressed his dismay that his prospective son-in-law had become unexpectedly ill and had not told them. Still, Jeffrey could think only of three things. Adopted, twelve, and Memphis. His son.

"Good heavens!" Mrs. Hamilton walked back into the room. She rushed to Jeffrey and placed a hand on his shoulder. "You're sick, Jeffrey, and you sat through dinner so bravely. See this, Father?" She looked at her husband.

"What a stoic young man our Cookie has picked! He wasn't upset at her story at all. He was simply ill. I know Cookie will be so relieved. Come, Jeffrey. Let's put you on the sofa until you feel better."

As she helped him stumble into the living room to lie on her $10,000 sofa, her words could be heard prattering all the way into the dining room where Betts was cleaning up the remains of Jeffrey's meal.

"I cannot believe how wonderful you are, Jeffrey. Who else would have sat through that entire dinner while feeling like you did? You are an absolutely perfect young man, and my Cookie is so very lucky. I am going in there to tell her that very thing. Perhaps the next time she goes to see her uncle and aunt in Memphis, you can just go along and meet her little boy. They live on Perkins Extended, right off Poplar. Cookie knows. She can get you there. Why, they even have a pool, and you can swim with him, right there in the back yard, all night, if you wish. Wouldn't that be fun? You never know what could come of an experience like that. You might find a family you never knew you had. Cookie is so fortunate to have found such a perfect young man."

Jeffrey's thoughts were quite different, though. He's twelve, and he's in Memphis. That and DNA test. What if someone asks for one?

Exhausted, he finally dozed on the chenille and brocade of Mrs. Hamilton's very expensive sofa, and his sleep was fitful. He kept meeting himself at twelve years old, and each time he would ask himself if he were his father. He kept telling himself no, and every time it broke his heart. Yet, in spite of the pain, he could not stop himself, and he began yelling no over and over, wishing his twelve-year-old self would go away, and each time, all he wanted to do was cry.

JOHN'S POCKET vibrated, and he set his fork down on his plate. As his coat sleeve shifted, one cufflink caught the light and sparkled. The restaurant had filled, and there was no way to answer this call here, especially as the establishment had a firm rule against private phones at the dining tables. However, his appetite was long gone, and when his electronics beckoned, he felt compelled to attend. Who knew how important this call might be?

"Two Points, it's my phone." He flashed his boyish grin and winked, patting the pocket of his neutral, cutting-edge suit. While very tasteful, the cut was in the latest sartorial style, an edgy one that only those familiar with current fashion trends would recognize. It added to an air of affluence that John felt exemplified God's blessings to his chosen people, or that's what he wanted people to believe. For John, his clothing helped make him into the man he wished he could be, rather than the man he sometimes knew he really was. Pushing his chair back, he stood and strode quickly to the bar where phones were out en masse—and even encouraged—as house betting on televised games with patrons' phones had become a very popular pastime, raking in even more profit than what the restaurant provided.

John pulled out his phone as he stepped through suited power brokers and western-attired landowners alike. Even a number of women were punching in numbers on their hand-held devices, either laughing or cursing when the final results scrolled across the television displays. Reaching a relatively quiet area of booths covered in deep-brown distressed leather, he looked at the display in his hands to see who was calling, but only the number was there. He accepted the call and put his phone to his ear.

"John, here."

The device was silent for a moment, and then a rustling noise was heard. John fiddled with his diamond cufflinks as he waited. He loved cufflinks and even had tie tacks to match, all in diamonds. The more the better, he thought with smug satisfaction.

"Sorry, John. It's Kaffe. Give me a moment."

Silence reigned for another space, and the honk of a horn could be heard over the phone.

"Kaffe?" John twisted one cufflink just to see it sparkle.

"There. I'm in the truck, John, and I was being cut off. I know this is bad timing for me to call, because I've probably caught you at lunch, but I wanted to let you know. Keith's headed out to the Kincaid's lake house."

"Keith Richardson?" If Keith Richardson was headed to the lake house, John suspected he knew why, and he needed to get someone out there fast for intervention's sake. He felt the returning pressure at the back of his head, and he took a deep breath to help himself push it aside.

"What other Keith do you know?" Carlson "Kaffe" Rodriguez sighed loudly. "Yeah, he overbooked his day yesterday, taking on an interview for a prospect up at that new high rise complex down on the river. It ran all day, and he didn't have time to get out to the Kincaid property. It seems the sprinklers aren't feeding up from the lake properly. Sharon called it in on Friday . . . or maybe it was Thursday. I don't recall, and the paperwork's back in the office. Anyway, do you know if anyone's out there today? Being Sunday, he thought he might have the place to himself."

"Sprinkler work on a Sunday, Kaffe?" John's voice was flat. With Sharon holed up at Little Elbow Lake, Keith wouldn't have the place to himself at all, and God knew, that old romance didn't need to flare up again.

Kaffe let out a series of mild profanities. When he quieted down, he immediately apologized. "Sorry. Idiot Sunday drivers. You'd think they could see my truck. It's got four doors, it's bright red, and it's taller than anything else on the road. They must be blind. Anyway, does he need to stop somewhere to get a key to get onto the property? I've not been out there since the security installation was completed, and I'm no longer sure about access procedures."

John looked up as a waiter in a very crisp, pocketed apron approached him with a drink menu, and he waved him away, pointing at his phone. The man nodded with a smile, slipping the leather-bound tome back into one of his pockets and moving on.

John was glad for the distraction. He was pretty sure Keith Richardson knew just who he'd find out at the lake. After all, Keith was in Trooper's inner circle . . . sort of, anyway. The man was more in Sharon's inner circle, attending any social or church functions where she would also be present. It had never been a problem before Sharon moved full-time to the lake house. Keith had come to the mansion for dinner parties, golfed with Trooper, and even spent time with the family at the lake house, swimming in the pool and enjoying time with the children. During all those times, he had been . . . well . . . supervised. Today at the lake house, there was no one around to provide that service.

John pressed his fingers into the back of his neck, pushing hard. He could have done without this call. Even so, this was what he did, so it might be time for him to check in with Sharon to see if she could use his help for the afternoon. After all, Keith's interest in the lake house might be totally innocuous. Maybe. Still, it wouldn't hurt to make sure.

"John?" Kaffe pressed him for an answer. "A key? You are still there? I don't care to talk to a dropped call."

"Oh, yeah, Kaffe. Sure, Keith can get onto the property. It's all on keypad, now. Let me give you the codes. I'd be surprised if he doesn't have them already."

"He might at that. He said he wasn't worried about access, that he's been out there several times over the past three months tweaking the landscaping infrastructure. However, given that I've not been there since the gate went in, I wanted to be sure."

"Then you think you don't need them?" Just for a moment, hope rose that Keith would not actually have access. If he called, John could warn him away. "You can have Keith ring me if he gets there and is locked out."

"Hey, you'd better give me the codes anyway, just in case. That way I won't have to bother you again."

"Sure. Here." It was a nice try, anyway. John rattled off the two temporary construction codes he'd loaded into the system, hating the idea that he hadn't known about the earlier visits out to the lake property. "Several times he's had to be out there, right, Kaffe? I guess I should have checked the log."

"Maybe." Kaffe paused, but then his voice took on a puzzled tone. "Never had a series of issues like this before. The supplier must have shipped us some faulty irrigation equipment. It just shows how important extended warranties are. Everyone should have them on everything they own."

"Sure." The word was an easy response, as John drummed his fingers on the leather tabletop. The surface ate up the noise, and he supposed that was exactly why it had been designed that way. The whole place was muted, moneyed, and very high class. He just hoped that out at the lake house, Keith and Sharon went for at least two out of the three. Muted and very high class, enough so that they didn't do anything improper. Moneyed? The ministry was struggling with that right now, so he'd let that alone.

"John, is everything okay? You seem distracted." Another honk came in over the phone, and Kaffe cursed again. "I've got to get off this freeway. Why do they build them if no one can drive on them? I'm sorry. I've got to go, John. Thanks for the codes. I'll get them to Keith. Later." His voice was gone.

John stood, and he looked at the electronic device in

his hand for a moment before slipping it into his pocket along with several other similar devices. Then, he glanced up at the well-dressed people around him, the women in their jeweled accoutrements, and the men with high-polished shoes and vested suits. In them, he saw things he knew might or might not be there. Illicit desires, porn or gambling addictions, or even spousal abuse that occurred behind closed doors. How easy it was to dress in one's finest and brave the world with a smile, while inside, a maelstrom oozed through one's soul.

He knew how people could hide what they really were. He did it every day. Putting his smile back on his face, he stepped back into the subdued atmosphere of the restaurant, striding confidently up to the linen-covered table, and seating himself once again across from his closest friend. When Trooper looked at him quizzically, John smiled and picked up his fork, placing the meat he had already cut into his mouth.

"This is the best, Trooper. We should come here more often."

"More often?" Trooper chuckled. "More often than twice a week? I know a distraction when I hear one. Who was on the phone?" His plate was already gone, and he had a steaming cup of coffee in its place. He raised it to take a sip.

"Landscapers. I need to head out to Little Elbow for a short time once we leave here." John made his words light and offhand. He had to. Trooper didn't need to know about this.

"Landscapers?" Trooper's broad forehead frowned.

"Keith, you mean?"

"Nah." John's reassurance was easy and believable. "That was Kaffe on the phone. You've met him, Keith's partner. He was already in the company truck and needed the codes to the gate."

Then it struck John what he'd just told Trooper. If Kaffe had the truck, what could Keith possibly have planned to do at the property? Surely he would take the truck if he were there to work on something. John's heart began to pound with anxiety, and he knew he needed to get away soon, for Sharon's sake as well as for Trooper's.

Trooper's face relaxed. "Kaffe." He chuckled. "I like him. Sure, John. You head out to the lake, and I might head home for a while. Maybe the twins will be there. It's been months since I've played a good game of pickup with them. They'd enjoy that." He looked at his watch. "It's even early enough I'd still have time to shower afterwards before evening services. Do you think my bum knee will take it?" He paused for a moment with a grin, watching John halfheartedly slice another piece of his steak. When John didn't respond, his smile faded. "John?"

"What?" He didn't look up.

"Do you think I give my boys enough of my time?"

John finished slicing the meat, and he raised it halfway to his mouth. He hated that question. He knew Trooper didn't give them enough time. Cody and Casey needed face time with their father, and that didn't mean wandering the upper tiers of the auditorium while Trooper ministered from the platform. They needed him at home, sitting around the house, unshaven, and in his pajamas. They needed him to be at their games, to see them win—and lose. He remembered one time Trooper had engaged in a disastrous verbal fight with his daughter, then accepted an out-of-town speaking engagement, just to avoid attending her upcoming birthday party. Look how Lindsay had turned out. No, his boys did not get enough of his time, not by a long shot. How did he say that, though?

"They're good kids, Two Points. You don't have to worry about them." He looked down to his plate, however. It was a half answer.

Trooper tapped the table to get his attention. "That's not what I asked, John. I'm an important man with an influential ministry. Everyone tells me what he or she thinks I want to hear, and I need someone who tells me what I need to hear. You've been that for me. Don't turn sissy on me now."

Sissy. That got John's attention, and his eyes jerked to Trooper's. The word hit too closely to home, and his stomach twisted. Was that how Trooper saw him? A sissy? This man was his hero, a man who had been a high school basketball star, who could have gone to the pros. His only disqualification had been a bad knee injury received during that final state championship game, a game that he had continued to play in spite of the pain, and he thought of him as a sissy?

John took a drink of his water and swallowed, his emotions compromised. He felt belittled, and he wondered if, to Trooper, he really looked like a sissy, a man who couldn't even remain between the breasts of the woman he'd married without imagining his best friend in bed with his own wife.

Then, Trooper's hand clapped him on the shoulder, and the lanky man laughed. "Come on, John. I'm teasing. Seriously, though, answer me honestly. Do you think I spend too little time with my boys? Cody and Casey, I mean. I see Jack at the church each day. If I married that boy, I'd see less of him than I do now." He took a deep breath. "They're seventeen, you know. That's an important age. That's why I want to play some ball with them, remind them I'm still their father."

"They do miss you." He could say that without stepping too hard on his friend's pride. "Casey, especially. He lost Jeffrey when his brother moved out ten years ago, and then Lindsay was gone seven years later. They've been alone for three. Yes, I think Casey misses you most."

"Not Cody?" Trooper's eyes became very intent. "The boys are identical. How could one need me more than the other? Even at seventeen, people have a hard time telling them apart, so why just Casey?"

John chuckled and toyed with his steak. The first part of his answer was easy. "Everyone is Cody's friend. You've seen him around the church. He doesn't meet anyone, but they're a best friend immediately." Before going on, he clicked his tongue against his cheek. This second part of the answer would hit closer to home. "You are the one who's Casey's friend. You, Two Points. He admires you. He misses you." He hoped Trooper took that well. Here in public, it was hard to tell. All this was still Trooper's public face, and he wore it well.

Trooper abruptly stood. "I will go home. You head to

the lake to help out Kaffe, and I'll play a game with my boys." He grinned and held his hand out to shake. "You've been a big help, John. Without you, I'd be dead in the water. I owe my family to you."

John smiled and returned the handshake, but as he watched Trooper walk boldly toward the exit, taking just a moment to speak to the maître d', he considered the truth of the man's words. If John didn't get to the lake house before Keith, Trooper might be deader in the water than he thought. It was all up to him, now.

He raised his hand, and their waiter immediately walked to the table to lay a leather-covered folder at his side. John opened it and signed his name. There was no bill inside. Copies of what they'd ordered and how much it cost would show up in the restaurant's monthly statement. It would all be taken care of by the accounting department at the ministry.

Standing and adjusting his jacket to hang properly, John headed for the exit. As he reached the door, the maître d' looked up and his face brightened.

"Did you enjoy your meal, Mr. Winston?" The maître knew all the regulars, and he always spoke to them by name.

"Excellent, Jorge. I'll see you on Wednesday. Remember to have round for Mr. Kincaid."

Jorge laughed and shot John a mock salute. "Of course, Mr. Winston. Always."

The elevator ride to street level was long, but that was fine with John. He was alone the entire way, and it gave him time to think. He thought about Trooper, the man he had grown up with, the man who had turned his Christian walk into a massive, financial behemoth, and then there was Sharon, his wife, a woman who lived in a separate house, fighting her manic-depressive demons. Jeffrey came next in his thoughts, the impossibly handsome young man who epitomized the Kincaid ideal of perfection, while in contrast, Lindsay his sister seemed about to self-destruct. The twins? John considered them. Trooper had just asked him about the boys. Where did they fit? They trailed friends with them wherever they went, as if the Kincaid name meant nothing to them. No one could deny they were Kincaids, though. They were their father's doubles, rubber stamped even to the outstanding skill with which they floated across the basketball court. If they could avoid serious injuries, they might actually have a chance at the pros, fulfilling the dream their father had been forced to let go.

The elevator door opened just as Keith crossed his mind. The way John saw it, the man was still star-crossed in love with Trooper's wife, and sometimes John suspected there might be some level of affection that Sharon returned. Had they been intimate? John didn't think so, not in the nearly thirty years of Sharon's marriage to Trooper, and that was the status quo he intended to maintain on this sunny Sunday afternoon.

For some reason, there was one additional friend that never crossed John's mind. Joanie. Joanie Zigler. She was only twenty-four, but she had become a regular in Trooper's inner circle. John had never understood that. She was clearly uninterested in the spiritual side of

Trooper Kincaid Christian Ministries. As far as he knew, she had never attended a service. Perhaps that was why she slipped his mind. She did attend any and every non-church function that Jeffrey was at, however, even those at the mansion. That should have sparked some interest. It should, even though it never did.

One more thing. There were packages, small and discretely wrapped. John had seen one, once, when Joanie had slipped it into Trooper's hand. That really should have sparked some interest, but alas, John loved Trooper, and as The Bible says, love overlooks all flaws, even when it shouldn't.

Chapter 9

"CHRIST!" Keith Richardson cursed.

A truckload of teenagers was just ahead at the gate to the lake house, and he pulled his custom-painted gold luxury SUV onto the side of the built-up gravel drive. He braked hard, his wheels dropping precipitously off the edge, barely avoiding a brushy stand of shrub. His cup tumbled forward, spilling his coffee onto the console, and he flailed at Trooper for not putting in curbs. Someone could run off and be stuck permanently. He grabbed a matching terry towel he kept in the vehicle just for occasions like this, and he blotted the coffee up as best he could.

"Oh, well," he mumbled aloud, guilt breaking beads of sweat on his face. "If the coffee shorts any of the electronics, maybe the warranty will cover whatever breaks. Dear God, I hope they haven't seen me." He thought of the

Angus steaks in the back, packed in dry ice. Would that ever be patently obvious! He needed to turn his truck around and make a quick exit.

When the call had come into the office the previous week, it had been Sharon on the line, and Keith's legs had melted. It had been picked up by voice mail, so it was only a recording, but even so, the sound of her voice had been the ripple of her fingers on every nerve cell in his body.

Keith, or Kaffe, if you're there, I need you to come out and look at the irrigation system. Everything around the place seems so dead. Can you come out and see if you can liven things up a bit? I'm here all the time except Sunday morning services. Thank you, Keith. Kaffe, too, if you get this.

He had read innuendos into every word of her message and was now convinced she was ready to consummate every desire he had ever felt for her. Now that he was here, he knew his presence shouted that out. He felt exposed, with her boys and their friends in the way. Once he was gone, however, no one would be the wiser.

Before he could move, the passenger door to the black Ford opened, and out stepped the tall and lanky form of one of the Kincaid twins. Keith had to be amused at the long legs and arms. If this were one of his and Sharon's kids, the boy would look normal, tightly built and no taller than five ten or so. No. This boy was his daddy made over, a rubber stamp that had left no details out on the second go round, and he was grinning like a monkey, as he walked toward Keith. God, he wished he didn't have to talk to this boy! Sharon was the only one he wanted to see. This boy would probably *smell* it on him.

He touched the switch on the interior's leather-covered armrest, and the window disappeared into the door. He pulled his gold-plated aviators from his face, laying them on the truck's dash. He smiled brightly, and he held out his hand.

"Hey there, kiddo. Cody or Casey?" In spite of how he felt toward Trooper, the boys were likeable young men. And to offend them was a roadblock between him and the woman who'd once professed her love toward him. He dared not risk that, not if he wanted a future with her.

"Casey, Uncle Keith. Are you trying to get in, too?"

"Your mother called. It's the irrigation system." At least that was honest. Still. *Uncle.* How he hated that title tacked onto his given name! God help him! He cleared his throat. "I can come back later. I'm sure the plantings won't die for lack of one day's water." His body was still coming down from its strongly elevated jolt of libido, and he didn't need to be around Sharon's children, for God's sake. What if they really could smell it on him?

"Stay, Uncle Keith. Everyone's here for lunch. Mom's cooking." The boy put his hands on the truck's window ledge, and he leaned down to peer inside. "Anyway, you can't go, now. We need you."

"So, tell me, Casey." An unexpected whiff that reminded Keith of Sharon made his groin ache. The boy's musky, athletic smell had just enough of his mother in it that he knew he wouldn't tell him no. "Why do you need me?" He reached for his shades and slipped them back onto his face, and he was surprised when the teen popped the door open without asking.

"We're stuck." He looked over at the laughing crowd in the back of the truck and grinned. "We think Mom's changed the code or something, and she's not answering the phone. Can you come try it for us?"

By now the door was completely open, and the boy was pulling him from his SUV. He put it in park and killed the engine before climbing out. Casually, he walked by the black truck, rapping his knuckles on the hood and waving at the mirror Kincaid sitting inside. The gaggle of teens in the back were talking loudly, and at one point, two boys gave each other a "high five" accompanied by a quick laugh. Flipping the cover open, he tapped the keypad several times, and the numbers lit up green. Immediately, the great iron gate smoothly moved aside. The crowd in the back of the truck clapped and cheered, rocking the big F250 from side to side.

Cody's window was down by then, and he pumped an arm outside the window. "Way to go, Uncle Keith! We're in!"

"I'm riding with Uncle Keith," Casey called to his twin. "See you at the house."

Cody waved, hitting the starter, and the truck roared to life. Revving the engine several times, he took off with spinning tires, throwing gravel back along the empty driveway.

Casey ran past Keith, slapping him on the shoulder as he did so. "I'm driving, Uncle Keith." He jumped into the SUV, landing in the driver's seat.

"Hey," Keith called out, more than a little irritated.

Liking the boy was one thing. Giving him carte blanche with his vehicle was another.

"Can I, Uncle Keith? It's just down the driveway. Come on. I've never driven your car before." He held out his hand for the keys, cocking his head sideways with a grin.

Keith was charmed enough by the boy that he laughed. As he climbed in on the opposite side, he motioned toward the dash. "Just push the starter. It's keyless." He cringed when the tires spun, jerking the big vehicle sideways for a moment, and only relaxed when they were through the gate. At least the boy's driving kept his mind off Sharon. He could be glad for that.

TROOPER pulled up to gate leading to the Stone Creek house and punched the Navigator's opener button. The massive metal and wooden gate at the end of the drive, larger than even the one at the lake house, slipped silently out of his way. He eased through and considered what he'd built. The quarter-mile drive wound through groups of well-tended trees that dappled shade across acres of tended lawn. It even looked refreshing, although Trooper's truck showed it was nearing ninety.

He loved this place he and Sharon had put together. The house sat tucked into a rise, seemingly slashed in two by the unlikely thrust of an ancient rock promontory jutting vertically from the hillside. The garage with its four doors was to the left of the promontory, and to the right, the massive, multistory horizontal structure of the house hovered far out over the creek. It was three stories near the promontory, slimming to one where it pushed out to hang in the open air. From the road, the building seemed to float, attached to the earth by no more than a single wall. Trooper knew otherwise. The mechanical rooms, together with massive anchoring beams, pushed far into the rock substrate of the hillside. Along with the concrete tunnel connecting the garage and the house, it all served to cement the structure into the hillside for all time. The house with its massive expanses of concrete floors and flat steel ceilings would hang above the creek until the very promontory into which it was anchored turned loose of its moorings and crashed down the hillside below. That house symbolized God's hand in Trooper's life. It was a gift to one of his Favored Children.

He nodded in satisfaction as he started the enormous black truck up the drive. Soon, Sharon would realize the errors of her ways, and when she did, she would know that the medication she refused to take was one of God's gifts to this world. God worked that way. He provided the things that made life more enjoyable. If good Christians didn't take advantage of what God's goodness provided, then suffering was surely their lot, whether they were Children of God, redeemed by His Mercy, or not. After all, didn't the Good Word say that it would rain upon the just and the unjust? The just simply had to know how to get out of the rain. Sharon would figure it out eventually. Until then, Trooper still had his youngest children at home with him, and this afternoon, he planned to give his attention solely to the twins. They needed him. He felt good about that, refreshed, even.

As he eased the Navigator up the smooth asphalt to the front of the garage, he saw the basketball goal pulled out. He smiled. His boys were already home, and a game had been put into play. How he missed doing that as a teen! Before his knee had blown out during the state championship, he had lived in his parents' drive. His boys were just like him, and he loved them for that.

When he opened the door, though, pulling his massive machine inside, he was surprised not to see the black F250 the twins shared. He shrugged. Cody was the social one. He was likely off with his friends, his excessive energy wiring him up once again. Besides, although he knew it was unfair to play favorites, he did enjoy his younger son more. Surely he would find Casey on his bed with a book or in the theater watching television.

Hitting the button to close the garage, he reached to his side and opened the door. He paused for a moment, waiting for the running board to automatically extend, and then he stepped to it, and finally placed his feet on the floor. He waited as his slim, tight-fitting, auto-darkening glasses lightened enough for him to see. Moving through the underground tunnel toward the house, he had no sense of it being a tunnel. It had plaster walls and a nine-foot ceiling. There were doors for storage and shelves for display. It seemed so much a part of the house that Trooper often forgot the rock promontory bearing down directly over his head. At the end of the corridor was a small table, and he pulled his glasses off to lay them carefully aside.

Stepping into the main body of the house was when

the reality of the residence's construction was evident. There had been no windows in the tunnel that cut through the promontory. It was carefully boxed in and cozy. Plentiful recessed lights in the ceiling had provided the only illumination. When he reached the house proper, though, it was as if the world opened up. Broad expanses of gleaming marble stretched before him, open and flat. Overhead, the expanse of ceiling exactly matched the reach of the floor. Connecting the two were walls of load-bearing, structural plate glass. An eclectic mix of furniture studded strategic points, with muted fabrics and Oriental screens giving a sense of containment. The far bank of the creek with its flowering shrubs shimmered under the dappled sunlight filtering down through the trees, and it was cool in the house, mercifully, quietly cool.

"Casey?" Trooper paused, not hearing a reply. "Cody?" He began walking from room to room. The house was large, so it took him a while, but he soon found the building was indeed quite empty. From the theater room to the indoor tennis court, each vacant space brought a renewed sense of urgency to him, and he soon realized he would find no one at all. He had sent John away, he had the entire afternoon to fill, and he had to do it alone. He had felt *good* at giving this time to his boys. Now, he had no one.

He walked to one of the great windows offering a view of the burbling creek below, and he placed his head against the glass, looking down. He did not like this, this being alone, and he was truly alone. Even the tick of his Rolex screamed its accusations. Sharon was gone. His boys had left him. The empty room surrounding him screamed that he was stranded, abandoned, left behind by everyone he knew and had once cared about.

All he wanted to do was get away. Not even God seemed interested in coming around any longer.

He didn't know when that had happened. It wasn't as if he had gone to bed one night knowing God was real and awakened the next morning with a note folded and placed neatly on his Bible telling him, "Sorry, Son. You are on your own, now." Yet, the end result was the same. He had been on his own for years now, running solely on the massive momentum of his ministry, and he felt that if he slowed down even for a minute, it would all come crashing down around him. Some days he could barely bring himself to go through the motions anymore.

He reached to the phone in his pocket, and after a moment's hesitation, he moved his hand away, not wanting to give in to the overwhelming temptation that this loneliness washed across his soul. Yet, he felt like he was drowning in this life he had built, and tears began to drip from his chin.

"God, I did all this for you. You know I did. Why did you abandon me?" Sobs began to wrack his frame. Then, slowly and with resignation, he reached for his phone once again. He thumbed the screen and tapped an innocent-looking icon. Slowly, he put the device to his ear. After a moment, it picked up, and he whispered his words into the room.

"Joanie, it's me. I'm out. Can you bring me something? Now?" He sniffled as he waited for a reply. When it came, he tried to put on a brave face, knowing only his reflection was there to see. Yet, that face staring back at him made it important. What he saw was what he would become. It was Biblical truth that resonated even for the unchurched and godless. "Yes, I'm alone. Jeffrey? No, I haven't seen him since leaving the church. Why?" There was another pause, giving him time to wipe his eyes on the sleeves of a suit that cost more to clean than most people paid for a suit in the first place. "I understand. Four hundred cash. I have it. The gate will be open, so you can just drive on in."

He pushed *end* and held the phone at his temple, as he leaned into the glass. He pushed hard against it, hoping vainly it would shatter, and he would tumble to the rocks far below. It wouldn't, though. He had built the house well, and structural glass doesn't shatter easily at all.

He didn't react as the phone slipped from his hand and clattered to the floor.

"God," he whispered to the window once again. "Where did you go? I can't do this alone." However, he heard no answer, not even the sound of his tears.

Chapter 10

"OH, HOW EASY!" Lindsay flipped through her mother's medicine stash, picking up containers to check the labels, putting most of them back. "Rozerem, Ambien, and Lunesta. And to think I thought I'd have to buy over-the-counter. Mother, thank you, thank you, and thank you, once again." Her words were whispered, but the smile on her face was very real. Her father would be devastated.

She closed the mirrored panel, watching the cache of drugs disappear into the wall, as the door became simply another of the panels stretching over the long counter. The only tell-tale sign of the cabinet were the tips of two hinges, one at the top and the other at the bottom, and, of course, one of Lindsay's fingerprints.

She dropped the three bottles into a small shoulder bag she had dug from the back of her mother's closet, one that was slightly more orange than red, and she set it aside.

Then, unclipping a pair of skinny jeans from a hangar—
ones with the fewest rhinestones possible—she slipped
them on, sliding them over her hips, and snapping them at
the waist.

Shaking out the loose peasant blouse she had found,
she laughed. "Mother, this proves you have no taste. It's
perfect for me, though." The blouse was pale green,
interwoven with orange thread.

"Lindsay?"

She was startled by the voice.

"Are you dressed, yet? I'm starving. I'm laying out
some food, and you need to come out and let me see what
you picked to wear. Hurry, now."

"Sure, Mother." She slipped the blouse with the orange
threads over her head, and she felt the ring she always kept
on a chain around her neck. It was the only piece of
jewelry she owned, one from a friend she had known long
ago. Then, she brightened her expression and opened the
door to face her mother.

"Lindsay, you look so . . . so fresh. That green . . . and
oh, you do love orange! Was that really in my closet?"
Sharon looked embarrassed.

"At the back, Mother." She laughed. "I love it."

"Keep it, then. It's yours. Now, let me show you
something I dug out just the other day." Sharon grabbed
her daughter's arm, and she tugged until Lindsay moved
forward.

"Fine, Mother. I can follow you on my own. I do know
my way around this house, if barely."

"How, Lindsay?" Sharon stopped and narrowed her

beautiful eyes at her daughter. "Have you spent even one night here?"

"Well, not since you moved in, Mother, but yes. Several."

"Oh. Then you must come stay with me when you get out of school. This place is wonderful, and no one bothers me out here, and I mean no one." She moved forward to a door just down the hall. Turning, it was obvious she fought to keep a grin from her face.

"What, Mother? Just show me." Lindsay remembered the purse in the bathroom. It was out on the counter, exposed, and in that moment, she wanted to keep her mother occupied with this new thing.

"Remember when you were thirteen?" Her mother opened the door a crack.

"Mom!" Lindsay sighed. Thirteen took her back, and it wasn't pleasant. "Every girl remembers when she was thirteen. It's the worst year of any girl's life, ever. Who can forget?" That creek and her picture in the paper. God refusing to notice what she'd done. It had haunted Lindsay throughout her entire thirteenth year. It had been awful.

"You danced with your father that year, remember? We weren't supposed to have dancing in the church, but you wanted it so badly, and your father gave in." Sharon reached inside the closet and pulled out an elaborately fancy dress. "A lot of people were very unhappy with your father about that. He was nearly forced from the church."

Lindsay took the dress and ran her hand down the shoulder, remembering how it had felt that night. It had been the church's annual father-daughter banquet, and she had felt beautiful standing there with her father, him holding her hand, the only ones in the room dancing. She had thought they were the only ones because she was so special. She looked at her mother, and she felt moisture in her eyes.

"He was nearly forced from the church?" Her words barely escaped her lips. "That was the most wonderful night of my life. Why would they do that?" She had loved her father that night, and for months afterwards. Then, he had slipped back into his church world, and he had left her alone once again.

"Your father loves you, Lindsay. I know sometimes you can't tell, and he doesn't take time for you like you need, but he does love you."

Lindsay's response was sharp. "He loves his church, Mother. Nothing comes between Dad and that International Faith Center. Tell me differently, and I'll call you a liar." She turned and crushed the dress to her chest, leaning back against the wall. She felt more tears filling her eyes, and she didn't want to cry.

"Lindsay!" Her mother's voice was quick, but her tone was not. "That wasn't always true, you know. Besides, we've all played a part in what we've become. But," and her voice brightened visibly, "Casey asked me to turn the pool on."

"No!" Lindsay turned to her mother, distracted from the dress as her mother's pronouncement had no doubt intended.

"Yes, and I have already done so."

"Did you tell those brothers of mine not to bring their

hordes of friends along with them? You know how they are. Cody, especially, and Casey copies everything his brother does." First the dress, and now this? She felt devastated.

"Honey, I just said I'd turn the pool on. How can I tell them who they may or may not invite over?" Sharon pressed her lips together, suppressing a smile. "Besides, company will buoy my mood for a bit longer, especially the twins' sort of company. That's why we built this great big house. For people."

"Thank you, Mother. I hope you have plenty of food on hand to feed half the junior class." She sighed and touched the ring at her chest. "Sorry, Grant," she whispered.

"What, Lindsay?"

"Nothing, Mother. Is anyone else coming?" Dad, maybe?

"I don't know, Lindsay. Possibly. I can't get anyone else on the phone just now. When I was downstairs, I accidentally dropped my phone into the pool. How do you feel about taking a dip?"

Lindsay laughed. Her mother seemed to have forgotten something very simple.

"There is a net. Rescuing your phone is something we can do without the need for either me or you to take a 'dip,' as you so aptly put it."

"Oh!" Her mother's face brightened. "Well, isn't that good news?"

JEFFREY was mired in quicksand, like a great fist of

sucking mud squeezing him tightly. If he held very still, he only sank slowly, but when he struggled, it boiled around him, growing ever more viscous. His chest tightened as if his heart would explode, and he wondered why those standing all around him refused to notice that he desperately needed help.

Just out of his reach, slightly elevated, stone paving covered the ground, and on wooden benches, men in leather-and-metal skirted uniforms sat around the rough-walled plaza, lifting cup after cup of foaming liquid to their lips, laughing at something that was scheduled to occur. He didn't know what, just that it was horrible, and that he could stop it if he wanted. How, he didn't know. Yet, that knowledge was as sure in his head as if it were written on the backs of his hands.

Then, coming up a side street, a robed figure walked, covered from head to toe in rough linen, hooded, and bowed under a great, wooden cross carried over one shoulder. Soldiers slashed at the figure with lashes, and blood dripped from the hem of the garment. Appalled, Jeffrey cried for the cruelty to stop, grasping for the stone paving just out of his reach as the quicksand bubbled around him. His voice pleaded for the men sitting around to do something.

It was as if they couldn't hear him. Several of the men pointed to the figure as they stood with their cups in hand. Then, with laughs that were filled with cruelty, they spit in their drink and threw the contents on the creature bowed underneath the cross. The shrouded figure convulsed as if in additional torment.

"Let him free!" It was a man. Somehow Jeffrey knew that, even as he called out. He pleaded for mercy. Whoever was standing there didn't deserve the cruelty the men were heaping his way.

Finally, one of the leather-attired men, a massive brute of a fellow, knelt by Jeffrey's side, and he reached far over the quicksand to grab the front of his shirt. With a mighty tug, he lifted him free of the quicksand, and he held him in the air for a very long time as those standing around continued to abuse the poor creature holding the cross, kicking at his legs until he could no longer stand. Then, with a cruel laugh, the man who held Jeffrey pushed him to his knees in front of the crushed and bloody figure. Two of the uniformed men grabbed the robed figure by the shoulders and roughly yanked him to his feet. Jeffrey cringed as he heard the wretched and abused creature inside cry out in pain.

"You," the uniformed man who had pulled Jeffrey from the quicksand pointed a beefy finger his direction, "are the only one who can save this poor wretch." His voice was like thunder, and Jeffrey felt the stones beneath his feet quiver. "This person says he is the son of his father. Will you offer proof and take him for your own? Only you can guarantee his life."

"Proof? What proof can I offer?" The blood had pooled underneath the robe, and Jeffrey knew the sufferer inside couldn't last much longer. "I have nothing to put forward as proof."

"You. You have yourself. We will take *you* for proof." The rough-spoken man with the voice like thunder leaned into Jeffrey's face. His breath steamed with the foul odor of decay. Then, the man stood and laughed harshly to the sky before turning back to him. "Tell us he is the son of his father, and he will be set free. Then, you may care for him and salve his wounds."

"How will I know whether he is the son of his father?" By this time Jeffrey was even more frightened than he had been while in the quicksand. He didn't know what was expected of him. Whose son? What father?

"You will know if he is who he claims to be. There will be no doubt. Deny him, and he will hang in shame for all eternity." The man yelled, "Remove his hood!"

"No!" Jeffrey covered his head, cowering, not wanting to see. Then, the man grabbed his hair, yanking his head back, and forcing him to look at the uncovered figure standing before him.

"What do you say?" The words were roared into the street, and they echoed from the stone walls.

Jeffrey cringed in horror. There, standing before him, wearing a crown of thorns on his head, with blood running down his face, was himself. As the broken man whispered, "Please, help me," Jeffrey began to violently shake his head no, unable to pull the word from his constricted throat.

The man at his side cried to those standing around, "He denies the son. Throw the betrayer back into the pit. On to Golgotha with this wretched one!"

Then, suddenly, Jeffrey was on his hands and knees, and directly in front of him was the base of a wooden cross. With his heart driving fear hard into his chest, he lifted his head to see who hung above him. There, with his arms and his legs tied with ropes, hung the man he had seen earlier, and with horror, he realized the blood from the man's crown of thorns dripped directly onto his own hands. He lifted them to his face, and his body began to shake with the enormity of what he'd done, when he could have so easily set him free. He tried repeatedly to wipe the blood from his hands, but each time he looked, the stain remained on his skin.

Then, the handle of a long knife was thrust against his palm. The big man breathed his foul breath onto Jeffrey, as he spoke to him, "You can cut him down. All you have to do is admit he is his father's son."

Panic overwhelmed Jeffrey. "No! I don't know him. Please leave me, and take your knife away." With those words, he dropped the blade and scrambled jerkily away from the scene of brutality, running from the blood he could not remove from his skin. A short distance away, he stumbled, and before he could rise again, the sky darkened, and great rumbles of thunder split the air. He quavered as he knelt with his arms around his head, and finally, a broken child's voice cried into the darkness.

"My father, why have you abandoned me?"

Jeffrey, afraid and smelling his own stink, turned to the figure suspended on the wooden cross, only to find the man was not a man at all. He was a boy, twelve years old. He fell to his side, and frantically, he began to plead, "You aren't my son. You can't be mine. No! I don't have a son."

"Jeffrey, wake up!"

He couldn't, though. He was back in the pit of

quicksand, and the world had closed in around him, with darkness as his only companion.

"Jeffrey!"

He knew that voice.

"Mother, get a wet cloth. He's burning up and covered with sweat. Jeffrey, you must wake up."

Cookie? She couldn't be here.

"What does he mean?"

"Shush, Cookie. Just help him awaken. He's very sick, and people say strange things when they have a fever. It's nothing."

Then, like a bolt of lightning, Jeffrey sat straight up, his eyes wide, grabbing the front of his shirt and gasping for air. He searched frantically for the uniformed men, and seeing the familiar faces, he grabbed his fiancée's arm.

"They're not real? The soldiers, the boy?" He swung his feet to the floor, shivering uncontrollably. "I wasn't there?" He leaned forward, his breath coming in ragged gasps.

Mr. Hamilton reached to pat him on the shoulder. "You were ill and had a nightmare. That's all. You yelled something about not having a son, but it wasn't real. Somehow, Cookie's story got mixed up in your mind, and you thought the boy she mentioned was your own. He couldn't be, though. We all know that. Now, Mother's coming with a wet cloth, and I'll get you a glass of milk. We'll take good care of you, Jeffrey. Don't you worry about that."

He looked at Cookie. He could still feel the sweat of his nightmare on his skin, and he couldn't shake the intensity of what he'd imagined. He motioned to her and patted the sofa cushion next to him. When she sat down beside him, he put his arm around her and pulled her close. The dream had ripped him in two.

"I'm sorry, Cookie. I know I must not smell very nice." He tried to smile at her, as he felt his eyes swell with tears.

"What is it, Jeffrey?" She reached to his face and wiped one tear away, but before she could dry her hand, there were more than she could remove. "Was the dream that bad?"

"Bad enough to destroy my life. Dear God, it was bad enough to destroy my family." He pulled her closer and buried his face in her hair. "I hope I never do what that dream showed me I might."

Cookie rubbed the front of his shirt, gently drying her fingers. "If it was really bad, I know you never could, Jeffrey. Never."

His tears began to flow again. "That's just it. I think I already may have." Then, he could say no more, as his body shook with stabs of wrenching emotion.

Chapter 11

"MOM!"

One half of a pair of enormously tall, leaded glass doors flew open, revealing an uncluttered expanse of flagstone paving that stretched around a grand double staircase. The twin flights of log steps led the eyes up to a landing that disappeared into high-ceilinged hallways. Skylights covered the dark-beamed ceiling.

The space made a perfect basketball court.

Cody Kincaid threw himself into the massive log structure that comprised his parents' lake house, his basketball doing a rat-a-tat on the stone floor. As his friends filtered inside, his hand never slowed, his legs taking him a full 360 degrees once, and then again. He called out into the house, his words the same as those of any seventeen-year-old anywhere in the world.

"Mom! Come see this!"

However, there was no answer. Then, he located his brother walking in with his Uncle Keith.

"Casey, heads up!" With a quick flex of toned muscles, his big hands released the ball his brother's direction, aiming directly at his head.

"Done!" Casey dodged, laughing, as he plucked the orange ball from the air. He bounced it once, then sent it flying to another of their friends across the room.

"Do you think your mother would approve?" Keith looked outside for a moment at his SUV parked to the side. When he'd seen Cody fly into the garage with tires squealing, he'd wanted his truck far away. Now, all four garage doors were down. Shaking his head, he pushed the front door closed.

"Maybe not." Casey winked at him, as he called to his brother, "Cody, do you think Mom wants us to play in the house?"

"Of course not. That's what makes it so much fun."

By that time, three of the boys were scrambling for the basketball. A redheaded girl stole it mid-dribble, and they were off after her in a fit of yelling.

"Sharon?" Keith moved to a doorway at the side of the stairs, calling inside. "Your boys are here. You need to take care of this."

One of the girls, petite with dark freckles, tapped him on the shoulder. "Have you been here before? I need to change, and I don't know where the pool is." Smiling, she held up a blue and white bag bound with yellow piping.

"The pool's downstairs, Lauren." One of the twins leaned in, answering for him. "We have plenty of changing rooms. You can use any of them. This is my Uncle Keith. He knows where everything is."

"Thanks, Casey. I'll show her."

"It's Cody, Uncle Keith, but that's okay. I'm heading up to my room to change, now." He leaped for the stairs, bounding up them three at a time. He turned to yell at his brother, "Hey, Bro. Get yourself up here. It's pool time!" Then, he let out a hoot that would have done credit to an adrenalin-crazed owl. Ducking his head into each opened door, he yelled as he did so, "Mom! Lindsay! I know you're here. I saw your car inside the garage. Where are you?" His voice faded into the depths of the cavernous house.

With a stride to equal his brother's, his younger twin was soon up the stairs and down the hall.

"DID YOU find Mom?" Casey dashed down the hall, his feet carrying him the direction he had last seen his brother. He rounded a corner into the upstairs great room to see him stepping out of the room they shared when they were here, looking down at his waist, and attempting to untangle the strings on the front of a brilliantly red pair of board shorts he had slipped on. There was a giant yellow flower on one leg.

"I quit looking." The knot had Cody preoccupied.

Casey leaped his direction, his hands out to slap him on the shoulders. Just before he connected with his brother, he called out, "Heads up, Cody!"

"Idiot!" Cody shoved him backwards onto a sofa and returned his attention to the obstinate strings at his waist.

121

"Hey! I resemble that!" the fallen boy called out, laughing.

"Get dressed. Mom said she'd have the pool on. There's a suit for you in our room."

"We're eating first. Uncle Keith's here, and all your friends—"

"Our friends." His brother's interruption was quick.

"Okay. Our friends. Brady and Matt didn't bring suits."

"Mom keeps extras. Are you dense, all of a sudden? Come on, Case. Let's get in the pool before we eat. We'll throw the girls in if they won't get in. It'll be fun." He had mastered the strings, finally, and he leaped in front of the sofa to land at his brother's feet in a crouch, yelling "Pants!" His hands grabbed the legs of his brother's chinos, pulling on them suddenly and hard. He wasn't successful in getting them more than partially down, though.

"What are you doing?" Casey shoved him away with his foot, yanking the waist back up. "Give me a chance."

"Sure." He let go. "See, I do love you, Brother." He helped him to stand, grabbing both sides of his face in his big hands. "I was only *teasing*."

"Sure," Casey mumbled.

"Then get changed." Cody patted him on the cheek. "You can't swim in your pants."

"Is there another pair like the ones you're wearing?"

"Only a pair with a pink flower." Cody slapped his shoulder. "Special for you, Brother." He began to dance away, doing an imitation of a boxer with a punching bag.

122

"Float like a butterfly; sting like a bee." He shifted to a pretend jump shot and called to his brother, "Pink's for girls, Case. That's why I left you the pink flower." Then, he laughed and shadowboxed his way out of the room.

Casey yanked off his pants in frustration and threw them after his brother. Then, he gritted his teeth and frowned, pulling his shirt over his head and holding it in his hand. He didn't want to wear a pink flower when his brother had on a yellow one.

With a sigh, he walked into the bedroom, resigned to being called a girl for the afternoon. The red board shorts were out on the bed, flower down and out of sight. When he flipped them over, a grin worked across his face. Working the cords quickly, his feet bouncing with relief, he ran from the bedroom all the way to the landing. He threw himself against the railing, looking around until he located his brother. Cody was trying to tap the basketball from another boy's hand, and he called to him to get his attention.

"Cody! See? I've got a yellow flower, too."

"Bro," his brother called, pointing to his own yellow flower, as he tugged one side of his shorts. "Of course you have a yellow flower. You and me, we're exactly the same." Then, he grabbed the basketball from the boy at his side, bounced it once, and fired it at his brother. At the last moment, just before impact, he called, "Heads up!"

His warning was unnecessary, though. Casey had seen it coming. Now, if only his father would come to the lake to join them. Then, Casey knew, everything would be perfect.

"AH, NOT GOOD." John frowned.

His Porsche burbled beneath him, the sound oddly out of place in the quiet countryside. However, it wasn't his car that bothered him. He was at the gate to the lake house, and checking the memory, he could see someone had already entered using one of the temporary construction codes. That meant Keith.

A breeze shifted the bulk of an overhanging tree growing next to the keypad, moving one low branch perilously close to the hood of his car. Cringing, and relieved when it drew back without marring his paint, he reached inside his pocket for a pen. It was more than a pen, though. He pushed a button on the side, and a red light glowed. He whispered quietly into the end before slipping it back into his pocket.

"One tree at gate, Little Elbow Lake, Private Drive No. 27. Trim branches seriously up. Priority." Those not needing the keypad probably hadn't noticed the branch. John had refused the magnetic tag, though. His entrances onto the Kincaid properties were tracked religiously to nip his impulses before they became even more. He wanted to be tracked.

He closed his eyes for a moment. The base of his head had begun to throb once again. He had refused to have it checked. He wouldn't, either. After Aunt Bessie gave in and went to the doctor, her end had come too quickly; he refused to let anyone toy with his mind. Doctors were always alarmists, and besides, the pain always went away . . . eventually.

He let out a breath and reached for the keypad to enter his private access code.

Watching the decorative wrought iron gate silently move aside, he shifted his transmission into drive, and he listened for the subtle alteration in the sound of the engine. He enjoyed this car, even though it cost nearly what the ministry paid him in a year's salary. With pleasure, he gently touched the gas, and his tires crunched forward on the crushed gravel drive.

Winding through the trees, he finally spied the house down the hill. First, he saw its great peaked roof with its open fretwork of logs extending high into the surrounding canopy of trees. Just beyond, glimpsed through openings in the greenery, the surface of the lake shimmered in the late midday sun. Farther yet, the far shore of the Green Fork seemed to glow with the brilliance of the midday sun, as it rose sharply from the blue expanse of water.

Where the graveled drive wound past the front of the house and down to the massive garage, he could see all four garage doors were closed. Only one vehicle was visible. There was really no need to check the guest house farther down. The one car he could see was the one he had come to find. Keith's. He pulled his pen from his pocket and pushed the button.

"One fifty-seven, Sunday afternoon. One car present, a gold Mercedes GL550, prestige plates GOGREEN, belonging to Keith Richardson." He returned the pen to his pocket and slipped his own low-slung sports car next to the GL550, forcing it between the Mercedes and a large tree. That was the best he could do to claim the need to

125

exit together, giving John a valid reason to pull Keith away.

As he contorted his body to squeeze out of the tight space, a bolt of pain shot from the top of his shoulder into his skull. He pressed a hand to the back of his neck, holding it a minute before closing the door. He squeezed his eyes shut, adjusting to the torment. Dear God, it had never been this bad before. Then, with a resigned sigh, he stepped out and into the heat of the day.

Walking up the front path, he did notice the plantings seemed a little limp. Then, puzzled, he knelt to retrieve a wrapper. It was from a chocolate bar, and that surprised him. Sharon might be off her medication, and she might be moody, but she would never throw chocolate wrappers in her yard. He turned to look around, searching for anything else he might have missed.

That was when the front door flung itself open, and one of the twins, bare-chested, wearing a red swimsuit with a yellow flower on one leg, burst onto the porch, startling him. He was holding a basketball high over his head. John hadn't seen the boys' truck, and that in itself was surprising. Even if they had parked in the garage, they were notoriously careless about putting the door down.

Almost immediately, three other teens tumbled out after the mystery twin, leaping on him, and taking him down flat of his back. With two boys holding his arms, they successfully wrestled the ball away. Laughing, they jumped away, dribbling the ball back inside, and leaving the laughing Kincaid lying where he had fallen.

With the exuberant energy he'd seen from the boy,

126

John was fairly certain this was the older of the two brothers.

"Cody?" He called to him, waving his hand. The boy twisted his long frame around, propping himself up on one elbow.

"Uncle John?" He laughed, a pleased look spreading across his face. "Good guess. How'd you know it was me?"

"Because you're you, Cody. Who else would you be?" He walked up and threw out his hand, pulling the boy to his feet.

"Um, Uncle John, I might be Casey." He grinned.

"Nah. I'd know the difference." It made a difference to this twin when people recognized his individuality. John had learned that long ago.

"Dad doesn't."

That hit John like a fist in his gut. The boy was right, though. "He loves you, nevertheless."

"He buys me stuff. He loves the church. Anyway, how'd you know it was me? I really want to know."

John threw his arm across the boy's bare shoulder, and he pulled him down to whisper into his ear. "You, Cody, are much better looking."

"Yeah, right!" The boy grinned. "Come on in, Uncle John. Everyone's here. Sort of. Mom and Lindsay are supposed to be here, but no one's seen them yet. You'd better get ready, because we're swimming later. Oh, and Uncle Keith's here. He came out to work on the irrigation lines or something. You'll probably want to see him. Let me call him for you." He leaned in through the door, and he bellowed out his words, "Uncle Keith! You've got company." For a moment, silence reigned.

John chuckled. "That wasn't necessary."

At the top of the stairs, Keith stepped out on the landing and waved, starting down when he saw John.

"It worked, didn't it?" The boy grinned, then he leaped to grab the basketball from the hands of one of his friends, and he passed it to his brother. "Take it up, Casey. We'll win this game, yet."

Casey did take it up, too, shooting the ball to the top of the stairs, where it bounced off down the hall. "Two points!" His yell filled the room, and all the girls cheered.

John smiled. Trooper would be proud. Two points, just like back in high school. These boys deserved their old man's nickname. The only thing was, Trooper wasn't around. He thought the boys were back at the mansion, and instead, they were here with him. Trooper, if truth be told, did need to spend more time with his boys. Just as John had told him, they really were good kids, but then, how would their father know? He was never around.

Still, he should be. All seventeen-year-olds needed their fathers, even when it seemed they didn't.

"MOTHER, be careful. You'll knock it in the drain. Here, let me have the net. I can get it, if you'll just let me."

Lindsay's voice reverberated in the hermetically sealed natatorium. Even the heating and cooling systems were completely separate to keep the moisture from the pool inside the basement, not in the rest of the house. That kept the sound contained, too, and voices always echoed

128

around the enclosure.

"Here!" Sharon handed her the long-handled net. "I'm exhausted. Perhaps I don't need a phone. Besides, it's certain not to work now. Do you think it's really waterproof? If not, I've drowned all my contacts." She chuckled at that.

"You have contacts?" That surprised Lindsay.

"It was a joke, Lindsay. Get it? Contacts? Water? Phone?"

Lindsay snorted, preoccupied for the moment with pinning the phone under the net. "Explain it to me, Mother." She almost had the phone captured, and suddenly the cleaner kicked on, setting up a current that kicked the phone just out of reach.

"There it goes, Lindsay." Sharon pointed to the black device now gliding across the bottom of the pool. "Like I said, I guess I don't need a phone. Besides, it's an underwater phone, now, and I certainly cannot talk on it underwater." She giggled.

"You have the house phone, Mother." Lindsay pointed to the wall.

"Pshaw. No one ever uses that. Give me the net. We'll not worry about the phone. It's just as well, since I never use it."

"The joke, Mother, explain it to me." Lindsay wiped her hand over her face and began to work the net once again. "What do you mean about contacts?"

"Eyes, Lindsay. Contacts go in the eyes where there's water. You know, if I have to explain my jokes, they're simply no longer amusing. Oh, what is that banging I keep hearing?" Sharon looked to the sealed glass door that led to the stairwell. The mechanicals for the poolroom were just beside it. "Do you think the central units down here are already on the fritz? They could be, you know. Everything else is. Even the irrigation isn't working—again."

"Got it!" Lindsay grinned. She could not believe how good that felt. Her life had been so gray since losing her brother to that Celadon, that *Cookie*, that she hadn't thought she could feel any pleasure again. Completing the phone rescue felt good.

"So, you think it might be the central unit?" Sharon frowned.

"Central unit, Mother? What are you talking about?" Lindsay lifted the net, shaking it to dry the phone. "Should we open the outside doors? If there has to be a party, they can have it on the deck outside. Maybe then the house will have some peace." She walked to the wall of glass doors. "Mom? What do you think?"

Sharon froze, and she put her purple nails to her chin. "Lindsay, I know that sound. They must be upstairs, already. Your brothers are playing basketball in the foyer again. I am going right up there to pinch their ears right off their heads." She didn't move, though. Instead, her eyes filled with tears.

"Mother, what?" Lindsay moved to her side, and her next words were falsely bright. "It's a log cabin. What can they tear up?"

Sharon smiled, but her tears still flowed. "Log cabin, my gold earrings—"

130

"Pearls, Mother."

"Pearls, then. You show me a log cabin that costs as much as this place did, and I'll show you a lake front palace."

"All right, Mother." Lindsay rolled her eyes. "It's a log palace. What can they tear up?"

"It's not that. I miss them, Lindsay. Jeffrey's gone and getting married soon, and you, well, you've been gone half your life. The twins have always been my little boys. Always."

Lindsay hugged her mother and laughed. "Little boys? What are they now? Six-two? Six-three?"

Her mother laughed and wiped her eyes. "Maybe six-four. It's not their size. It's the way they are."

"I think I know what you mean, Mom." Mom. She heard her use of the familial term. Oh, well. Her mother would appreciate the familiarity.

"Do you?" Sharon looked at her intently for a moment, and then she relented. "Maybe you do. I love Jeffrey, but he's so perfect, never making a mistake, always so handsome—"

"That's you, Mom. He gets that from you."

She chuckled. "The looks, maybe. He does get his looks from me, just like you, my beautiful Lindsay. I don't know where the perfect part comes from, though. His father, maybe."

"I agree, you know. Jeffrey is that. Perfectly perfect. He outshines all the rest of us." Lindsay remembered that day in the garage when she had climbed on her father's bike to rest her head against his back. Even his smell had

131

been perfect. Her brother had seemed a perfect, golden god to her that day. If he had offered her the moon, she would have believed he could have delivered it.

"Then, there's you, daughter. Well, you were grown at ten and old at fifteen. I never got the chance to really know you, did I?"

Lindsay knew she never would, either. For a moment she regretted that, but regrets were old news. Real life had stepped in long ago, and that's what she lived now.

"Move back home, Mom." Lindsay gave her mother another quick hug. "Dad loves you." And his church, but she didn't say that. Her mother probably knew it even better than she did.

"Not yet, Lindsay. Someday, perhaps, but not yet. Today's good mood will be gone with the sunset, and I'll be good company for no one. I know that. I just miss the twins, their things strewn about, and their easy way of making friends. I never managed that, did I, making friends? Where did my boys get it from? Jeffrey still has his old friends from college, you know, although he never brings them home with him. You know he's rooming with that Sean, now. Me? I can't even keep my own children around." Her sigh was ragged, and she wiped her eyes with her purple-tipped fingers.

"Mom, you still have your children, no matter what you think." Lindsay laughed about one memory. "Have you forgotten that Valentine's Day when we all brought cards to the platform and gave them to you? We were all coached on special things to say because it was live to the world. Casey couldn't remember his words, though. When it came his turn, he pulled a chair up and climbed on top. Everyone thought he wanted to be taller for the cameras, like Jeffrey. When he motioned you over, you thought he wanted to whisper in your ear."

Sharon laughed. "I did, at that. I had forgotten about it until now."

"He threw his arms around your neck and kissed you right on the mouth, smearing your lipstick, if I remember. The church went wild. Dad said one broadcast never brought in so many donations. No one can take that kiss from you. Not ever."

"You're so good for me, Lindsay. You are making this my best weekend, ever. You grew up entirely too quickly, but I love you so very much. Thank you." Sharon gave her a kiss on one cheek and patted the other with her palm. Then, she pressed her hands together and proclaimed, "Now, let's get ready for the party. Shall we open things up and head upstairs? Lindsay, you get the outside doors, and I'll open the stairwell. Everyone will be welcome anywhere in the house." The phone in her hand chimed a series of soft messages, and she laughed, her eyes twinkling. "Oh, I guess it really is waterproof. I have a text message from your brother. Guess which."

"Cody." Casey hated to text, claiming it hurt his fingers. Lindsay thought it hurt his brain.

"Now, I wonder. How did this thing receive a text underwater? That seems strange to me. Anyway, it asks where I left his eggs. Why, I haven't even cooked them, yet." Sharon looked at Lindsay and winked before swinging the stairwell door wide and hooking it with the floor's built-in latch.

Once she was gone, Lindsay moved to the bank of glass doors that formed the opposite wall of the basement. The doors unlatched without a fuss and slid easily into their recesses at the opposite ends of the walls, leaving a forty-foot expanse open. Beyond the adjoining deck was a green carpet reaching all the way to the lake at the bottom of the hill.

However, Lindsay didn't follow her mother upstairs. She leaned against one side of the opening to look out across the lake. It was a bright and sunny day, as perfect as they came, and it was a stark contrast to the darkness that had trapped her soul. She thought of her mother's words. *You're so good for me, Lindsay. I love you very much.*

"How am I good for you, Mother? What have I ever done to make you love me?" She knew there was no answer to those questions, and as she lifted a hand to brush her face, she felt a tear roll down her cheek.

It was more, though. Grant's note kept haunting the back of her mind, and for some reason his words and her mother's seemed the same. *I loved you that weekend. Thank you.*

Lindsay's next words, with no one around to hear, laid the real Lindsay bare. "Thank you for what, Grant? You still killed yourself. What good did my love do for you?"

As she stood there, her tears began to flow, and she couldn't even bring herself to raise a hand to wipe them away.

It was indeed a perfect last day to be alive.

Chapter 12

JOANIE'S red Miata purred as she sat at the gate of the Kincaid mansion. She had the top down, although the day had become entirely too warm. Yet, here in this rarified world in which the very rich lived, the trimmed trees and dappled sunlight made the day seem perfect. It was, too. Joanie was getting four hundred smackers for this little package at her side, and it was almost a full hundred percent profit.

She just wished Jeffrey was here. She saw him at family functions, and she had even spoken to him on occasion, but he was hard to pin down. Joanie was certain she was in love with him, though. Who wouldn't be with that gorgeous face and that perfect, blond hair? If he aged like his mother, he would be incredibly attractive for decades to come, too. She liked that idea.

However, she hated this house. Her eyes narrowed at

the flatness of it, and the way it seemed it might fall into the ravine at any time. Then, there was that rock sticking up out of the middle of it. Who would want a rock sticking out of the middle of their house? Rich people were crazy. They should live in houses with steep roofs, lots of chimneys, and fancy bushes all around, not flat houses that had rocks in the middle. She shivered as she eased the car up the drive. She got nervous jitters every time she was in the Kincaid house. She just knew it would slide off the hillside, taking her with it, and dear God above, she didn't want to die in a preacher's house.

Halfway up the drive, one of her phones rang. She fumbled in the seat at her side, shuffling through the four she regularly carried, until the found the one that demanded her attention. Slowing the car, she clicked the talk button and put it to her ear.

"Joanie." She didn't say anything else. If someone was calling on one of these phones, they weren't calling for a friendly conversation.

"Hey, friend."

The voice was a man's and ragged, but whoever it was, he was only a friend if he was buying. Joanie didn't have any other kind.

"Yeah, friend. So?" If he didn't identify himself, she was hanging up.

"Charlie." He paused as he coughed a few times.

She waited. A lot of her "friends" were like that. As long as they had the money, she didn't care. When he was silent for a time, she decided to move the conversation along.

136

"So, Charlie. How's business?"

"Low, friend. Running low."

His answer was vague, but that was because Joanie would cut the connection on him if he said anything that even resembled drug talk. She knew of people who had been taken down because of their cell conversations. Not Joanie. She talked in vague terms that would never stand up in a court of law. Her clients had to do the same, or she'd cut them off in a heartbeat. There were always more customers than dealers, so they had to jump when she said. They needed her more than she needed them.

"What's your nightmare?" Charlie didn't call very often, and she wasn't sure any longer.

"White, I think." His voice shook. It sounded like he'd been out a while. "Little. I don't remember much more."

"Ah." That could be eight different things. However, his description had been enough to trigger her memory. "Gotcha, Charlie. Fifty at Fourth and Vine?" When he rasped out his agreement, she clicked the phone off. Four-fifty. That would give her enough to pay her rent, and it was due two weeks age. She laughed. This was a really good day.

Now that she had Charlie lined up, she'd have to make this quick. At least old Troop had said the family was gone, so there was no need for chitchat. She could just collect and get on back to the part of the city where real people lived.

Pulling up to the bridge leading to the front door, she put the Miata's emergency brake on. She grinned. Wouldn't want it to roll off the side and into that creek down there. Might have mosquitoes when she had it hauled back up. Creeks always had mosquitoes. Always.

Then, before she got out, feeling an itch, she reached to her glove box and pulled out a package of sanitary wipes. Her heart beat faster as she hurriedly ripped one out. She knew an anxiety attack when she got one. Her response to it was uncontrollable, too. With her hands shaking, she worked the cloth inside her clothing down to where she never let any man touch her, and she wiped the memory of long ago clean one more time. It never came clean, though. It was never, never clean, and she didn't even remember who he had been.

When she had done the best she could, she pulled her hands free and stuffed the wipe into a disposable rubber glove she found under the seat. She would normally just throw it out the window, but here, she might be sued, that or ticketed, and rather than risk something so stupid, the glove could stay in her floor until she got back on the highway.

She grabbed the box at her side, and she hesitated before opening the door. This same stuff inside was why she didn't know who had violated her. She had been sixteen and high. God, she had been so high that weekend. She didn't even remember leaving her room. It wasn't until several months later that she learned she was pregnant, and she was so distraught, she climbed in the bathtub, and took it out herself with a wire hanger, nearly killing herself in the process. Afterwards, she had felt so ashamed, even though it hadn't looked that much like a baby. Her real shame had washed over her when her mother found her bleeding in bed, and at the emergency room, she'd been forced by her parents to tell the doctor she'd been attacked and raped.

Nowadays, she wondered why her parents had been so complacent about her self-mutilation. She wondered what they knew that she didn't. She'd never find out now, though. The week after she got home from the hospital, her father killed her mother, and then he turned the gun on himself. God, she hated her father. Maybe even her mother, too. However, it was hard to hate someone when you held her as she died, her blood soaking through your fingers, her eyes pleading with you to understand, until the pleading turned to a blank stare.

"Damn you," she whispered to the box.

No, Joanie didn't feel much sorry for anybody in the world. However, she would like to see that handsome Jeffrey again. That she would like, for sure.

"SHARON." Keith stepped from among the young people and greeted her as she reached the top of the stairs. "You *are* here."

She was beautiful, and his skin flushed as he reached for her hand. He could see it on his arms, and he could smell his sudden need for this woman. He hoped she couldn't, not with this crowd of high school students at his back.

Then, she reached and kissed him on the cheek. His skin burst into flames. Trooper didn't deserve her, and he hadn't for the nearly thirty years since he'd stolen her away from him.

"Keith, welcome. I see you came to join our little party." She patted his cheek, her voice very bright. "All you've done lately is work on my place, and not one time have you come in for a visit. I still remember high school, you know, and we were very close. Trooper won, but I still enjoy your company. Now, come to the kitchen. You can help me feed my boys and all their friends. You will stay to swim with us, won't you?" Her fingers still rested against his face as she waited for an answer, but her smile had already begun to fade to hollow.

He sighed. He could see the signs. Sharon might be having a good day today, but she was afraid of losing it. If she did, then no one would find her pleasant company. His hopes of an assignation were fading quickly, although his libido hadn't quite gotten that message yet.

"Keith?" She patted his cheek again and then dropped her hand. "Stay if you want. I have extra suits. The twins love you, you know. Stay for them. I really do have to get some food ready. My boys are hungry hounds." She giggled nervously. "That was a joke, Keith. I'll be in the kitchen." Then, she called louder to the boys dribbling the basketball on the flagstone floor of her foyer, pointedly including the girls standing around in small groups. "I'll be in the kitchen whipping up something to eat. The pool's open, and I have my phone out of the bottom. It still works, too." She held it up, laughing.

Keith stood mesmerized as she fairly ran for the kitchen.

ALL THOSE years and four grown children, and she still

enjoyed the smell of that man. She knew exactly what that smell was, too. That's why she had run. It was wrong, wrong, wrong, and she hoped he didn't follow.

Dear God! She closed her eyes when she reached the kitchen. Please don't let him come in here. She leaned over and placed the side of her face on the cool surface of the granite countertop.

"Sharon?"

"Go away," she barked. She jerked her head up, and in that moment, she recognized John. She turned around, placing her hands over her face. She had wanted Keith, and now she felt found out.

"Seriously?"

"You may stay, John." She turned to face him, her heart still racing. "I'm sorry. I didn't realize you were here. Is Trooper coming? I'm not sure if I have any round steak. He may have to survive on apple pie. There's some of that in the freezer. I think I might also have cheese in the fridge." She laughed, and she heard just a touch of hysteria in it. She knew she was rambling, and she couldn't turn it off. "Can you tell? My day's crashing around me quickly."

"It doesn't have to." He stepped to the counter to stand just across the island from her. He was still in his suit from that morning, and he reached to her, almost touching her. "Pretty dress."

She glanced down at her clothing and looked back up, horror crawling all over her. "John! All those children out there, and I'm not even dressed. This is my slip from this morning. My heavens! It was just Lindsay and me, and we

141

were down in the basement getting my phone out of the pool. I didn't even know they were here. I have to find something more appropriate to wear."

"It will be fine, Sharon. Perhaps you should have changed; however, those kids will soon be running around in less at the pool."

She put her hands to her head and began fluffing her hair, but then she dropped her arms, resting her hands on the cold granite. "That can't fix my slip, can it, John?" She tried to smile, but she couldn't hold it. It was Keith and her slip, and dear God! Keith would surely know she had on only a slip!

John touched her arm with a quick motion, and then he pulled his hand back. Sharon stopped, oddly reassured, and looked at him, studying his face.

"What you have on is fine, Sharon. I shouldn't have said anything. This is more of a dress than some people wear to services on Sunday mornings. Relax."

"You think so?" She smoothed the front with one hand, and she smiled. Her eyes felt raw, though.

"Are you all right?"

"I . . . I just want this day to be fun for the boys. I really do, John. You know, I almost lost it there. For a moment, I felt the despair, and I don't want it today. Dear God, I don't want it to come today." She placed her hands to the sides of her face and patted her cheeks, then slowly let them slide down her neck. "Why doesn't God heal me of this awfulness, John? Then I could go home. I still love Trooper, you know. I really do, even if he doesn't think so."

"What about Keith?"

Her eyes jerked to his, and she cringed when she saw the expression on his face. It wouldn't be like John to stop with that one question.

"Does he fit in anywhere?"

"You know better, John." Her words lashed out, her voice almost strident as she answered him, her hand slapping the granite surface of the countertop stretching between them. She knew she was telling the truth, but she also knew the verses she had learned as a child. Just to think something in her heart was to have done it. By that measuring stick, she might as well sew a scarlet letter on the front of all her clothes.

"I trust you, Sharon."

His voice was barely more than a murmur, and she looked at him with a puzzled expression. Then, he nodded his head to the door.

"Mom?"

She glanced that direction, unsure which of her boys she was seeing. That dismayed her. Always, she had been able to tell them apart. She didn't know how. A particular expression, perhaps, or some subtle flaring of the nose. A difference in a haircut, maybe. This time, she had no idea, and suddenly she felt that if she called out the wrong name, this boy would disown her, run back to his father, and never want to see her again.

With her eyes wide, she looked at John in desperation. Help me, John, she silently pleaded.

"CODY?" John saw what was happening, and he stepped

143

in to rescue Sharon. He wasn't sure this time, either, but he knew what had just gone through her mind. She had spent too much time away from them. She was becoming another Trooper, trusting in her children's goodness, not understanding how much they needed their parents with them every single day. However, the boy would understand if his "Uncle" John called him by the wrong name.

"Sorry, Uncle John. I'm Casey. Mom, do you have any chips? Pizza, if you have that flavor."

Sharon flew to him, throwing her arms around his torso, and hugging his bare chest. Then, she began laughing and patted him on the arm. "Oh, Casey. I love you so much. Of course I have pizza chips for you, dozens and dozens of cans. They're right there in the pantry. Help yourself." She opened the pantry door and pointed to the first shelf. "Is there anything else you need?"

He grabbed two cans. "We're getting really hungry out there. Cody wants to swim first, so we're heading downstairs. Do you think you can bring something down after a while?"

"Oh, Casey, you know I can, my little love. I have lots of fajita fixings. Would anyone like that?"

He grinned. "You're the best, Mom. We're so hungry, we'll eat anything." He danced away, then stopped and held up the two cans of chips. "Thanks, Mom. I love you."

Before she could answer, he was out the door.

"He loves me." Sharon smiled at John, radiant. "My son still loves me. I feel good again, John. Casey's my son, and he loves me."

John tightened his lips, and with a determined step, he

took her by the arm and led her to her bathroom. He pushed aside a small orange shoulder bag and pressed the mirror just above where Lindsay's fingertips had rested earlier.

"John, what are you doing?" She frowned, and her voice quivered.

Swinging the mirror wide, he ran his finger along the containers, quickly skimming the medications. Finally, he reached one bottle at the very top. He pulled it out and closed the mirror.

"Here." He held it out to her.

She kept her eyes trained on his, though, and didn't look to see what it was.

"Take it, Sharon."

"What is it, John?" However, her expression said she knew. "Please, John. What is it?"

"Are you as blind as your husband, Sharon? I'm offering you your children back. Can't you see that?" He pressed the bottle into her hand and turned to face away from her, his own internal turmoil ripping at him. He knew what he was offering. He was offering her something that God had forever denied him, a mate and children. She had all those things, and she was willing to throw them away, a man she loved . . . a man John loved . . . and children who wanted nothing more than her attention.

"John." Her voice shook. "No. Please don't do this." She grabbed his hand and forced the bottle inside, wrapping his fingers around it. "God can heal me of this, if He wants. I don't need the medication."

He whipped around, and he held the bottle in her face.

His words were terse and filled with emotion. "You are losing your family, Sharon. You just stood in your kitchen, and you didn't know your own son. You have a man in this house who simply waits for your consent to make a mockery of your marriage." She began to shake her head in denial, but he continued, overriding her repudiation of his accusations. "You need this, Sharon. It is medication, and it works for you."

"I don't, John. Don't say that." Her eyes were red, and it looked as if she might cry.

He could see he hadn't gotten through to her. Irritated, he took his arm and swept the orange purse off the counter. It hit the wall, scattering its contents on the floor. He grasped Sharon's medication in his hand and slammed the bottle on the bare counter before releasing it and removing his hand.

He reached to his neck and grimaced. The pressure was back again, and it was fire shooting into his head. He breathed and pushed the pain from his thoughts. He would not give in to it now.

"John," Sharon began, and she hesitated, her face deflated. Her eyes darted around the room, finally resting on the purse and its contents scattered across the floor. Shaking, she knelt to pick them up and place them back on the counter. "Lindsay borrowed this purse from me today. I told her to take anything she wanted. I didn't need any of it."

As she started to return the bottles to the bag, he reached to pull them out of her hand. Glancing at them one at a time, he looked at Sharon hard in the face. He heard

Lindsay's words to him that morning. *You want me to wear summer this final time, John?*

"Your daughter has borrowed all your sleeping pills, too, Sharon. Why do you think she would do that?" He dropped them in the bag and held it out to her. "Does it tell you anything?"

"They're just sleeping pills, John. I use them myself, sometimes." Her voice shook, though, and there was desperation in her eyes.

"Do you use three bottles at a time, Sharon? Three?" He reached with a finger and touched the bottle of medication that she had refused to take over the past several months. "God has given you your healing. It's in this bottle. Your family needs you."

"Mom?" A voice drifted up from the basement. "Are the fajitas ready?"

Sharon pressed her lips together tightly, and then she leaned out the door and called brightly, "Almost." She turned back to John and smiled as she wiped her eyes. "It's only a little lie. I have to go, John. The kitchen needs me. I could use your help in there, though. Are you really angry with me?"

"I'm not angry with you at all, Sharon." He looked at the bottle on the counter and lifted his hand away, turning to the beautiful woman standing before him. "I'm frightened. I don't want your family to fall apart, and I'm watching it happen. I just want to help."

Sharon sniffled and pushed her hair back from her face. "The first step is to meet me in the kitchen. Before that, though, I have to use the bathroom. Will you excuse me?" She smiled as he stepped around her, and she gently closed the door after him.

TURNING on the water in the sink full blast, Sharon opened the cabinet and returned her bottle of medication to the top shelf. Picking up the purse, she opened it and looked at the bottles inside. Then, she carefully opened each lid, and from all three bottles removed every tablet except one. Replacing the bottles in the purse, she set it back on the counter. Holding the pills, her eyes welled up, and she hissed her words, refusing to admit what she knew was true.

"These weren't mine, John. They couldn't have been mine. Lindsay wouldn't do that to me."

With disgust, she flung the tablets in the toilet and pushed the lever to wash them away. Then, before joining John in the kitchen, she leaned the top of her head on the mirror and let her tears wash her eyes clean. She ran her hands over the smoothness of the countertop, thinking of the bottle John had pressed into her hand. She knew her answer wasn't inside that bottle. She didn't know where it was, but that was not it.

At a knock on the door, she jumped. With a bright voice, she responded, "Yes! I'm just finishing!"

"I need to know how hot to set the oven." It was John.

"Five hundred on broil. I'll be right there." She splashed water on her face, patted it with a towel, and yanked the door open to see him standing, waiting on her.

"Five hundred on broil doesn't sound right to me. Maybe you can help."

He was smiling at her, though, so maybe he really wasn't angry at all. "If you know, why are you asking me?" She walked past him toward the kitchen, still wiping under her eyes with her fingers.

"I couldn't think of anything else to say to get you out of the bathroom, and besides, I really don't know where all your things are. This is my call for help." He chuckled as he spoke.

She turned and pushed him playfully on the chest, and finally, her smile was real. She felt lighter inside. "If you ever get married again, your wife had better be a chef."

John just laughed, and after a moment, Sharon joined him, laughing until she had to wipe her eyes.

Chapter 13

"MY PHONE?"

Jeffrey's phone rested in Mr. Hamilton's hand, the screen flashing silently, somehow alien, intrusive and sinister. Jeffrey had just come from a world of leather-clad soldiers and children hanging on wooden crosses, a world where the streets were paved in stone, and it was acceptable to beat an accused man—or an accused boy— as he bled. Jeffrey's grasp on the world to which he had returned was still tenuous, at best.

"Jeffrey, I'm sorry, but this is the third time your phone has gone off, and it's been the same caller each time. Do you wish to take it?" Mr. Hamilton drew his hand back. "Ah, I see you missed this one, too. I can return it to the foyer sideboard, if you wish."

"Thank you. I probably should return the call." He drew in a deep breath and reached for the device. He glanced at it, keying the ringer volume up. Seeing the most recent three calls were unknown, he looked at Cookie. "May I?"

They were interrupted as a small shih tzu ran into the room, its toenails clicking on the hardwood, leaping onto the sofa to excitedly lick him in the face.

"Oh, Pooky!" Cookie reached to pull the animal away, as her mother came belatedly trailing in after it, a look of despair on her face.

"I'm so sorry, Jeffrey. I know you aren't well. I just opened the door to check on little Pooky, and she darted out faster than I could reach out my hand. Here, Cookie. I'll put her away again." Mrs. Hamilton rubbed her hands together and then clapped them to call the dog. "Pooky, come to Mimi. Be a good baby. You'll get fur all over dear Celadon's dress."

"Now, Mother. The dog is not a grandchild to be cajoled into obedience." Mr. Hamilton shook his head. "Just walk over and pick the animal up. It's simply a pet, after all. A very expensive pet, I might add."

"Not too expensive for me." She cooed as she bent over in front of the sofa, toying with the animal's ears. "Besides, I don't care about money. I love my little Pooky, and she's all I have, for now, anyway." Then, she winked at her daughter and made to pick the animal up.

"No, Mother. I'll hold her for a while." Cookie patted her mother's hands away and turned to the man at her side. "Go take your call, Jeffrey. It must be very important if they've called three times. Give me a kiss, first." She pointed to her cheek and tilted her head.

Jeffrey could still smell his nightmare all over him, but he did as she asked. As he leaned in to her, he inhaled the freshness of her scent. He shivered at the memory of the boy he had left hanging on that cross, and he felt the shiver continue down his spine. How could one moment in a person's life haunt him for so many years? He'd only been fifteen. How could he have known? He brushed his fingers along the sleeve of Cookie's tailored dress as he stood to find a place to make his call.

"This way, my boy. You may use my office. The house phone is on my desk, if you prefer." Mr. Hamilton pointed through a polished, wooden door. "Just pull the door to when you step through."

As Jeffrey reached for the knob, he could hear Mrs. Hamilton's words. "Cookie, dear. Your dress. Pooky will leave fur all over it. Let me put her away." Then, softer, as he pulled the door to, "Oh, my poor baby. Father wants to replace you with a real baby. Shame on him. He doesn't know just how much I love my Pooky, does he?"

Jeffrey had to smile as he clicked the door shut. Then, he touched the screen of his phone and looked at the number displayed there. It could be anyone. Was it important? He couldn't be sure, except it had been important enough for someone to try to reach him three times in a row. That made him curious.

Engaging the device to initiate the connection, he put it to his ear. He listened to it ring several times, and then a voice answered at the other end. The words carried a preoccupied air.

"Yeah. Buck, here. Hold."

Then, there was silence for a moment, and Jeffrey suspected he shouldn't have returned this call. "Buck" sounded like it could only be one man, and if this were Bucky Simms—a man he had never met or even spoken to—then there was trouble afoot. Bucky was a media hound, one that worked for the Chronicle, and in the past week, he had put it upon himself to take Trooper Kincaid Christian Ministries to task for some imagined flaw that seemed to him a cesspool of iniquity. No one at the ministry had any idea what it was all about, but Bucky Simms was not one to call up his targeted organizations for light conversation.

Before he could decide to hang up, the voice returned with excitement.

"Oh, my God! Is this who I think it is? You called back! Is this the real Jeffrey Kincaid? Tell me it is. I've tried everyone at the ministry, and no one will take my calls."

"Yes, this is Jeffrey. What can I do for you?" His voice was somewhat less exuberant than the one on the other end of the line, though, and his thoughts raced. If this were indeed Bucky Simms, this man's number had been tagged in the ministry's systems as a nuisance number. Bucky Simms' calls never rang through, dumping directly to voicemail.

Realizing that, Jeffrey relaxed a bit. This number hadn't gone to voicemail, and that meant it couldn't possibly be Bucky Simms.

"Oh, my God, man! You don't know how glad I am to finally talk to you. How have you been doing, Jeffrey?"

"I'm fine. How may I help you?" He struggled to remember where he might know this "Buck" from. The man spoke to him as if he were an old friend.

"My God, you don't remember me, do you? From church camp. We went to youth camp together for two years. Remember? Bucky. Bucky Simms. You were in my dorm when I was seventeen. The next year my baby sister hung all over you. You surely remember that."

Baby sister. Jeffrey's insides twisted, and he felt bile rise in his throat. Unsteadily, he sank into a chair beside Mr. Hamilton's desk. This couldn't be what it sounded like. He didn't know Bucky Simms, had never met him. He was certain of that. Twenty girls, thirty girls had hung all over him that final summer. Even if Bucky had been at camp, he wasn't someone he had known.

"Jeffrey? Did my call drop? Jeffrey Kincaid, are you there?"

"I'm here."

"My God, I thought the call dropped, and this is the most important call I've ever made. Hold on a minute, Jeffrey."

He was grateful for the pause. He had nothing to say. He heard the sound of rustling papers over the line. Then, he heard a slapping sound as if the man on the other end had hit his forehead with the palm of his hand.

"I am so stupid! God, my head is empty! Of course you don't remember me. I wasn't Bucky then. I went by Benjamin. You remember now, don't you? I slept on the bunk right over yours. You were just a skinny little kid, and I kept short-sheeting your bed all week. You can't

154

have forgotten that."

"Benji?" The short-sheeting Jeffrey remembered. Someone named Benjamin, no. He had slept underneath a Benji. He had worshipped the older boy and hadn't known how to show it other than to give him a horrible nickname. It had certainly gotten him the attention he'd wanted, including a head dunking in the toilet.

"Oh, God, I'd forgotten. You got so angry with me that you called me by that awful name all week. It was a dog's name, and you said I was a big, ugly mutt, so I was just a Benji to you. You do remember! I have so got to get together with you, and now, too. Let me look at my schedule for a minute. Hold on."

More papers rustled, and Jeffrey could hear drawers being opened and closed. Then, Bucky came back on the line. "I knew this appointment book was somewhere. I just finished lunch here at my desk, and it got mislaid underneath. You know, I've had to call you on my personal phone. Your ministry has my office number blocked, well, not blocked, but it might as well be. I immediately roll to voice mail, and no one returns my calls."

"I, um, have heard of that happening sometimes." Jeffrey felt his neck warm.

"You have, huh?" Bucky chuckled. "Let me check my schedule and find an opening I can fit you in."

Jeffrey felt ashamed. He had no doubt Bucky knew he was being avoided, and he seemed to harbor no ill will about it. He reassured himself it hadn't been a real lie.

"God, I'm swamped this week." Bucky could be heard

flipping pages. "My sister died several years ago, by the way, if you haven't heard. Brain aneurysm. Who would have guessed, and at twenty-three? You probably didn't hear anything about that, though. Why would you? Today, Jeffrey. It has to be today. I have deadlines hanging over my head like a Gulf Coast hurricane, and I'm locked in on each one. No flexibility, but that's newspaper life. If what I suspect is true, it's big, and you will want to know. Trust me. It'll change your life."

"Um, sure. Today, you say?" *It'll change your life.* Jeffrey almost dropped his phone when he heard those words. A chance meeting in a pool had changed his life. What now? "Can't you just tell me over the phone?"

"It's too big. This is not an over-the-phone matter. You wouldn't propose over the phone, would you? Or tell someone their spouse just died. No, this needs to be in person."

Now, Jeffrey was so rattled, he could barely think, and he rubbed his hand over his face. "Can you help me out with what this concerns? I'm a little confused, here." He was more than a little confused. He was in a cold sweat. Then, the house cooling system cycled on, and chilled air swept down his back. He shivered.

"Like I said, this is too big for the phone. Name a place. Oh, and someplace we can be undisturbed for a few hours. Not my office, though. People are in and out of here like it's Grand Central Station. Got any place in mind?"

Not his apartment. He shared it with Sean, his old college roommate, to halve the cost, as well as to stay grounded to the real world outside of the ministry. The place in Stone Creek? The twins would be there, along with anyone they could find to drag home with them. His mother was holed up at the lake house. However, no one used the guest house, and it was very private. He'd need to drive right past the lake house to get there, but at the moment, it was the best he could come up with.

"Jeffrey? Are you shutting me out? This isn't something you should let go. Come on. Work with me." Bucky's voice carried a note of desperation.

"No, no. I'm just thinking." He was thinking of a number of things. His mother living at the lake house, and the medication she refused to take. His sister, who barely seemed to be part of the family anymore. His father. The twins, normal, thank goodness. Then, there was the boy, twelve, and in Memphis. Which of those cesspools was this newspaper reporter dragging him into? Even worse, he knew his participation was voluntary, if he met with this guy. Dear Father in Heaven, what was he thinking?

"Okay, Jeffrey. Do you have a place, because I know a little motel down in Southside. It's a trifle seedy, and I think hookers frequent it, but I can rent it by the hour. We could meet there, if you want."

"Southside?" He couldn't imagine meeting in Southside, and he was certain his dismay carried in his voice.

"God, Jeffrey!" Bucky laughed. "It was a joke. Loosen up. Still, we do this tonight, or if not, someone loses out forever. You're crucifying me, man. Name your place."

Crucifying me. That stuck an unwelcome chord in Jeffrey. It made him think of that boy on that cross. "My parents' guest house." The words poured out of his mouth.

"It's never used. No one will bother us there."

"Great, Jeffrey. Give me a time and a location."

"Little Elbow Lake, Private Drive No. 27. Follow West Lake to Green Fork Cutoff. Give me an hour."

"Gotcha. I've got a meeting I've got to catch the tail of, but I'll be there. Oh, and one more thing."

Before Bucky could tell him, Jeffrey heard someone in the background call the man's name. Bucky responded to the unknown speaker, "Just a second. I'm coming, Craig. I had a call come in, and I had to take it." Suddenly, the phone clattered, and everything went silent.

"Bucky?" Jeffrey was glad there was no more food on his stomach, because that queasy feeling had taken over.

"God, I'm sorry. I had the phone with my shoulder, and it fell. I'm really sorry, Jeffrey. I've got this meeting, and I've got to go. One hour."

"Bucky!"

"Yeah, Jeffrey?" The urgency in his voice made it clear he really needed to get off the line.

"You said there was one more thing." He wasn't sure he wanted to hear it, but he was even surer he needed to. His stomach demanded it.

"Oh, yeah, I remember. He sure looks like you. See you in an hour."

"Who looks like me, Bucky?" His question went unanswered. The phone had gone silent, and he looked in dismay at the display. The numbers clicking off the call's time flashed at him, no longer changing, and he knew the conversation was over.

In spite of the silent phone, he knew who looked like

him, though, or at least he thought he did. He tried to remember the girl's last name from that long-ago summer, but he'd pushed that from his mind years ago, if he'd ever known it at all. Could it have been Simms? Youth camp was a first name camp. Who needed last names for friends who would be gone on Friday? Live in the moment. Live for the week. Live for half an hour in the pool. Jeffrey hadn't even known Bucky's last name that first summer he'd attended camp. Benji. That's all he'd known him by. Benji, the dog-faced boy.

"Jeffrey?"

He jumped at a knock on the door, grabbing his phone and standing. "Coming. I'm finished, now." It was Cookie. She couldn't find out about this.

"Is everything okay?" The door opened a crack, and she peered through. "I don't mean to intrude, but after earlier, I'm just worried about you."

"Everything's fine." He pulled the door wide. She had changed to trim slacks with a top stitched in a coordinating color. She was shockingly beautiful, as always, but at that moment, he could only see a dark cloud of disaster gathering before him.

"Are you sure?" She touched his face and handed him a shirt she held in her hand. "My father's. He thought you might want to put it on."

He smiled gratefully and took it from her hand. "I have to head to the lake house, Cookie. Business. I need to leave now. It's unexpected, and I'm sorry." He kissed her on the forehead. "I'll head in the other room and slip this on before I go."

159

"Will you be long? I could ride out with you, if you like. It must be beautiful out there this time of year. I could sit by the lake, and I wouldn't be any bother at all."

She smiled and brushed her hand across his arm, and as he watched her fingers move across his skin, all he could see on his hand was the blood in the dream that he hadn't been able to wipe away.

"Besides, hasn't your mother been spending time there? I would love to see her again. It's been months. Let me go with you. I can even drive my own car, if you think you'll be long."

"You want to see my mother?" He didn't want that. Not at the lake house. She barely held herself together for the Sunday morning services.

"Please, Jeffrey? Look, I even changed."

He finally noticed, and he knew she needed him to see, because he hadn't noticed the first time.

"Mother was right, and Pooky did get hair all over my dress. This is brand new, and I know your mother loves clothes just as much as I do. We could talk the latest fashions. It would be wonderful. Please say yes, Jeffrey."

"Well," he started, and he knew he would give in. He knew why, too. His mother might be able to brighten herself for Fashion 101. "Sure," he said. "We need to leave now, though. I want you to ride with me. I will not have you taking a second car."

"Oh, I do love you, Jeffrey. Thank you." She reached up to kiss his cheek. "Use my father's bathroom to change. You may choose from any of his colognes. He's said he doesn't mind at all." She giggled, and Jeffrey adored her for it. She was the most thoughtful person he knew.

She had also managed to distract him for a moment from the disastrous events of the day, and he would be glad to have her along. He just hoped his mother felt the same way.

LINDSAY stood at the lake's edge, just having made it out of the basement before the party moved downstairs. She looked out over the water, tuning out what little pool noise could be heard over the waves lapping the shore.

"Lindsay?"

Startled, she jerked erect at the sound of her name, pulling herself from the tree against which she had been leaning. Turning, she saw Keith. A slight breeze blew a strand of blonde hair into her face, and she reached a hand to pull it aside, tucking it behind an ear.

"Oh, Keith. It's you. The party's inside." She pointed back to the house. It was, too. The friends Cody and Casey had brought out with them could be seen in the pool, and the sounds of their roughhousing drifted across the yard and down to the lake. They used their friends as buffers. Even she could see that. She didn't say it, though. Keith was smart. He probably caught on.

"Right. Your brothers. I'm quite aware of that. I can hear them even from here. Too bad. It would be peaceful, otherwise." He reached an arm to a low branch, using it to support his weight. He casually leaned against it, and the leaves just overhead rustled.

"The sounds of teenagers living it up." Lindsay laughed.

"It's pretty out here." He shifted one hand to the tree she had been leaning against, and he looked out across the lake. "You're lucky your parents have this."

"Right." She smiled, but it was humorless. She hated herself. She hadn't even stayed in the basement to greet her two brothers. She had watched them from a distance, their matching board shorts making them the same as they leaped into the pool, sometimes dragging others with them, and at other times jumping in alone, their arms and legs spread wide to achieve the biggest possible splash. She had determined which was Casey, though. He jumped differently, less carelessly. He was her favorite of the two, the one she preferred to talk to. He was more introspective, more like her, and he understood her better. He was the one she would miss most.

"Why so sour?" Keith looked at her, pursing his lips. "At least you don't have to pay for all this. That's a good thing, right?"

"This is a man-made beauty, Keith. Uncle Keith." She laughed when she said that. "You hate being called that, don't you?"

"Sometimes."

"All the time, you mean. Do you love her?"

Keith turned her direction with a frown. Lindsay reached for a leaf on one of the trees and pulled it loose. She smoothed it carefully between her hands, stroking it with fingers that were worthy of a fashion model, long, slender, and even. Her nails were short, though, evidence that she had no patience with needless tweaking to her looks.

162

After a moment she held the leaf up to catch a ray of sun, and with a short bark of a laugh, she let it go in the breeze, watching as it fluttered to the surface of the water and began to float away.

"It will eventually sink." Keith's voice was even, but it carried a hint of condemnation. "It would be better to leave it on the tree where it can provide nourishment for the rest of the plant. Pull too many off, and the tree will die."

"Will it die if just one's gone?" She reached for another leaf and rubbed both sides of it with her long fingers, but she didn't pull it loose. She looked at him and smiled.

"Not even if you pull two, Lindsay. You can pull another, and the tree will survive just fine."

"What if a tree has just six leaves?" She leaned back against the tree again, aware of the sound the lapping water made. The wind was blowing the waves away from the shore, but they could never leave for good. The water had to return to fill the void. Could she do this for good, leave, not caring if the void were ever filled? She had the means, now. Three bottles full.

Keith snorted a short laugh. "Six? What tree has six leaves?"

"My tree, Uncle Keith." She grinned at him, although it was more of an impish smirk than an actual grin. "My imaginary, six-leafed tree. If I pluck one leaf and throw it away, will my tree die? You are the trained expert. This is what you do for a living." She turned to look him full in the face. "Be honest. Will my tree die?"

He shook his head and laughed. He reached to a different tree and twisted one leaf until it came loose in his hand.

"One leaf." He held it out to her. "It's still alive, even now, you know. However, this leaf will die. No matter what we do, this leaf will die. It will use up the nourishment inside its cells, and it will die. The other side of the coin is that the tree can no longer draw sustenance from the leaf. However, I'm not answering your question, am I?"

"No, you're not, my sweet Uncle Keith. Thank you for trying, though." She turned back to watch the leaf from earlier. It was just visible far out in the water. She hadn't really expected him to understand, anyway.

"I wasn't finished, Lindsay. If your tree is very healthy, even with its six leaves, removing one will do only minimal damage. It will suffer, show stress, and perhaps stop growing for a while. However, it will recover. That's a healthy tree, remember."

"A sick tree?" She didn't look at him, and her voice had no emotion. She didn't want to hear this part. She had asked, but she didn't want to hear his answer. She already knew.

"A sick tree? Hm. If the tree is already sick, one leaf might make the difference. If you pluck that leaf, you've just killed the tree. It might look fine for a while, but eventually the other five leaves will start to yellow, dropping one at a time, and before too long, the tree will be dead."

She snorted softly, and before she could catch herself,

it turned into a sour chuckle. Then, she ran one hand through her hair. She didn't say anything else, though. If she said what she thought, it would hurt too much, and she didn't want Keith to see that.

"What, Lindsay? You seem very sedate today."

"My poor brothers. I'm very sorry, Cody and Casey." She took a long breath and whispered, "Especially you, Casey. I am so very sorry."

"Lindsay, are you all right?"

"My tree is very sick, Uncle Keith. You've not answered the real question, though. Do you love her? It's just me out here, and I keep secrets very well. Whatever you tell me today will be wiped away tomorrow. Feel free to bare your soul, and your deepest confidences will die with me. Literally." She turned to him and smiled, and she made sure her smile was real and beautiful. She had that knack, no matter how she felt inside, to be real and beautiful on the outside. She knew that everyone was fooled, even John, and he knew all her secrets. Well, almost all. Not the one in the purse she had borrowed from her mother. He would, though, soon enough. It would be too late, then. It was too late, now. It had been too late for a very long time.

When Keith didn't answer, Lindsay prompted, "Are you in love?"

"With who, Lindsay?" He looked decidedly nervous.

She laughed. "All right, Keith. I won't push the question." She turned at the sound of a voice calling her name.

"Hey, Lindsay! There you are! Fajitas are here! Uncle

165

Keith! Come on up and get some!"

She could see one of her brothers standing in the doorway, directly in the middle of the forty-foot opening where she had pushed back the glass doors. The sunlight was coming through the deck above, shining in bands across his skin. He was covered with water, and he sparkled in the sun. She smiled at the long limbs and narrow waist his height had given him. It must be Casey, she thought. He was the one who would think of her. He looked wonderful standing there in his bright red trunks, one leg wrapped with a brilliant yellow flower. In that moment she loved him more than life itself, and it broke her heart to know she planned to leave him alone. But then that was the whole problem. She loved him more than life itself. She didn't love life at all.

"Let's go, Lindsay." Keith reached to take her arm. "Let's go have fajitas. You've got a brother who loves you, and he wants to share."

"I love him, too. I just wish I loved me."

"What was that, Lindsay?" He started to turn to her.

However, she didn't get a chance to repeat herself. As they watched, two of Casey's friends ran up beside him. One grabbed the plate from his hand, and the other tackled him, one arm around his waist, taking them both into the pool. Keith laughed, and he reached for Lindsay, motioning for her to hurry up.

She did follow, but her heart wasn't in it. She had other things on her mind, and every one of them was in her mother's purse, that orangey-red shoulder bag sitting on the bathroom counter.

166

Then, she frowned. She had forgotten to move it, and now look at the crowd in the house. She felt a flash of panic, and then she let it go. It would still be there, or it wouldn't. If it was gone, there were other ways. Instead, she would spend the next few hours enjoying her wonderful brothers, because she would never see them again.

Chapter 14

TROOPER swung all six feet of the massive metal and glass front door closed. Counterweights helped the eight-foot tall door swing smoothly and easily. When it aligned with the matching door at its side, small motors whirred, and the threshold lifted a quarter inch to seal the frame airtight. Trooper didn't pay attention, though. He had hoped Joanie would stay for a while, just for a physical presence in the great emptiness of the house. He would have been glad to discuss the weather, his next purchase, or even his son, Jeffrey. He was lonely. There was no one around to trigger his public persona, no one to see his presentation of the Trooper he needed the world to know, no one at all. He had no audience, and with no audience to see and believe in what he wished them to see, then all Trooper had left was what he really was, and that was alone.

Through the metal and glass that made up the door, he saw the petite young woman climb nimbly back into her car, not even looking back at the house to wave in farewell. A small puff of smoke at the tailpipe told him she had started the engine, and with a quick flash of brake lights, the red convertible wound its way among the trees and was gone.

With his eyes closed, Trooper held the box to his face and breathed deeply several times. He didn't want what was in this box. He wanted what had been his thirty years ago, or perhaps twenty or fifteen. Yes, fifteen years ago. Then, Jeffrey had still worshipped his father, and Lindsay had been an adoring little girl. The twins had been small, still, and it had taken the four of them, Trooper and Sharon and the two older children, to corral their shenanigans. It had been exhausting, and Trooper had loved every minute of it. Now, what did he have? This big house with its indoor tennis court, a four-car garage, and a good dose of loneliness. Even his youngest sons had abandoned him.

Stepping into the living room, he broke the seal on the package, and he lifted half the lid. He paused, remembering all the calls the ministry had received the past week from that man at the Chronicle, Bucky Simms. He had quite a reputation for unmasking things organizations tried to keep concealed. In spite of his encouragements to John, Trooper knew the ministry *was* overextended, and seriously. But there was no way Bucky Simms could know about Joanie.

A buzzing sound from the other side of the house called his attention, and he sighed. Setting the box on a side table, he stepped toward the kitchen, rummaging through the remains of the breakfast the twins had left scattered on the counter. Finally finding the source of the noise, he picked it up. It seemed one of the boys had left a phone behind. He pressed the button and held it to his ear.

"Dad! Uncle John said you'd be there. Come out for fajitas. Mom's cooking, and we're all in the pool."

"Um, whose phone do I have?" Someone should have been asking for one of his sons, not one of his sons asking for him. "Anyway, how'd you know I'd be the one to answer this phone?"

"Dad, it's mine. I forgot it this morning, and I'm using Cody's. Only three of us live there, remember. Cody and I are both here."

That hurt him. Sharon had been gone only three months, and now she didn't live here. He hadn't thought of it in exactly those terms.

"I came to see you, and I missed you, Son. I thought you'd be home this afternoon, and I wanted to play a little ball with you." He sighed, unable to keep up his pretense. "Oh, well. The house sure feels empty. I guess you prefer being out there with your mom. That's okay. Some other time, Son." He was about to end the connection when Casey's voice stopped him.

"Dad, don't hang up. You've got to come. Will you, Dad? Please? We've got a basketball, and our friends are in the pool. There are lots of things to do. I'll even play golf, if you want. Please, Dad."

Trooper thought of the box he'd just had delivered, and he thought of the woman he'd hoped would stay just for a moment. Now, he had his boy on the phone begging for his attention. Casey didn't even like golf.

"Have you asked your mom?" He wasn't sure he'd exactly be welcome. He heard water splash in the background, and another voice, one that was the same as the one on the phone, yelled for everyone to watch out. In that moment, Trooper wanted what he heard at the other end of the line.

"Dad, I don't have to ask Mom. I'm asking you. It's fun. Come out. I want you around."

You're the one who's Casey's friend. You, Two Points. He misses you. John had said that to him just today. In spite of himself, Trooper smiled. "Is your Uncle John there? Did John put you up to this, Casey?" It would be like him.

"Dad! He's upstairs, and I haven't seen him for an hour. I'm asking. Me. Casey. Would you rather I come home? I drove Uncle Keith's Mercedes down the driveway to the house. I bet he'd let me use it. Mom could bring him to get it later."

Keith? John had said Kaffe was headed out to the lake property. Keith shouldn't be out there with Sharon. Something welled up inside Trooper's chest, and it was hard. Desperate, even. He would go.

"I will come out, Casey. Thank you for calling. I'll bring your phone, too." It would provide a good excuse in front of Keith and Sharon, a dutiful father returning a son's misplaced phone. Dear God, how had he let this happen?

Casey laughed. "I don't need it, Dad. I've got Cody's.

171

You keep it with you. Then I'll be able to call you anytime. I'll see you in a few minutes." Before the connection broke, Trooper heard him yell, "Hey! Dad's coming!"

Cheers erupted in the background, but equally important was one particular voice among the crowd. It was a victory whoop, and Trooper knew it must be Cody's.

"Way to go, Casey! Way to go!"

Trooper clicked off the phone. He looked at it, its glossy black screen now blank, and he set it on the counter, resting his hand beside it. The granite was cold and smooth, and it pulled the heat out of his hand, giving him a chill for a moment.

God, where did you go? I can't do this alone. Hadn't he said that just before he called Joanie? He tapped the surface of the phone, remembering a Bible lesson he hadn't taught in a very long time. Was his own son an angel sent to answer his prayer?

"Thank you, God. I'll try to believe." He tapped the counter beside the phone three more times, then he picked up the device and slipped it into his pocket. "I will carry it, Casey. Call me anytime." He knew the boy couldn't hear him, but he'd thought God couldn't, either. Casey had called, though, and just in the nick of time. He'd let God take the credit for that.

Just now, however, he had a family to go see.

Chapter 15

"OH, LINDSAY! Keith! You've found us. Come on in. John and I are preparing fajitas."

Sharon felt her insides go soft, and tingles covered her from her spine to her fingertips. With the sounds from the pool echoing up the stairwell and into the kitchen, she hadn't heard them approach. She and John both had their hands in the food, slicing up additional items for the oven, and she set the knife aside. Her hand was shaking, and she knew she dared not try to cut with it in this state. She knew what state she was in, too. A Keith state.

"John." Keith held out a hand, awkwardly dropping it when John held his up covered with fajita fixings. John didn't speak.

Sharon felt the sudden tension in the room, and she spoke up. "You must forgive me. Earlier, I didn't realize I still had on my slip from this morning." With her heart pounding, she realized she still had it on. Quickly, she rinsed her hands and wiped them on a towel. With a nervous gesture, she patted her face, then adjusted a shoulder strap. "Would this be a good time to change? Lindsay, can you help John?" She grabbed her daughter's arm and pulled her to the counter. "We're a bit low on meat, dear. I hadn't planned for so many. Just slice the strips thinly, and we'll be fine."

She was very flustered. In spite of John's talk, Keith had that effect on her. It was out of her control. All she could do was run for safety.

"I have meat, if you need more, Sharon." Keith jerked his thumb the direction of the door and began to back that direction. "May I? It's in the truck. It won't take me a minute to bring it in."

John laughed. "I'll go with you, Keith. Lindsay, take a knife and work on the meat. Keith and I will be right back. Just let me wash up, first."

Sharon stood at the door for a moment as he flipped on the water and cleaned his hands, making sure to apply soap twice. After a moment, she realized he intended to ensure time for her to exit the kitchen before he headed outdoors with Keith. She caught Lindsay's eyes, and she felt her face warm. In that soul-baring moment, she turned and ran, certain she would never make it through this day at all.

STEPPING outside into the early afternoon sun, John paused, grabbing Keith's arm.

"Yes, John?" Keith looked at the hand on his arm.

174

"My truck's this way." He made to walk forward.

"I know where it is, Keith. Uncle Keith." John smiled, using his foot to lift a flowering shrub off the path, his reference to Keith as an uncle a very clear barb that there were children inside the house who knew him as one. The shrub shifted back again when he moved his foot. "The plantings look a little dry."

Keith chuckled. "That's why I'm here. Sharon called, and I came out to look at the irrigation system." He nodded to the gold Mercedes. "This way, John."

"I know, Keith. You've got me blocked in." He didn't move forward, but instead knelt to inspect the shrub.

"Ha! You weren't even here when I arrived. Come on, John. Sharon needs my meat." Then, he reddened and coughed. "Fajitas, and all that."

"Not yet, Keith. Come down here and look at this bush. You need to see this." John fingered one leaf as if he had found something there.

Keith knelt beside him, reaching to touch the shrub, then pulled his hand back. "What's going on here, John?"

"Very good, Keith." John's tone was that of a college professor praising a star student for a correct answer. "You've just asked my question for me. You do remember that Sharon has twin sons in there, seventeen-year-old twin boys that look just like their father, a well-known minister." He released the shrub and turned to him. "How about Lindsay, Sharon and Trooper's daughter? She's twenty-one. Beautiful, isn't she? Jeffrey's not here, but he loves his mother very much. How badly do you want to hurt those children? They call you 'Uncle.' Do you know

175

why, Keith? Because they love you. What's that worth to you, the love of four wonderful children?" He turned back to the shrub and reached for a wilted bloom, lifting it to his nose and drawing in the odor.

Keith snorted. "What are you saying? Trooper and Sharon are my friends. They have been for thirty years. I've watched their kids grow from babies, and I've been part of their lives, every one of them. That's all." He stood and took a step back, his feet crunching against the crushed granite path.

John just smelled the flower as if Keith had said nothing. A bird landed nearby, and as quickly, it flitted away. From the back of the house, the sound of laughter could be heard from the pool. A huge splash made John smile. Teenagers only saw the moment. If *now* was enjoyable, then the world was theirs for the asking.

"It's warm out here, Keith." He continued to hold the bloom in his hand as he spoke.

"Yes, it is, John. May I get the meat and take it inside?"

"Listen, first. This bloom. Even though it's wilted, it just opened today. I'm sure of that. It only opens when the weather grows hot. The heat brings it out. This is a bloom that's enticing in the heat of the moment, so to speak, but when the heat cools, the intense beauty, the attraction of the bloom, fades away, and all that's left is something dead. The shrub lives on, though. Sharon and Trooper's marriage still lives, Keith. Is enjoying the flower in that one moment of heat worth it?" He stood, his point made. He didn't look at Keith, though. Keith was a smart man.

They remained there, side-by-side, for several moments before Keith spoke.

"You can have the meat, John." His voice carried anger, but it also told of defeat. "I can see I have you blocked in. Perhaps I should go."

"Keith, you are an honorable man. I've known that for thirty years. I appreciate this." John turned to him, reaching out his hand to shake.

Keith stood for a moment before reaching into his chest pocket and pulling out his gold sunglasses. He slipped them onto his face, and after a moment, reached to take John's hand, gripping it tightly.

"It's hard, John. You know I've loved her since high school." He kept his grip on John's hand the entire time.

"The right thing is often hard." He remembered the gate tag he refused to install in his car, wanting his movements tracked. "Let Kaffe come out next time. Will you do that?"

Keith stood for a moment more, and he pressed his lips together. John couldn't see his eyes through the lens of the sunglasses, but he bet they were red. Finally, Keith gave a quick nod and released his hand, turning with a quick stride to walk to his truck. John just stood and watched. When he got there, he opened the back and pulled out a Styrofoam chest, setting it on the drive by John's car. Then, without further recognition that John was standing there, he climbed into the Mercedes. The brakes flashed, and for a moment, the tires spun. Then, as if he had managed to leash his anger once more, the brakes flashed a second time, and the huge SUV slowly pulled away. The gravel underneath the wheels crunched softly until it was gone.

John sighed. He liked Keith, some, at least. He didn't hate him at all. He did hate that this situation had forced them to this. It felt grimy on his skin. It felt really grimy on his skin, and it wasn't the sort of grimy that one could just wash away. However, at least it was done.

With a heavy sigh, he walked to the chest and picked it up. He stood for a moment in the dappled sun, and he enjoyed the sounds of being outdoors, the birds and the leaves rustling. He smiled at the other sounds, the laughter from the back of the house. He was surprised, though, when there was a sudden whoosh, and sprinkler heads popped up all over the yard. Just one, however, right where the wilted bloom drooped onto the walk, didn't.

That was when he realized Keith perhaps wasn't as guilty as he had thought. Still, John had seen them together, and he knew the signs. They were the same ones he fought so hard to hide when he was alone with Trooper. He wasn't angry with Keith at all. Rather, he felt very sorry for him, because he knew what it was like to be in a position where he could do nothing at all, and not even God seemed willing to help.

He made it back to the house with the steaks, but he was wet by the time he got there. It seemed that in spite of the one malfunctioning nozzle, the rest of the irrigation system worked very well, indeed.

"YOU SHOULD have been there, Jeffrey."

"Been where?" He turned to Cookie, clearly preoccupied with his thoughts. They were together in his Escalade EXT, a giant of a truck that had been handed down from his father. It was black, the only color his father drove.

She chuckled.

"In Memphis. You would have seen." She played with her ring, leaning her shoulder against the man she intended to marry. She looked up at him, seeing the stress in his damp hair and flushed skin, suddenly wishing she hadn't said anything.

"Tell me again about Memphis. I think I missed part of it at lunch." He reached over and took her hand in his. He grasped the ring's band, and shifting it slightly, he made its colors flash. "How much did the boy look like me?"

"I love you, Jeffrey." She did, too, and with all her heart.

"That's nice." He laughed. "Where did that come from?"

"Were you really sick today?" She snuggled in closer, wanting her question to be an easy one for him to answer. She needed the reply to be simple.

"I think so." He smiled and squeezed her hand. "Why do you ask?"

"I don't know." She did, but the answers might not please her at all. "You seemed fine before. During dinner, you remember. It started with my story. He looked so much like you, Jeffrey." She paused, untangling her hand and resting it on his leg, palm down.

"How much, Cookie?"

Her heart turned over, dread somehow tingeing the

179

moment. The charm was suddenly missing from his voice, and his words had gone flat. Once again, she had said the wrong thing.

"How much did he look like me?"

"I'm sorry, Jeffrey," she whispered, rubbing her hand over the fabric of his pants. "I should have left it alone. It's just that," and she looked up at him, pleading with him to understand, "I love you so much, and he was just like you. I couldn't help but fall in love with him, too. You should have been there, Jeffrey. You should." She dropped her head again.

"It's okay, Cookie. You tell me all about him, and I'll just listen. No questions, just you talking. Will that do?" He put his arm around her, pulling her in close.

She did talk of the boy, his pale hair, his golden skin, and all the expressions on his face that had made her think of Jeffrey. It was also listening to the boy; he had talked exactly like Jeffery did. Even in the way he carried himself, she had seen Jeffery sitting beside her the entire service.

THE MORE Cookie said, the more Jeffrey was convinced. With each stroke of her fingers across his leg, he remembered how his moment of eternity in that pool that night had ended in one brilliant flash of light. Only, it hadn't ended, not for him and not for her. He had left life in her, and she had faced that alone. She had lived through childbirth, enduring the disgrace of her family and the pain of giving up her baby.

His baby.

Dear God, he prayed, Why did you let me enjoy it so much? Now, he didn't know what to do, and it was tearing him up inside. In that moment, he remembered what Bucky had said. *He sure looks like you.* It seemed he'd heard those words before, and on more than one occasion.

Dear God, he prayed, what would I do with a twelve-year-old?

JEFFREY didn't realize it, but with that simple prayer, at that very moment, he had cast the die. It hadn't finished rolling, but it was on the table, and soon it would come to rest. It was a terrible risk, but then so was a fifteen-year-old climbing into a darkened pool with a girl he hardly knew. Sometimes the die is tossed, and it takes years before the result is known. About twelve years, not to be too exact. About twelve years and nine long months.

Other times, it takes about thirty minutes. That was exactly how far he was from the lake house at Private Road No. 27.

Exactly thirty minutes.

Chapter 16

MUSIC BLASTED from beneath the deck of the lake house, and bare arms and legs, wet and glistening, were everywhere. The pool was filled with teenagers. More precisely, it was filled with boys, and the girls were in a tight group off to one side.

Cody rushed up behind his twin brother, wrapping his arms around his neck, nearly tumbling both of them into the water. He pointed with his long arm, and he leaned his wet face against his brother's cheek as he shared his plan.

"You see Emily?" He panted with exertion. He'd been chasing the girl for the past fifteen minutes. She had managed to elude him so far.

"The pink suit, right?" Casey had her picked out in a heartbeat. She was the prettiest of the girls, and her suit fit her very nicely.

"She's fast. I need your help. Every time I get close to

her, she's gone. Her friends help her, too. They get in the way and grab my arms. You're going to have to help me."

"How?" Casey frowned.

"For this to work, brother, we are each other, see? Sometimes I'm me, and sometimes you're me. Other times I'm you, and then you'll be you. Is this making sense?" Cody wrapped his arms around his brother's chest and pulled them tight several times in rapid succession, laughing, licking water off his face, being stupid just for fun. "Understand?"

"We talk to each other, you mean?"

"Yeah. I'll call you Casey, and the next time I'll call you Cody. You do the same to me. That way, Emily won't know who's who, and we'll close in and grab her. Ready?" He drummed his palms on his brother's chest, grinning, and he stepped away to the side of the pool, motioning for his twin to head the opposite direction.

"Hey, Casey. I hear you called Dad. He's coming out, you say. That right, Cody?" Cody grinned and pointed to his brother.

"That's right, Casey. You know, Cody, I think we've got the best father in the world. I hope one of us can be as good a basketball player as he was. Do you think we can, Casey?" He nodded at his brother for him to take his turn.

Those around the pool watched the display of thespian skills with interest. Once it started, no one could tell which Kincaid was which. They were just two identical, red-suited boys, exactly the same height, with exactly the same voices. Even when they raised their arms to point, or lifted their feet to take a step, their muscles flexed in exactly the same way. Pretty soon, the audience grew amused and began to laugh.

It took several more flip-flops in the banter before the boys reached the end of the pool where the girls were sequestered, and when they did, they broke their act apart and rushed for their target at the exact same time. Seeing two red-suited seventeen-year-olds coming at her from opposite directions, Emily didn't know which way to run. For that reason, she didn't run at all, and when the boys got to her, she grabbed the one she thought was Cody, laughing and fighting him as he hauled her toward the pool.

The only thing, it wasn't Cody at all. He was left with his mouth hanging in surprise as his brother landed with his girl in the center of the pool, erupting a moment later in a spray of water with her still in her arms. Just as soon as Casey showed his face, his twin brother leaped from the side of the pool directly onto his head and pulled him away from her. By the time he let him loose, she had already climbed out and run to her friends.

With a scowl on his face, Cody swam over and grabbed his brother around the neck, holding him from behind. He growled into his ear, "Did you enjoy that, grabbing my girl?"

Casey twisted his head to look at his brother's face, and he grinned. "You mean grabbing *my* girl? I sure did, *Casey*." Then, they were underwater again, the two boys tangled up as one.

When they finally came to the surface, however, they were laughing once again.

TROOPER'S Lincoln Navigator sat at the turnoff to the family's property, the engine running. Glowing numbers on the dash told the truth of the heat outside. It was pushing one hundred.

However, it was seventy-two degrees inside. As the outside temperature display climbed another notch, the low-pitched hum of the air conditioner's fan motor shifted, and the volume of air from the vents increased.

Trooper reached and adjusted one vent to the left of the steering wheel, as he chewed the inside of his lip. He didn't know whether to be relieved or upset. He had just seen a gold Mercedes coming off Green Fork Cutoff where it intersected West Lake, and it had been traveling too fast. His first response had been one of unbridled anger. He had glimpsed the shine of gold-rimmed glasses on the driver, and he was certain it was Keith.

Now, recalling that instant of recognition and perceived betrayal, Trooper felt anger surge once again. His breathing deepened, and his face grew hot. Glancing at the temperature display, he reached to the dash and touched a control, watching the numbers dip to seventy, then, with another movement of his fingers, it suddenly showed sixty-eight. He didn't feel any more comfortable, but the chill in the air took the heat off his face.

After a moment he lifted his foot from the brake and let the big machine crunch down the drive toward the oversized iron gate. Bringing the black Lincoln to a stop before it triggered the gate's sensors, he looked at the iron wall blocking his path, now unsure of his welcome. With

Keith gone, his driving reason for coming out had evaporated. What would he now find on the other side? That morning in the service, Sharon had been beautiful and engaging, even interacting with him from her seat in the front of the audience. While the rolling of her eyes had not exactly been playful, she hadn't looked away, either. More than a few times in the last three months, she had hurt him by refusing to look at him, cutting him off with her expression, and almost destroying his focus on God's Word. This morning had been good. What he could expect away from the church, however, was a different matter altogether. The last time he'd come to see her here, he'd left angry, calling her deplorable. She had been, too, unbathed and wearing clothes that were more in need of a garbage bag than a washing machine. Without the cleaning service he insisted on each week, there was no telling what the place would be like.

He picked up his foot and inched forward once again, stopping just as quickly, and then he shifted violently into reverse, convinced he shouldn't have come.

His outside mirrors automatically angled down to help him back up, but rather than helping, it prevented him from seeing anything except what was just beside the truck. Hitting his steering wheel in frustration and shaking his head to clear vision that was suddenly blurry with anger, he spun the wheel and trounced the gas overly hard. The powerful motor under the hood roared, spinning the drive train entirely too quickly in the loose gravel, and the big truck jumped, sending gravel flying. Catching even Trooper off guard, the unwieldy machine flew backward in a careening arc, vaulting the back wheels off the drive, and sending the rear end of the truck directly into a dense stand of brush. The sound of shattering glass brought home what had happened.

Glancing in the outside mirror, he growled and threw the transmission into park, watching as the glass ovals mounted on the doors quietly moved back to their proper position. The reflections were filled with large branches gripping the back of the SUV like caressing fingers.

He was angry and yet relieved at the same time. Back at the mansion, he had perceived the phone in his pocket as his entry pass back into life. Then, he had seen Keith, and his motivations had shifted. Now, he had an equally good reason to head back to the city. He had damaged the paint on his glossy black SUV, the back window was shattered, and no doubt he would find more damage than that when he pulled forward. Even his son couldn't fault him for not staying.

"Sorry, Casey," he muttered. Then, as if a hand lifted from his chest, he laughed, suddenly out from under the responsibility of reengaging with his family, and he realized the air from the vents was too cold. Adjusting the temperature once again, he pressed his foot to the brake and shifted into drive. Hitting the gas, he prepared for the big, rear-wheel-drive machine to surge ahead, leaping forward onto the built-up gravel drive. Instead, while the back wheels spun and dirt flew, it was as if something held him in place. He punched the gas harder, and the truck shivered, the back end dropping even lower as the wheels dug into the dirt.

"What, God?" Trooper slammed the gearshift into park and sat, his breathing fast and hard. He hit the steering wheel twice and ranted, spewing his anger against the Maker into the interior of the truck in an abusive volley of vitrified fury.

"Are you satisfied? I have services in three hours, you know. How am I to get to the church if I'm stuck out here? God, are you listening? You can't do this to me." Then, in frustration, he threw the transmission back into drive once again and slammed his foot to the floor. The rear end shimmied fitfully as the truck's wheels spun, and dirt flew to the side. However, when he finally admitted defeat, the truck still sat in the exact same position, with its front wheels on the gravel drive, and its back end wedged firmly into that stand of brush.

Throwing open the door, he paused to give the step along the bottom of the door a chance to descend, then he placed his foot where he knew it should be. He was caught off guard when his foot met open air, and he stumbled from the truck. He looked to find the center of the truck on the ground, preventing the step from extending. He kicked the step, or as close as he could get to it, then growled when he realized he had marred the toe of his shoe. Kneeling at the back of the truck, he found why he hadn't been able to move. When the heavy SUV had launched off the drive, it had come to rest on a stump that was now wedged inside the back bumper mounts. Each spin of his wheels had hollowed out the dirt, dropping the big machine lower and lower onto the stump, and now it was wedged so tightly it might as well be permanently attached.

As he stood, the phone in his pocket turned awkwardly, and he reached inside to adjust it. The surface was smooth and cool in the afternoon heat, and he pulled it out. Its glossy black face mocked him.

He loves you, Trooper. He wants you with him.

However, he wasn't sure he believed it. Phones lied. People lied. Sometimes, he felt like God lied. He certainly didn't feel loved at the moment. His eyes grew gritty, and he muttered, "He loves his brother and all the things I can buy him." He squeezed the phone in his hand and leaned inside to the truck to kill the engine.

However, the phone wasn't through with him yet.

Call him, Trooper. He was willing to come to you. He's there, just through that gate.

"And so is Sharon. She's run from me, out here hiding in the woods. She's the one my family loves. Not me." He climbed to sit in the Navigator's black leather seat and leaned forward with his feet on the sill. The door hung open, and he reached one hand to push on it gently, watching it bounce back and forth, returning to him each time.

Are you sure, Trooper?

Then, he remembered his box back at the house. It sat half opened. He had forgotten it when Casey called. He had been so relieved to hear from his son, so pleased that he was still loved, that he was *wanted,* that he had put everything else from his mind. He had needed what he had heard over the phone, and now all he wanted was to run from it. He was frightened. He wasn't a father, anymore.

189

He had become Trooper, the acclaimed televangelist, known for his ability to change people's lives. He had lost Trooper, the father, Trooper, the husband, Trooper, the man who loved God even more than he loved his ministry. He had lost himself, and he didn't know how to find his way home.

Are you sure, Trooper?

He looked at the phone and the face he saw reflected in its glossy surface. Home was on the other end of this line. He had heard his son speak to him, and his son had begged him to come home. With determination, he touched the power button, and the screen lit up. Navigating the unfamiliar device, he finally located a list of recent calls. It made him laugh. He'd forgotten how little Casey cared for operating his phone. There were only three numbers there: Cody's, his mother's, and his father's.

"God love you, Casey. More than anyone I know, God love you." He reached and tapped Sharon's number. That's who he needed to talk to. His wife. However, when it picked up, it wasn't Sharon on the phone at all.

"John, here. Yes, Casey. What do you need?"

Trooper could hear Lindsay in the background, and the clanking of cooking utensils littered John's question.

"John. It's Trooper. Can you come down the drive? I'm stuck, and I could use some help." As soon as he spoke, he realized just how much of a double meaning there was in those words. He had become stuck over the past few years, and not just here alongside the driveway. He could use all the help he could get, especially to fix his family, whatever that might entail. If he could trust anyone, it was John.

"Stuck, Two Points?" Water could be heard running, and then it quickly shut off. Lindsay's voice murmured something that Trooper couldn't catch.

"John, it's hot out here. I'm off the drive just past the gate and very stuck." He suddenly realized how hot it really was, and the black vehicle was making it worse. He stood and walked to a patch of shade under a nearby tree, his feet kicking up dust at each step. A small bird skittered away, stopping nearby and chattering at him. It was painfully obvious not even the wildlife wanted him around today.

"Two Points, did you see Keith?"

"In passing." He didn't care to get onto that topic.

"So, you know he was here." The words were flat coming from the small, black box.

"Can we talk about Keith later? All I need is a ride. The truck's stuck out here in the driveway."

"How—" John began, but he was quickly interrupted.

"If we're going to take time to discuss this, I need you to hold on, John. It's gotten really hot, and I need to take a minute to pull my jacket off." Trooper put the phone in his pants pocket and slipped off his coat. Draping it over one arm, he fished the instrument out once again. "Now, that's better. Where's Sharon?"

"Changing clothes, Two Points. Lindsay and I are slicing up some, um, Angus, I think, for fajitas. Right, Lindsay? This is Angus?" Lindsay could be heard agreeing with him. "I'll be right there. Keep cool."

Trooper clicked the phone off, holding it in his hand

191

for a moment. Then, he tossed it in the air, easily catching it before dropping it back in his pocket.

"Keep cool, John? You bet." He pulled a white handkerchief from his pocket, pressing it to his face. "Just tell me how."

But he already knew the answer to that, and he climbed back into the Navigator to start the engine, slamming the door to shut the heat away.

"YOUR FATHER'S here. I wonder why?" John clicked the line off, turning to the girl at his side.

Lindsay laughed. "Not because we're his family, that's for sure." With her knife, she deftly sliced the steak in her hand into several long strips. "I wonder how Mom'll take it. He's invading her hiding place. Where will she run to next?"

"Home to your father, I wish." John spoke very frankly with her. She expected it, and he knew he would get the same in return, whether he wanted it or not.

In response, she held up one slice of the steak she had just cut, and she looked at it intently. "You know, John? This looks like a bunch of bull. You know better than to tell me you wish that." She looked at him and smirked.

He closed his eyes with a grimace, as a wave of pain lanced into his head. "Don't, Lindsay. Whatever you think, that was over nearly forty years ago." He sighed, his face tight. The pain was making it so, but the girl was so perceptive it sometimes unnerved him. He tried to smile.

She stepped to him and patted her hand on his cheek. With unexpected tenderness, she looked into his eyes. Her own were red, and she whispered to him softly, "John, when you love someone, it's never over, not even after forty years. Only death gives you freedom from love." She removed her hand, and when she looked at him, she giggled girlishly. "I seem to have smeared bull all over your face. I'm so sorry, John. Let me help you clean it off." She reached for a towel, and stepped to wet it in the sink.

"Lindsay, don't. Please." The pain throbbed, and he could barely keep it from showing on his face.

She turned to him with a surprised expression. "You like your face covered in bull?" She leaned back against the sink, holding the towel to her chin. "You do look kinda cute that way. I do believe we should just leave it. Dad might think you look cute, too. If he's really hungry, he might just, you know—" She giggled, pausing, and it was laced with hysteria. "—lick it off." Then, she whipped around to face the sink, the towel at her side, and she began to cry. "Oh, I am so mean. I'm sorry, John. That was awful of me." She turned to face him, putting a bright, very believable-looking smile on her face. "You, John, are the one person I should be nice to. You are as honest as you can be, and you try so hard to do the right thing. Be my friend for this day, John." She stepped forward and began to clean his face. "I want to remember you as my friend."

"I know about the pills, Lindsay."

She sighed, continuing to wipe the side of his face. "And you are my very best friend, John. You never tell my secrets, do you?"

193

He grimaced, but it was for the pain in his skull. He felt sympathy for his Aunt Bessie.

"Don't let me down, John." Lindsay gave his face one last, very firm stroke, her voice harsh, and she threw the towel in the sink.

"I love you, Lindsay, and I have for twenty-one years. Have I ever told you that?" He watched the beautiful girl in front of him, hoping he was getting through. He wasn't sure anymore.

She laughed. "More times than my own father. Look at you. You're not even upset at me, and I've done my best to flay you to the bone. You should have been my father, John. You love me. I can honestly admit I believe you when you say those words to me. Thank you." She stepped to him to kiss his cheek just where she had wiped away the remains of the steak. Then, as she finished, she licked his cheek and backed away, laughing. "There. That's the last of it. Now, my father won't be tempted."

"Girl," he smiled, "you cannot believe how much I love you. I want you around for a very long time."

"Go, John." She patted his chest. "My father needs you. He's out of your presence for one afternoon, and his world seems to be crumbling around him. You know, I think he would love you, even if he knew. He really is a good man."

"Just not a good father?" He watched her eyes. They brightened, and he knew she was through being honest.

"Well, we can't have everything, can we?"

They both looked to the door to see Sharon prance in wearing a terrycloth robe.

"There's more steak? Good! Where's Keith?" She smiled brightly, and her skin was flushed.

John shook his head, unable to deal with Sharon's obvious interest in Keith, and he walked to the door, calling out, "I'm headed out to the driveway to pick up Two Points. I'll be right back."

"Trooper's here? Where's Keith?" Sharon suddenly looked bewildered. "I put on my best suit. I want to swim."

"Oh, Mom." Lindsay went to her and put her arms around her mother.

John paused at the door, holding it slightly open and watching the two women. Sharon was so transparent, and she was lost without Trooper. Lindsay pulled her mother close and then kissed her on the cheek.

"Uncle Keith got the sprinklers going again, and he had to go. You should have seen Uncle John. He was outside, and he got all soaked. I laughed and laughed. You would have loved seeing him run through the water, Mom. Thanks to you, I'm having the best time of my life today. I will never have another day better than this."

John watched Lindsay lean her face into her mother's hair and draw in a deep breath. He remembered how she loved the smell of her mother's hair. She had always loved the smell of her mother's hair.

He gently closed the door and headed down the walk. Out there, somewhere and for some reason, waited Trooper. It was John to the rescue, once again.

Chapter 17

THROUGH the ironwork of the gate, even before it opened, John could see Trooper's Navigator. He shook his head. The front was nose up on the drive, and the back was wedged in the trees. At his approach, the gate slipped out of the way, and he eased his Porsche through, slowly pulling up to where Trooper was waving from inside the truck. He rolled down his window.

"Hey, there's a party going on in the house behind me. They let just anybody in. You want to crash it?" He grinned in greeting. As Trooper exited the truck, he didn't look very vibrant. His coat was slung over one arm, and old sweat stained his shirt.

"Is there air conditioning?" Trooper trudged around the front of John's car, dropping heavily inside.

"There are better parking places up at the house, Two Points. You do remember that. Sharon would let you borrow one." He said it lightly, but his barbs were pointed.

"Back off, John. Right now I'm barely here." He sighed and flipped the air on high. "I called Joanie, you know." He turned his head and looked out the window.

"Joanie?" He did not like the sound of that at all. It smacked too much of Sharon and Keith. "Why Joanie, Two Points?"

"She gives me help. It costs, but she gives me help. I needed help today." He closed his eyes.

"Sex, Two Points? She's younger than Jeffrey." Dear God, he thought. Please no.

Trooper laughed, and he looked at John. "If you think that, then maybe my revelation won't be quite so shocking. No, Sharon's the only person who's ever shared my bed, John. You of all people should know that."

John knew that wasn't exactly true. Someone else had, too, just never when Trooper was awake. However, that had happened decades ago, and that old tent was ancient history. Then, he realized what Trooper meant. Joanie and her little brown packages. That could only mean one thing, and in a rush of understanding, everything came clear.

"Are you high, Two Points? I'm not taking you in there to see your boys, if you're not clean. Face me. Let me look in your eyes." Those words were not light at all, and the barbs were razors.

"I'm clean." He turned to face John. "See?" He leaned his head against the seat. "I didn't think you had figured it out, yet. Now, I have nothing else to hide. Can we go?"

"Go? There's more you haven't said. Why are you here?"

"Casey called. Before."

"Before what?" John loved this man, but he had no patience with anything like this. Trooper should know that, too.

"I didn't take them, John. Joanie brought the pills, but Casey caught me in time, and I'm clean. So, there. Can we go, please?" He closed his eyes.

"Where, Two Points?"

"The party, John. What is this, throw your best friend on the grill time? I'm here because Casey invited me out, no other reason."

John just let the engine idle, not yet sure Trooper needed to enter the gate. "I didn't know Casey called. I'm sorry. I thought you came about Keith. He was here."

"Yeah, that, too." Trooper looked at him and actually smiled. "Casey told me his Uncle Keith was here, and that decided me. I had to come."

"Not because your son invited you, though." The barbs were back.

"No more hard questions, John. I told you before, I'm barely here."

"And leaving?" When Trooper looked at him, he pointed to the Navigator stuck in the trees.

"That's another hard question, John. Yes, and leaving. Can we go to the house, now?"

John drove forward, though, taking a left on Green Fork Cutoff, and quickly revved the engine up to quite an excessive speed. Practiced hands tapping paddles on the steering wheel forced the engine to scream in protest, and the RPM indicator flirted with the red line. He didn't say anything to Trooper. In moments, the sleek automobile had turned the trees into a picket fence.

"John!" Trooper sat up, grabbing his friend's arm. "Stop this. I want to go to the lake house."

"Do you?" He slammed on the brakes, and just before the car ground to a halt, he whipped the wheel sideways, forcing the Porsche into a neatly executed 180. It shook once before it settled onto the surface of the road.

"Dear God, John!" Trooper held onto the console and door, and he turned to him with a frown. "What was that about?"

"Why do you want to go to the lake house?" John had just come from there. Trooper's family was in tatters. His wife was interested in another man, and his daughter was collecting sleeping pills from her mother's stash. The man should feel lucky his three sons seemed even reasonably stable. "Why, Two Points?"

"Leave it alone, John. Just take me there, and I'll get a ride back with someone else." He sank into his seat, defeat all over him.

"I'll take you back, Two Points, but not because I'm happy with you." During the very public lunch at the steak establishment earlier that day, John had been polite, skirting his concerns about Trooper's family. However, in private, he intended to be very specific, especially after witnessing what he'd seen since coming out this afternoon.

"You don't need to be happy with me. You just need to help me out. Can you do that?" Trooper's voice was tired.

"I am helping you out. You're just not listening."

Trooper didn't respond. Instead, he turned his head to look out the window at his side.

"Two Points?" John ventured a truce. He knew he'd pushed his friend awfully close to the edge. He released his foot from the brake, and the powerful car surged forward.

"What now, John? Do you intend to abandon me, too?" Trooper turned from the window, pressing his mouth together. After a short silence, he whispered, "Do you?"

John laughed at the audacity of the question. "After forty years? That's how long it's been since that first camping trip. Do you remember, Two Points?"

"The first one?" Trooper finally smiled. "How could I forget that one? The snake."

"The snake?" John had actually forgotten the snake. It came back to him in a flash. It had been cold, and they had carried sleeping bags that first trip. As a joke, he had put a plastic snake in the foot of Trooper's bag before they went to sleep. In the middle of the night, Trooper had grabbed his arm, whispering frantically that there was a live snake in his sleeping bag. John had promised him that he knew how to handle snakes, and if Trooper would lie really still, he would crawl down and get it. He had, too, crawling down in Trooper's sleeping bag, right on top of him, to get to that plastic snake. He had pretended to wrestle with it at first, but it had been his unexpected closeness to Trooper that had kept him from simply backing out of the sleeping bag with the toy. The roughhousing had only stopped when Trooper flew out of the bag in panic. From then on, John had known without a doubt how he felt about his friend.

"You saved me that night." Trooper grinned at the memory. "You've saved me other times, too. I trust you, John. You know that. Even now, even today. Even when I don't like what you have to say to me. That's why you're my closest friend, and that's not going to change."

"A plastic snake, and I'm your friend forever?" John laughed at that idea, as he slowed to turn onto Private Drive No. 27.

"I didn't know it was plastic, then. Not until the next morning. I was terrified that night, and after you zipped our two bags together, I felt safe, finally. You do that to me, John, make me feel safe. I think I can face my family, now. Thank you." Trooper laughed as John squeezed by the stranded Navigator. "I may need a tow truck."

"You may need a new truck, period." He edged by the massive front bumper, frowning as it came perilously close to the glass.

"Just not a new friend."

John smiled. "Thank you, Two Points."

As he pulled up and punched in his code, Trooper cleared his throat. John looked at him. "You can have a tag for your car, John."

"So I can crash it into the ditch?" He grinned. "Then I'd still have to punch in a code, and what good would that do?"

Trooper laughed, looking in the mirror at the front of the vehicle balanced on the edge of the drive just behind them. "I guess you're right about that. What good would that do?" He faced forward, his voice brightening. "On to the house, driver."

"Yes, sir," John replied with a grin. He reached a hand to his neck, working it absently. Then, as he drove down the driveway, the open fretwork of logs at the peak of the roof slowly came into view. The trees were flushed with green, and past the house, the lake sparkled.

"It's beautiful." Trooper motioned with one hand. "Look at all that. When I see it like this, I know how much God loves us."

Good ole Two Points is back, thought John. I don't think he heard a word I said.

At least he'd said them. Maybe, just maybe, someone would listen to him today. Dear God, someone needed to.

"THEY'RE here, Mom." Lindsay ran her hands under the water, looking out the window as she did so. She shook them dry before shutting the water off, reaching to a towel at her side. She felt her mother walk up to her side.

"I don't see your father's truck."

"Maybe Dad was still in town. It took them long enough they could have made it in and back, and with time to spare."

"Perhaps. You know your father when he's with your Uncle John. Nothing can tear them apart."

Lindsay glanced at her mother, surprised at the layers of meaning in those words. Then, she laughed. She was hearing what she wanted to and nothing more.

"I'll finish this, Mom. Spend time with Dad." She pushed her to the door, refusing to take no for an answer. "Go out to greet them. Go."

Sharon laughed, and it was high-pitched and a bit frantic. She peered through the door but didn't open it. "Are you sure, Lindsay? I have on this old robe. What would he think?"

Lindsay remembered her little six-leafed tree. It was struggling to survive. Keith and her mother were evidence of that. Suddenly, she needed it to survive. She needed that very much. If her parents were to make it through the upcoming shearing, they had to find each other once again.

"Just go." Lindsay opened the door and gave her mother a push. Then, just before she got away, she reached to her and placed her hands on her shoulders, pulling her close to whisper in her ear, "You don't need this, Mom. I'm helping you, remember." Without further words, she reached around her waist, loosened the tie, and slipped the old terry robe from her shoulders.

"Lindsay!" Her mother turned her head, but Lindsay was already closing the door, waving at her mother and blowing her a kiss.

SHARON may have been appalled, but she shouldn't have been. She was quite stunning, and it was clearly obvious why Keith had been in love with her all those years, why he was still in love with her, in spite of John's cautionary warning. Four children had done nothing to detract from her waistline, and her legs were as long as they had ever been. The suit she wore may have been a one-piece, cut in a tasteful manner, but as its shimmery surface sparkled through the colors of washed purples and blues, and then deeper into cherry reds, she put many a twenty-year-old to shame. She knew it, too, but this was Trooper she would be facing. It had been three months since he'd seen her dressed in something so revealing, and she was as nervous as the first time they'd been together on the night of their wedding. What if he didn't approve, if he looked at her haughtily, or even called her deplorable? He had, and not so long ago. She didn't want to be deplorable. It was just that when she fell into that deep hole the weekdays seemed to dig for her, she couldn't find the other side of deplorable. Today, she wanted to be magnificent. She didn't feel it inside, not yet. She had lived too long in deplorable to find magnificent so easily.

She did have mind enough to kick her house shoes aside as John's little Porsche pulled up at the end of the walk to let Trooper out. He didn't have to do that, but that was John, always doing the little extras for Trooper, and she appreciated it. Now, though, she especially appreciated the opportunity to have her husband to herself just for the short walk up to the house. She could charm him. She was sure of it.

She called to him as he opened the door.

"Trooper! I'm so glad you came out today." She realized she had no idea just why he had come. Her words could skirt around that little omission, though. "The boys want everyone at their little swim party. Look!" She raised her arms and twirled around, showing off her suit. Even if she didn't quite feel magnificent, she had played the part often enough that the motions came very easily to her. "I intend to jump in, too. See? Bare feet? Everyone's down at the pool."

She twirled once more, waiting nervously on an answer. Once, she would have trusted in his reactions. Now, she wasn't sure. Instead, he sat for a moment and looked her, holding the door open.

"Trooper?" Sharon paused in her display, her expression falling. She could feel deplorable knocking. "Lindsay's here, Trooper." If he didn't want her, she at least had three children she could offer. Surely she could tempt him with something.

"I heard her over the phone." He didn't climb out, though.

"Come in and see Lindsay. She's in the kitchen preparing fajitas. Our Lindsay, cooking. You have to see it, Trooper. The twins are downstairs." She ran to the car and took his hand, lifting it to her mouth to kiss his fingers. He had liked that when they were first married, for her to kiss his magic basketball fingers. He hadn't played anymore by then, but he had liked to be reminded that he had once been very good. "Of course, Trooper, you have to brave their twelve little friends if you go see the twins. You know how they are, always bringing a mob with them wherever they go."

"I know, Sharon. They've been living with me."

His words sliced into her heart. It was clear what he meant. They hadn't been living with her.

"Please, Trooper." Her eyes pleaded with him. All he had to do was climb out. Then they would be a family again. "Please?"

John pushed him on the shoulder. "Remember, I'm helping you, Two Points. Go. Tell her how beautiful she

205

is. Now."

How Sharon loved John for those words!

Trooper turned to him, and he snorted a laugh. "You are the best kind of friend, John." He grabbed the roof of the car, and he pulled his lanky frame out, wrapping one arm around Sharon's shoulders. He leaned into her neck, and pulling her hair back, he kissed her just where her neckline turned into her shoulder.

"Trooper, I have missed you." She wrapped her arms around him and held him tight.

"You are beautiful, Sharon. You've never been more so."

"Come in, Trooper. I really am glad to have you here." She leaned to the car before she closed the door. "You, too, John. Thank you for everything. Do not leave, either. Everyone stays."

He saluted her and motioned for her to close the door, waving his thanks when she did.

She heard him pull away as she turned with her husband, and suddenly, seeing the water drops covering the plantings around the house, she felt guilty. She needed Trooper to understand about Keith. She wouldn't have let it go anywhere. She wouldn't have intended it, anyway. She had just been lonely.

"See? The sprinklers are working again. Keith came out today, and now they work perfectly." She smiled, reaching to one flowering shrub leaning onto the walk. "See? It's perking up already." It was the only one not doing so, but it would. She was sure of that.

"Kaffe was supposed to be here." Trooper sounded

sour.

"Oh?" She was bright, still, and she smiled. "I didn't know. They are fixed, though. That's what counts. Go in with me, Trooper. Come see Lindsay." She took his hand and pulled his arm like a little girl urging on a wary brother. "You can't back out now. Not when you're this close."

He turned from her to look back the direction they'd come. Sharon saw John standing by his car, waiting. At her side, Trooper sighed. Then, he turned and squared his shoulders.

"I am close, aren't I, Sharon? Well, we mustn't lose touch with our family. Where is that charming chef of a daughter of ours? I want to see this, our vegetarian daughter preparing fajitas." He held out his arm. "Madam?"

Sharon laughed. She had seen the change. He knew there was a crowd inside, and he had slipped on his public persona. She would rather have had the Trooper that was pleasant and attentive because he loved her. However, in his absence, at least this Trooper would be good company. After all, she had all week to be lonely. Today was for having fun.

"Lindsay!" Sharon called to her daughter, knocking sharply on the door as she entered. "Your father's here. Come give him a hug, and then we're on the way to see the twins. Say a prayer for us when we go down." She winked at her daughter and kissed her on the cheek. "We might not survive all their friends, not all in one room at the same time."

"Hello, Dad." Lindsay glanced at him briefly and

207

looked away, using the knife to slice a strip of steak.

Please, Trooper. This moment is up to you. Sharon willed him to respond. She couldn't help him out in this.

"Lindsay." He hesitated and then spoke something safe. "You look as beautiful as your mother. You do know that, don't you, Lindsay?"

He smiled, but to Sharon, it was a smile of relief, not one of an anticipated greeting for a favored daughter. Lindsay was silent as she continued to slice away at the meat. Sharon felt the tension, certain that this moment could cause everything to fall apart, and she mustn't let it happen.

"Lindsay, aren't you going to answer? Your father is here to spend the day with us." She wore her brightest and most compelling smile, pleading for her daughter's cooperation.

"Well." Lindsay set the knife down and wiped her hands. Then, she went to her father and touched him lightly on the face, looking up into his eyes. She smiled, and it looked like love. "The boys are in the pool, Dad, and they really want to see you. Go on down, why don't you? I'll finish this up and bring them down when they're done." She turned to her mother. "You, too, Mom. Go with Dad. You need each other. Now, I've got fajitas to prepare." She waved her hands and shooed them away.

Sharon pulled Trooper to the stairwell, grateful that Lindsay had at least played along. She knew her daughter didn't understand Trooper, but politeness was second best. Sometimes, that's all there was.

It was at the top of the stairwell that it got interesting,

208

because the boys were playing some sort of game involving loud, bantering phrases. Sharon and Trooper stopped to listen, and when they did, two seventeen-year-old voices came across loudly and clearly.

"Hey, Casey. I hear you called Dad. He's coming out, you say. That right, Cody?"

Trooper looked at Sharon with a puzzled look on his face. When he started to speak, she put a finger to her lips.

"That's right, Casey. You know, Cody, I think we've got the best father in the world. I hope either one of us can be as good a basketball player as he was. Do you think we can, Casey?"

That was when Sharon saw Trooper's eyes begin to turn red, and he began blinking away the tears. She reached to him and linked her arm in his. "Let's go down, Trooper. They're our boys. They need to see you."

His response was ragged. "Even more, I need to see them." He smiled, but it was through tears.

Moving down the steps, a series of two splashes got their attention. Trooper looked at his wife. "The boys?"

"Probably," she smiled. "There are suits. Change and go in with them. They would like that."

Reaching the basement, the twins were together in the middle of the pool, wrestling with one another. Sharon saw Trooper's face light up. She hadn't forgotten how he loved having two identical children, ones that no one could tell apart. He used to tell them they gave him twice as much love. Now, she was convinced he needed some of that back. She begged her sons to pay him some attention.

He walked up to the edge of the pool unnoticed.

"Boys!"

His voice got their attention, and they turned to look. "Dad!" They shouted his name as one. Then, they turned to each other in glee, and the mischievous glint in their eyes was the same.

Trooper waved when they swam over to see him, but Sharon couldn't fight a smile. She had seen the look on her sons' faces, and she knew Trooper really shouldn't stand so close to the edge of the pool. Two against one was horribly unfair, especially as the two in the water were exactly the same size as their father, and more than thirty years younger.

With a huge splash that not even Sharon anticipated, Trooper went for an unexpected dip in his own pool. She leaped back, laughing. The twins had given their father the best kind of attention, and she was certain things would only get better.

They could hardly get worse, could they? She was confident of that.

Chapter 18

JEFFREY turned onto Private Drive No. 27 to see a silver Corvette immediately in front of him. It was parked in the partial shade of an overhanging tree, and it was in his way. It wasn't what he had expected to find, a newspaper reporter driving a low-slung, high-powered car like that.

He turned to Cookie. "That must be the man I'm meeting." He picked up her hand off his leg and squeezed it tenderly.

"This is really just business, Jeffrey?"

"Just business." He kissed her on the forehead and then raised her hand to kiss it, too. "You are beautiful, Cookie. Thank you for coming with me. I love you."

"I love you, too, Jeffrey. This man you're meeting is blocking the drive. Has he ever been out here?"

"I'm sure he hasn't. I'm the one who suggested the lake house." There had been no other logical choice, not on such short notice, but he let that go unsaid. "I can pull around, I think."

He turned the wheel, hitting the gas, and he felt his left tires drop off the edge of the drive. He grinned when the Corvette's brake lights came on, but once he was completely off the gravel, the man ahead of them seemed to understand. The reporter rolled his window down and motioned Jeffrey's big truck past.

"Lean out the window and wave for him to follow me," He hit the button to roll down the passenger's window. She did so, and as she leaned back to him, he rolled the window up and grabbed her hand again, catching it before she placed it on his leg.

"Ready to get back on the drive again?" He gunned the engine, forcing the wheels to jerk onto the elevated surface. He laughed. "Think that little car could do that?"

She pulled her hand free and slapped his leg, laughing, leaving it there once again. "Drive, Jeffrey. He doesn't have to. He'll follow us."

Catching his first sight of the Navigator backed into the brush, Jeffrey immediately hit the brake. "Hold on to your dipstick. What's this?"

"Isn't that your dad's truck?"

"It seems so. I didn't expect him out here, and especially not parked right there." He pulled up to the Navigator and inched by very carefully. "However, maybe he's not the one who drove it out. The twins, possibly. I can't imagine Dad driving that badly. Not ever."

"He would loan it to them?" Cookie laughed, looking behind her to see the small sports car creeping equally cautiously past the truck.

"He might, if they were bringing a crowd. I'm sure someone at the house will have an idea about what happened." He pulled up, and the iron gate blocking their way began to swing open.

Once he pulled through, he watched in the mirror, driving slowly to ensure the Corvette made it through, and the gate shut behind it.

He braked at the front of the house. "I'll let you out here by the walk, and you can wave our little guy along. I told him we'd meet at the guest house."

"Little guy?" Cookie chuckled. "He didn't look all that little when I waved to him back there."

"All right, wise girl. Little car. How's that? I'll let you out, and you wave his little car along."

"I'm so lucky to have found you." She reached and kissed his cheek before patting him on the leg.

"I hope so, Cookie." His eyes were on the car in his mirror.

"I know so. Oh, look, over there. I don't know that car. A Porsche, is it? Does your mother have a new car?" She pointed.

"A Porsche? Give up her BMW? Hardly." He glanced in the guest parking area. There was only one car there, and he knew whose. "It's John's."

"Your Uncle John?" She sat up to get out, reaching beside her for her purse.

"Yes, my Uncle John. He's just my Dad's old friend, though. I don't know if you've ever been told that." He eased the Escalade forward a few feet and stopped again.

"At least if Mom's gone, you can be sure of John for company. You'll find him very charming."

"I remember," she laughed. "I met him at your church one Sunday. He seemed as if he could run the entire service if he wanted."

"I think he could." Jeffrey grinned. He knew John actually did. He reached one hand to his mouth and blew Cookie a kiss, as she opened the door and jumped down.

"I'll be sure to send your little man along." She giggled girlishly and closed the door.

Jeffrey had an uneasy feeling, however, even as he smiled. This might be the last day she would be his. It had been that kind of afternoon, one where every bad thing in his life had come back to haunt him all at once. He didn't want to lose Cookie, yet he suspected he might have already done exactly that.

Still, he had a reporter to meet. There was a show to put on. He pulled into the guest house drive just as if the world were all he wanted it to be, and he parked confidently and with no hesitation. Stepping from the truck, he already had a smile on his face. It was a family trait, and he was as skilled at it as any of his siblings.

"Ah, Mr. Kincaid. Pretty girl. Bucky Simms at your service." The man stood from his car, holding a hand out, and as Cookie said, he was not a little guy. His size was just not in height. He was as broad as he was tall.

"Mr. Simms." Jeffrey held his hand out, although unwilling to be too chummy. He had yet to find the Benji he remembered in this man's face. "That pretty girl is my fiancée."

"Congratulations, then. May I call you by your first name? I used to, and I certainly did on the phone. However, if you would prefer something more formal—" He shrugged.

"Jeffrey is fine. And I may call you Bucky?" He smiled, determined to relax. He had to, or he'd soon break out in a cold sweat, as he had in Mr. Hamilton's office earlier. When Bucky nodded his head in agreement, Jeffrey frowned. "I don't recognize your face. I'm sorry if that sounds stupid of me, but the Benji I knew was thin and wiry."

Bucky just laughed. "I *was* very thin back in high school. However, I hit thirty, and I have a desk job, mostly anyway, when I'm not out chasing stories."

"Stories?" Jeffrey froze. He knew he shouldn't have met this man out here.

"Wait." Bucky laughed. "I know dismay when I see it. This is no story. This is very private, very discreet. That's why I wanted a place like this." He clapped Jeffrey on the shoulder, as an old friend would.

Up close, Jeffrey realized Bucky was actually taller than he was. When the man turned his face to the side, a remnant of the old Benji came out, causing Jeffrey to grin in relief.

"I remember you, now. Your face, anyway. I can see the old Benji. I couldn't find you before."

"Oh, you can find me now?" Bucky pursed his lips. "Most people find me quite well without having to think about it. It's not like I'm hard to see." He laughed. "I guess I was pretty cruel to you, short sheeting your bed

215

every single night. You were just a kid, and I should have cut you some slack."

"And I worshipped you that week." That raised Bucky's eyebrows. "I just didn't know how to tell you, so I teased you. My apologies for that." It was the truth, and Jeffrey felt himself begin to relax a bit. It didn't seem that this big, gregarious man had brought any ominous bombs to drop on him, not any that he could sense, yet. "Come on, and we'll go in."

"I'm on your heels. Get it? Benji's the name of a dog, and I'm on your heels?" He slapped him on the back and guffawed.

Jeffrey looked at him and grinned, and he reached to the keypad at the door, typing in his code. Then, the door clicked open, automatically turning the lights on in the building, and Bucky cooed.

"Man, would I ever like a place like this! You know, I moved here from Austin after my parents died. I never knew they had places like this around here, or I'd have looked longer before buying my condo. How many of these cabins does this resort have? I mean, can just anyone rent them?" He stepped inside and looked around, glancing at the log walls. After a moment, he turned his eyes to the ceiling that soared overhead, and doors on the upstairs landing indicating additional rooms. Through an enormous back window, the lake sparkled in the mid-afternoon sun. "Wow! What a view! That's got to be worth at least a million dollars!"

"Six, but no one's counting any longer."

"Six? Million?" Bucky walked to the window. "To live

like rich people! Wow, even if for a weekend." He turned back to Jeffrey. "I didn't catch the name of this place. What's this resort called?"

Jeffrey was embarrassed, and he cleared his throat. "Well, it's not really a resort, not like you're thinking. However, you may call it Green Fork if you like."

Bucky laughed. "Green Fork, like you eat with? Funky!"

"Funky?" He was really starting to like this guy. "No, not fork like you eat with. That water out there is the Green Fork that branches off Little Elbow Lake." He motioned to two leather wingback chairs in front of a fireplace. Flames were flickering inside.

"Nah, not a fire!" Bucky knelt in front of the opening. "With the heat outside? These are real flames."

"Lighten up, Bucky." Jeffrey got that phrase from his father. He'd heard him say it a hundred times. He went to a switch on the wall and flipped it, dousing the flames. "Everything in the guest house is tied into the keypad. When someone logs in, the system boots up his or her preferences. It's more welcoming that way."

"Oh, man. You log in?" He hit his head with the heel of his hand. "This is so 007."

"It's not a big deal. It helps us keep track of who's been here. Can we sit before we talk?" Jeffrey's jumpy feeling hadn't completely faded, and he didn't want his knees to give him away. He dropped into one of the chairs.

Bucky did likewise, although more carefully, and in that action, his demeanor changed. For just a moment, he looked around the room, tapping the arm of the chair.

217

Then, he leaned forward to look directly at the man he'd come to see. In that one motion, it was as if he tried to read his character in his eyes. "I'm sorry for not being more forthcoming. I had to watch you a few minutes, just to see your face."

"Why? Should I begin to worry?" Jeffrey had already done so, and he felt sweat prickle his skin.

"I've got a hard reputation in the news field. That's how I got my nickname. Bucky. I got it because I buck the system, you see. They tell me no, and I jump up and prove the answer is yes. That's me." He sat back as if his announcement were over. He smiled for a moment, and then he let the warmth fade from his face. "You probably know that. It's why my phone never got answered at your father's church. His ministry. Sorry. His very big ministry."

Jeffrey's eyes narrowed involuntarily. "Is this about the ministry?"

Bucky sighed, and his eyes reddened. "It might be easier if it were. Remember, I told you my sister died?"

Jeffrey nodded, suddenly frightened. He blinked several times, and he felt his throat constrict.

"And that you looked like him?"

Jeffrey felt sweat tickle his armpits. There were pins and needles in his legs, and he could barely sit still.

"Who did you think I meant?"

Jeffrey took several deep breaths, and he turned to look out the window for a moment. For a fraction of a second, he felt the room close in, and he wanted to get up and run away. This man sitting across from him was

218

asking questions he would expect him to answer. It terrified him. Yet, his world had not changed. Not yet. The sun still sparkled on the lake, and the trees rustled in the breeze. His black truck sat outside, waiting on him to drive it back into the city. His fiancée was still his fiancée, and his prospective in-laws still thought he was wonderful. Tomorrow morning, he would wake up and go to work at his father's church, and the same people he had known for years would call good morning to him. Nothing had changed, and yet, he knew it had. As of this moment, nothing was the same. Nothing.

He turned to look at Bucky, to find him patiently waiting on his answer.

"Memphis."

Jeffrey knew that word summed up the roiling turmoil inside his mind better than any other. Besides, he didn't know the boy, had only Cookie's unsure recollection of the boy's name as Jackie or Jack. In the battering of information he had taken in today, he could only picture that the boy was in Memphis. He knew where he was for the first time in nine years. He hadn't even known Jackie—or Jack—was alive the first three.

Then, he could sit no longer, and he stood, walking to the window. He let his gaze drift to the water. From this window, it was just possible to see the back of the main house, and he was surprised to see the basement wall open. His mother must be swimming. He hoped Cookie enjoyed visiting with John.

Finally, he turned to Bucky, and he knew his eyes were red. He could barely keep the tears blinked away. He couldn't speak through the cotton filling his throat.

"Smart man." Bucky's face was somber, and he watched, with his eyes trained on Jeffrey. "No one knows about Memphis. How did you learn that?" He leaned forward. "Tell me, Jeffrey Kincaid. How do you know about Memphis?"

He moved to stand at the back of the chair he'd just vacated. "Perkins Extended just off Poplar." He remembered Mrs. Hamilton's directions. "Do you know that address?" He held himself tightly together. He felt wound like a top, and he was afraid he would come loose at any moment, his self-control shattering all over the room.

Bucky frowned. "I'm guessing Perkins Extended is a Memphis address. I know Poplar runs through Memphis."

Jeffrey nodded with a tight smile. "My fiancée's aunt and uncle live there and have a small church in their home. My 'girl,' as you called her, was just there, and she sat beside this small boy that, in her words, was me. She met him in Memphis." Jeffrey closed his eyes, and he felt the tears begin to roll. He sniffled. "His mother was your sister?"

"My sister."

"Are you angry?" He deserved whatever he got. He knew that.

"Angry? God, no! Is that what you think?" Bucky jumped up to pull Jeffrey back to his chair, again taking the one across from him. "Man, I'm just glad to have found you."

"Glad? Why?" His face was tight, and he could hardly think, could barely keep his emotions under control. Then, he broke. "I was fifteen. I didn't even know what we were doing, sneaking into the pool that last night of camp. Yeah, at the end, I knew, but not before. I never intended for us to do what we did. You have to know that. Then, the next morning, camp was over, and I never saw her again. I can't even remember her name, Bucky." He looked at the man across from him, begging him for forgiveness.

"Rhianna."

"Rhianna." He remembered. Her name had rolled off his tongue all week, and he had said it to her again and again. "How could I have forgotten that? I did see Rhianna once afterwards, when I was nineteen. That was the only time. I saw her for maybe three minutes, and she told me she gave the baby up for adoption. I never knew before that."

"So, she did know you were the father." Bucky grinned.

"What do you mean?" Jeffrey frowned. "She never told you?"

"Like I told you, I watched you when I first got here, you see. All that rigmarole I did. I needed to know. However, I could tell as soon as you stepped from that truck that you were his father. I could tell." His voice was excited.

"You've seen him, then? Rhianna told me he was adopted out as soon as he was born."

"I'm a newspaper reporter." Bucky was obviously enjoying this part. "I investigate stories. Now, let me give you some background. You need to understand all of this, because I plan to ask you to make a decision before I leave here. You can say yes, or you can say no. Whatever you decide, I'll walk away and respect your decision, and it'll end with me. Got that? I'm Bucky, and I buck the system. That's what I'm doing right now."

"I don't understand, but if you want me to listen, well, I can do that." He took a deep breath. He wasn't sure he'd like what Bucky had to say, but if he could choose to walk away at the end, then he could afford to at least listen. That couldn't be too bad a toss of the die at all.

THAT WAS true, except that Jeffrey had tossed his die twelve years and some odd months earlier. A second toss had been made about thirty minutes before arriving at the lake property. That second toss was the one coming to rest right there in that guest house. Jeffrey didn't realize it yet, but the decision was made.

Dear God, what would I do with a twelve-year-old? It hadn't been a question. It had been a cry for help.

Chapter 19

"MRS. KINCAID?" Cookie knocked, and without waiting for a response, just opened the door. She was from a world of money and privilege, and that gave her a sense of confidence, one that helped her navigate among other people, that was unless those people were fiancés who seemed suddenly upset at an interesting story she happened to share. However, that had nothing to do with money and privilege. That had to do with love, which was entirely different. Jeffrey had told her to go on in, and that gave her tacit permission to enter. Also, those inside had to hear her, didn't they?

However, the person who greeted her was a surprise, indeed.

"Cookie?" Lindsay smiled broadly, and she turned from the oven to set a pan of sizzling fajitas on the hard stone counter. She pulled out a platter, and with a wooden spatula, shifted them over, poking at them to adjust them evenly. "Are you alone? If so, that brother of mine is as mean as they come."

"Yes and no. I'm sorry if I'm intruding, Lindsay. I begged Jeffrey to let me come, and we thought it'd be just your mother here. I wanted to visit. He's at the guest house." She paused, seeing lunch was being prepared, and she looked back through the door. Of course, Jeffrey was long gone.

She determined she would make herself useful, and she turned back to Lindsay with a bright smile on her face.

"MOM'S HERE somewhere." Lindsay wasn't happy to see Cookie at all. This threw a wrench into her plans. If Jeffrey had come with her . . . . She blinked away sudden tears, twisting around and reaching to the oven in order to fiddle with the controls. She took a moment to get her face under control.

She turned back into the room and wiped her eyes with the backs of her hands. "Oh, I hate doing fajitas! They always make my eyes burn. What about yours?" She looked at Cookie and laughed, the excuse a good one, if not quite true. She also had a good excuse to send Cookie away. "There's a party downstairs. It's a pool party, but you're welcome to join in."

"A party? Oh, I'd be interrupting. I should have had Jeffrey call first. I'm so sorry, Lindsay." Cookie looked at the prepared food, and she placed her purse at the end of the counter. "Let me help you. Do you need to transport that downstairs?"

Lindsay forced a chuckle. "I could certainly use help, of one kind or another." She smiled brightly, the one that everyone found so believable. Inside, she felt sick, though. It was only to have been her and her mother here, today. Now, here was this girl reminding her of the brother she adored, the one she was stealing from her. He had been her last lifeline. Once he'd announced his engagement, there had been no more point. If he was here today and made her fall in love with him all over again . . . well, complicated couldn't even describe what this day would become. It was supposed to have been easy. She didn't need complicated.

No, she wasn't happy to see Cookie at all.

"What do I need to carry?" Cookie reached for an apron on the counter, and she shook it out to put it on. "The extra plates?" She finished tying the strings around her waist and turned to wash her hands.

Lindsay stepped up and whispered in her ear, "Sweetie, you can carry the fajitas and drop them down the stairs for all I care. I'm a vegetarian. Besides, these are seconds. They've already had one go round. Just follow me."

Oh, she hated this!

Even so, she chuckled with false brightness and picked up the extra plates herself, cringing at how she would also hurt this girl at her side. She had begun to hope this branch of her little tree might survive. She no longer felt so sure.

"Lindsay, you are such a cut-up." Cookie's voice sparkled with enjoyment. "I'm looking forward to years and years of having you for a friend. Better than that, for a

225

sister. I've never had a sister, and now you're mine."

Lindsay turned away, her eyes tight, walking rapidly out of the kitchen. This was not what she needed. She moved to the stairway, making sure not to look back, the sharpness of anger making her steps hard. She didn't want this girl to make her feel loved and needed. Dear God, that was the last thing she wanted at this stage of the game.

By the time she reached the bottom of the stairs and readied herself to enter the party, her game face was back on, and she walked in, smiling bravely as she set her plates on a table. Several of the teenagers were lounging on floats in the pool, one of them being either Cody or Casey. A pretty girl in a pink swimsuit was at his side. Her mother had obviously just exited the water, and she stood drying her hair. She laughed at her father. He was fully dressed and dripping from head to toe.

"Mom, Dad, we have company." She turned to motion with her hand, her expression bright. "It's Jack's fiancée, Cookie." Just then, Cookie walked in with the steaming fajitas, and all the teenagers jumped up and cheered, rushing toward her as a mob.

"Hey," Cookie called, laughing, looking for a place to set the platter.

"I've got it." Ever gracious, her iron rein on her true emotions keeping them in check, Lindsay took it from her to set it beside the extra plates. Her next words were spoken brightly and with the illusion of true camaraderie. "You know how to make an entrance, girl. Welcome to the real family."

"You are so sweet, Lindsay. Thank you for letting me

226

help." Cookie touched her gently on the elbow, just enough to make contact.

Lindsay's chest throbbed, and she needed to get away from all this happiness, back to something less like a fairy tale. The sudden, sharp anger from earlier had crystalized and turned to dry dust in the face of the party atmosphere filling the basement, and she felt her tears about to burst. She rushed for the stairs.

"I'm headed back up." She was loud and bright to cover her distress. "Enjoy, Cookie. If you want, Mother can show you the extra suits. Watch it, though. These guys will drown you." She laughed loudly, and Cookie waved.

At the top of the steps, she paused to lean against a wall, and for a moment, she closed her eyes. However, the happy sounds from the pool echoed up to her. Desperate for peace, she stepped into her father's office, a room that was rarely used, and she was surprised to see John lying on the sofa.

"Taking a nap?" Her words no longer had the bite with which she had earlier attacked him. This morning, she had known what she intended to do, and she had been hard and careless. She hadn't cared who she hurt. The day had gotten twisted, though, and that made it more difficult. Not impossible, just more difficult. She was exhausted, nevertheless. She leaned over her friend when he didn't respond and quizzed him, "John?"

"I'm awake, Lindsay." He laughed, but it was shallow and weak. "Go look at the computer. I've pulled up the ministry email account. As of three this afternoon, there have been over ten thousand messages, all in one category.

It's later, now. There might be more." He kept his eyes closed, as if the light hurt his eyes.

"Are you all right, John?" She was concerned, and that wasn't fair. If she felt concerned, then it meant she cared. She didn't care about anything, anymore. She mustn't care.

"You know I had an Aunt Bessie, don't you?" He sighed loudly, as if that told the whole story.

"Not really. Why?" She sat in a chair opposite the sofa, watching him.

"No reason. Go look at the computer. It's interesting." He didn't even move his hand to wave her along.

"No thanks. I don't care about the ministry. Besides, the ministry gets ten thousand messages a minute during telethons. So? What could be so special about these?" She would like to lie down and hide, also. However, there was only one sofa in the room. "John, it's so unlike you to hog. Want to share? I think I need to crash, too."

This time he did wave her away with his hand, and he chuckled. "Not if you want to be amorous. I'm not in the mood." His words seemed bright at first, and then their strength faded. He continued, though, his voice softer, with a raspy crust at the edges. "The emails are about you. We could have made some real money, you know. For a small donation, and all that. Rather, make that a large donation. Go see, Lindsay. You're a hit. Listen, girl, there's a great idea here. Get budding designers. You wear their creations, and then, for just a small—" He coughed with laughter, his attempt at humor obviously draining him. "—oh, excuse me, a large donation, a copy of the item is in the mail on Monday. Everybody wins. Go see, Lindsay."

"You could just tell me what this is." She sat for a moment, watching him, finally deciding he wouldn't. He would make her do this. "If you insist, I'll look. The computer's up, you say? The screen's dark."

"Tap a key, Lindsay. It's like any computer. It likes to sleep. Tell me what you see."

She did, too. The emails were there, and her name stood out in yellow on every one. "John?" She looked at him. "What is this about?

"Your first hat, Lindsay. You wore your first hat ever this morning. Ten thousand people want one. They love you." He chuckled. "Hit the refresh button at the top. I've set it so only the ones about you pull up. See your name highlighted? I had it search to find you. Did you get more, yet?"

She sniffled. "A few." Seventeen thousand and some odd was the new total. That old hat John had covered her hair with. They all wanted one. Why?

"Did you see, Lindsay? From all over the world. Some even sent money. They went right to the ministry website and sent honest-to-God money."

"Why, John? Why?" This was another complication she didn't need. Seventeen thousand. "Why?"

"Come to me." When she perched on the sofa beside him, laying her arm across his chest, he opened his eyes for a moment and took her hand. "You can't love yourself, but everyone else does. Can you feel that? Ten thousand people love you. They want to emulate you. Your life is

229

important to them."

"Shush, John." She reached and wiped her eyes, understanding what he was doing. "Just shush. I don't need to hear this from you."

"You do, Lindsay." He rubbed his forehead, squeezing it tightly between his fingers. "Those ten thousand people aren't the important ones, either. You know that."

"Who is, John? You?" She smiled, but she felt the tears still seeping. She reached to place her hand on his face, shocked at how cool he felt. "Are you sure you're all right, Uncle John?" She surprised herself calling him that. She meant it, though. He was an uncle to her, even if he was no real relation at all.

"Not me, Lindsay. Think. You're not, you know, thinking." He sighed, but even now, his barbs were back, if muted.

"Who, then?" She felt a little better. That sounded like more of the old John; he was sparring with her.

"Those people downstairs. In the pool. Your family. You're important to them."

"Sure." She sniffled and wiped her face. "Then tell me, John. Why am *I* not important to me? If I were important to me, that might make all the difference in the world."

However, his face was twisted in pain at that point, and he didn't answer her at all.

Chapter 20

JACK SAT on the sofa, and he stared at the television as the image began to blur. His adoption records identified him as Richard Samuel Hall, adopted son of Craig and Julie Hall, now deceased.

He remembered nine, because that's when he'd decided to go by the name Jack. No one had understood "Jack," but he was an only child. His parents, as adoptive parents often do, indulged him regularly in such small things. That day, he'd ridden his bike home from school. Jack, still Richard then, had dropped his bike in the yard. Running up the steps to the porch, he had thrown his backpack to the side. He loved getting the mail, and today something was hanging on the door. He snatched the bag from the knob, and threw himself onto his backpack, the books inside making a perfect seat for a small boy of nine.

The bag contained a number of papers. Some were

heavy and slick, and a few were folded in half. Most had pictures, but one seemed special. It opened twice, and on the glossy front was a big stadium.

His mother, Julie, stepped out and knelt beside him, reaching to give him a kiss.

"Something from school, Richard?" She picked up several of the papers he'd looked at and already discarded off to the side.

"No, Momma. It was on the door. It's mail, and I got to read it first." He looked up at her and smiled, pleased that she hadn't been the one to open it this time.

"It's an invitation to a church." She returned his smile, flipping through the papers. "They have clowns on Sunday morning in their children's services. How nice!"

"Clowns?" He reached to see, and she turned the paper his direction. He laughed at the brightly colored actors standing before groups of cheering children. "Can we go see the clowns, Momma?"

She patted his head. "We have a church, Richard. Remember?" She laughed. "Besides, the children's choir sings in two weeks. You must be at our church to practice."

"Momma! Clowns! Please?" Holding up the glossy flyer, he added an extra layer of enticement to his words. "See? We can watch football, too."

"There's no football in that stadium, my little boy. It's a church, now. Someday I'll drive by and show you where it is."

"When, Momma?"

"Keep the papers, Richard. However, you have choir

on Sunday. I love you, Pumpkin." She stood with a smile and patted him on the head.

"Love you, Momma." Inside, though, he found something unexpected. He found himself. "Momma!" He looked up in excitement, but she was already gone.

The boy was only nine, but he was bright. Scattering the rest of the paperwork across the porch, he ran to his room, holding the treasured paper in his hand. He stuffed it far under his mattress where no one would find it, not even his mother when she changed the sheets.

Then came that Sunday morning when he was sick, and his mother stayed home from church with him. Sitting on the sofa, she turned on the television, keeping the sound down low, and there, right in front of her, was that stadium from the flyer.

"Richard! Come watch this. You can see your church after all." She picked up her soda and took a sip as a tall, lanky man gave a call for the people to close their eyes in prayer.

"What, Momma?" He was in his pajamas, and his hair was tousled. He crawled beside her to curl up with his head in her lap.

"The clowns you wanted to see. Remember? This is that church. It's big. I cannot imagine a church with that many people." She reached to the table beside the sofa, and she set her drink on a towel. Then, she reached to the remote to turn up the sound.

"Where are the clowns, Momma?"

"We might not see them, baby, but this is the same church. Let's just watch for a bit. I want to see this." She looked down and patted his little face, and she frowned a bit. "You're flushed, baby."

He pushed her hand away. "I always flush, Momma. Quit."

She touched his cheek again, only giving up when he brushed her hand away a second time. "All right, Richard. I'll leave you alone." She sighed.

He heard, and he felt for her hand. Once he had it, he pulled it to his mouth to give it a quick kiss, then pushed it away once more.

At that moment, something on the screen stole his attention, and he sat up to snuggle against his mother's side. It was the man from his picture, and he was on the television. He looked to his mother to point, but she had reached for her soda, and it had spilled. She was wiping it from the table. However, on the television, the man from his picture was talking, and a girl next to him called him by name. She called him Jack, and she reached up to pat him on the face. A smile grew on the man's face. The boy had seen that smile. It was in his school pictures and in the bathroom mirror. It was there in the reflections in the glass when he looked outside at night. It was his smile. Then, the image was gone, and the tall man returned to the television.

He rolled onto his back and let his head rest in his mother's lap. He stretched in his pajamas. She reached to place her hand on his stomach.

"I'm Jack," he whispered to her.

She looked to see what joke this was, only to find him serious. "Jack? Why Jack?"

"It's my name." He reached with his small hand, and he placed it on her cheek. He pressed his lips together in seriousness, and then let his face relax into an easy, charming smile.

"What is this about, Richard?"

"I'm Jack." Then, he grabbed her hand and kissed it once again.

She laughed. "I love you, Jack."

"Thank you, Momma. I like being Jack." He rolled over to stare at the television once more, hoping to see the man again. He didn't, though. The broadcast was over, and the next Sunday, he was singing with the children's choir. However, from then on, he went by Jack, and even though he had no more than the one picture he'd gleaned from all those on his front porch that day, somehow he felt different, as if he knew who he really was.

Today, sitting in front of the dancing animals, he had only the one thing that meant anything from his life with his parents. Everything else had gone in the fire, his schoolbooks, his video games, and his new gym shoes. Even the present he had mowed yards to buy for his dad's birthday was gone.

He still had the picture from all those years ago. He'd also written his name all over the paper, covering everything up but the man's picture. Jack. Jack Jack Jack Jack. The man on the paper must be his father. His *real* father. If the man in the picture were his father, he would come for him, wouldn't he? He would know his parents were dead, and he would come be his father again. Wouldn't he?

Tears filled his eyes as the animals skidded across the ice, chasing a funny little nut. His godmother walked in and saw the tears.

"Oh, you baby. You're missing your parents again. Let me get you some candy. Candy will make you feel better." She reached to a shelf and opened a box of filled chocolates. Most of them had the tops broken, and the fillings were clearly visible. "Here, Richard. I've already pushed the tops in so you can see what you want."

He looked away. "I'm Jack."

His godmother laughed, and it sounded kindly. "That's right. Jack. I forget you changed your name. If you don't want any of these, I'll just take one or two before I put them back." She patted his hand and stood to pop one of the candies into her mouth.

He stared at the dancing animals. He had never changed his name. He had always been Jack. It was just that no one ever knew. He's always been Jack. Always.

He missed his parents, though, and once again, the characters on the screen blurred, as the boy's eyes began to burn.

"BUT YOU'RE his uncle," Jeffrey pointed out. His heart was torn, because the ramifications were huge. On one hand were Cookie and his father's ministry. He had been groomed to take over one day. Then, there was the boy he had fathered in that pool so long ago. That boy was parentless, now, and very nearly homeless, to listen to Bucky. Jeffrey knew his choices, and neither path would be easy.

"And it would seem that you're his father." Bucky tapped his knee. "We could prove that with DNA testing, but that's not what I want. I won't ask that, not now, and not ever. I want you to take the boy because you want him, not because you're forced to care for him. And as far as your remark about me being his uncle? I don't know the boy at all. Of him, yes, but to know him? The boy's relationship with whoever he lives will be a blank slate, and that blank slate should belong to his father."

"You would take him, though?"

"Certainly. But that's not my point. I saw the boy just before he was sent to Memphis. In that moment, even before I knew he was my sister's son, I didn't see just the boy. I saw a skinny kid I spent a week with at youth camp one summer, one I'd short sheeted the kid's bed all week. And the kid was also one that my sister doted on the next year."

"You didn't tell anyone, though." Jeffrey held his breath.

"No. Is that what's worrying you?" Bucky laughed. "When the authorities showed up at my office, with documentation showing the boy was my sister's son, I already knew who the father was. Well, I couldn't *know*, but I was pretty sure. I cautioned myself that it had been nearly thirteen years, and I know from newspaper investigations that memories, even my own, can be notoriously inaccurate. I needed to see you to be for sure."

"She never told anyone." Jeffrey's words were a statement, but they also asked a question. It wasn't the first time he had said the words, and it still amazed him that he was being given the choice to walk away.

"Not who the father was, no, she never told, only that he had been a boy at camp. She was adamant about not telling. I really think she loved you with all her heart. She watched your family's broadcast every week after that, you see. I never put it together, not until I saw the boy. Then, bingo! Suddenly, I felt stupid, and I felt brilliant at the same time. That's when I started calling."

"And how. You have the ministry in a panic." Jeffrey felt himself smile.

Bucky continued, "I was about to give up on reaching you when I got this idea. You know there are digital phonebooks you can buy that have all the phone numbers in America. Well, I went online, and as it turns out, yours is not exactly unlisted, just hidden in all the ministry registries. I looked at it, and I pointed with my finger, and I said, by God, that's Jeffrey Kincaid! I'll bet, I said, and this was a good bet, that I have just found the same Jeffrey Kincaid from all those years ago. That was this afternoon, Mr. Kincaid, and now, look at me. I'm sitting here with the father of my nephew, and no one else in the world knows." He grinned, and he leaped from his chair, surprisingly agile for such a big man, pumping his fist in the air. "I'm that good, and you know it!"

He paused in his excitement and looked at Jeffrey. His next words were measured and serious. "However, if you want to walk away, no one else in the world will know. I don't attend anymore, but I know that in your line of work, this could cause you problems, being so involved in your father's church, and all. I also know that since the fire,

238

people have been hoping to come up with the boy's father. Even so, if you decide against this, I'm taking him. I assure you, he'll never know, and neither will anyone else."

"Does he know that? Not the part about me, but the part about you being willing to take him?" He wiped his hands on his knees and then ran them through his hair. Bucky had just given him another out if he wanted it. The boy would have a home. He glanced out the window and thought of Cookie in the house next door. "If he knows about you already, then I'd just be in the way."

"He knows nothing. I saw him, but only as a reporter. I only knew he was adopted and there were no relatives. They dug up his old adoption records afterwards, and that's when I got the call. He needs a father more than he needs an uncle, and that's why I'm here. The ball's in your court. If he comes to me, I'll love it. I always wanted a kid, but with newspapering, there's just been no time. However, for this kid, I'd make the time. You, though, need first choice in this matter. You also need to know I'm being pushed to take the boy as soon as possible. His godparents simply have no room, and," he chuckled, "they are very old. He needs somewhere to live. More importantly, he needs someone to love him."

"You could force a DNA test. Then I'd have to take him." That still worried him.

"I've already covered that. You have to do this because you want to. I do understand that this is sudden and very difficult. You probably want some time to think on this."

239

Jeffrey shook his head. "You have no idea." All this had hit him in one single day, and his mind was fogged with indecision.

"One more thing you might be interested in. His adopted, legal name is Richard Hall. Richard Samuel Hall." Bucky looked at him expectantly.

"Richard? My fiancée said his name was either Jackie or Jack. She wasn't sure which. Can you be sure this is the same boy?" The possibility both relieved him as well as wrenched him in the gut. He wanted to know his son.

"That's right, also. I'm pretty sure what I intend to say next might make a difference to your decision. I saved it until last, sort of, well, as a clincher." He had a full-blown grin on his face by this time. "It seems he started going by Jack at about age nine or ten. You know, he survived the fire because he was over a friend's house when his folks died, but he had something with him you might be interested in."

"And what was it?" Jeffrey's patience with intrigue had grown thin. "Spit it out, Bucky."

"Your church does fliers, right? Passes them out to houses?"

"Once a month. The youth take them out. I've done it several times. So?" He didn't see the point in this line of questioning.

"The boy had one of those in his backpack. One of your church flyers. He had written all over it." Bucky paused, one finger doing a gentle tap on his pant leg.

Jeffrey took a deep breath. "Just say it." He closed his eyes.

"He had written one word everywhere except on top of your picture. Know anyone on that flyer named Jack?"

"Dear God," Jeffrey breathed. "What will I do with a twelve-year-old boy?"

Bucky grinned. "I'm sorry, Jeffrey. What was that?"

"My family calls me Jack, Bucky. Only my family. It's been my nickname forever." Not even Cookie called him that. She had heard his family use that name around him, but everyone else, including Cookie, knew him as Jeffrey.

"No one else? That seems a really big coincidence."

"Oh, God! How could I forget?" Jeffrey leaned forward and put his face into his hands. "That night with your sister in the pool. I asked her to call me Jack. It was the last thing I said before we . . . I'm sorry." He looked up, realizing who was in the room with him. "I'm talking about this like it won't offend you. She was your sister. I am so sorry."

Bucky leaned forward and touched Jeffrey on his knee with his knuckles. "No offence. I'm telling you, she loved you." He sat back and grinned. "Do you think the boy knows who you are? He has your picture, and he's even changed the name he goes by to match your nickname. Makes a difference, doesn't it?"

"You knew this? You knew my nickname was Jack, and the boy had written it all around my picture?"

"Lucky guess. By the way, quit saying 'the boy.'"

Jeffrey snorted. "What should I call him? Richard? Or, Jack?" He was so jittery with the possibility that this boy was actually his that he could barely sit still.

"Better." Bucky leaned forward to punch him on the

241

knee. "Try 'son.'"

"My son." Jeffrey threw his head back in the chair and chuckled. It wasn't humor. He knew what it was. It was relief. "Jack, my son. I like that, Bucky."

He was elated, too. A decision had been reached, one that took those thirteen years of weight off his back. His elation was temporary, though, as all chemical or emotional reactions must be, including ones spent in a campground swimming pool, no matter how eternal those moments might seem to a fifteen-year-old boy at the height of his first embrace, but he couldn't tell that, yet. He just felt as high as a kite, and no brown boxes had been needed.

Bucky grinned back. "I like 'nephew,' myself. You and your fiancée will let me see him, won't you? I want to get to know my sister's kid."

Jeffrey's bubble of elation just shattered. "Cookie! Oh, Bucky! How will I tell Cookie?"

Bucky didn't grin this time as he answered, but he might as well have. "Very carefully?" Then, he smiled. "You might like this better. With Jack's uncle at your side. For the kid, we can do this, Jeffrey. Oops. *Dad*, I mean. We can do it as a team."

Dad. In all the years Jeffrey had imagined this boy out there somewhere, he'd never once thought of himself as a dad. A father, yes, but never a dad. His eyes found Bucky's face, and he saw excitement painted all over the man's features. He hoped he saw that on Cookie's face, because if he didn't, then he would have another choice to make, and he didn't think it would be any easier than this one.

"Okay, Bucky. Let's go find my fiancée. Let's see if she's still my fiancée after she hears the news." He stood and moved to the window, noticing movement at the main house. He saw a pair of red shorts dart out from the basement, and he knew at least one of his brothers was there. Then, in dismay, he saw his father run out, wet and fully clothed, to grab his brother, picking him up and dragging him back into the basement. He turned to look at Bucky. "It seems my fiancée's not the only one there. This might turn out to be a full family reunion. God help us."

"God help us. How appropriate, Jeffrey. I think your son's been praying that exact, same prayer. I think God's answering his prayer right now."

Bucky walked up to stand beside Jeffrey. A dripping, red-suited boy once again ran from inside the distant house, but this time he was chasing a pretty girl in a pink suit. Then, a second red-suited boy, also very wet, ran outside, working with the first to corner the girl. Finally, as one, they wrapped their arms around her. She clasped her hands around both boys' shoulders, and her legs flailed the air as they picked her up and carried her back inside.

Bucky grinned. "Any of those related to you?"

"My twin brothers." He turned and walked to the door. "We might as well go. At least this way, the whole family learns the story at once. Who knows, my sister might even be there, too." He laughed nervously. "I might be dead before this is over."

Bucky clapped him on the shoulder. "At least the newspaper will get it right."

"The newspaper?"

"Have you already forgotten? I'm a reporter. The Chronicle. We make the news."

"Good news, I hope."

"In this case, whatever happens will be good news." He grinned.

"Okay, newspaper reporter. Let's go. Sour milk never gets any fresher by putting it off."

"Hey, I ought to write that down. May I?"

"Sure." Jeffrey bypassed the cars and headed out across the grass.

"We're not driving?" Bucky jangled his keys, hesitating before walking off. "My car's right here."

Jeffrey thumbed toward the house. "You can do this, Bucky. You may soon have the leading story of the week. Prominent Local Minister Throttles Son. Fiancée Helps. You need to be there for firsthand observation."

"Hey," Bucky called to him. "Nice headline. If your father fires you, I want to offer you a job at the paper. You're good."

"Shush." Jeffrey looked at him, but he was grinning. "Be careful what you offer. I may come begging."

"And you will be welcome." Bucky sounded winded already.

Jeffrey was glad Bucky was out of breath. He was relieved to be able to walk in silence. In spite of his teasing, his back was damp with nervousness, and he could feel his prospective father-in-law's shirt sticking to his chest. He needed to get this over with, and he still didn't know if his new family would consist of two people

244

or three. Whichever it was, he was certain of one thing. One of his family members would be called Dad. There were no two ways around that, because one of his family members would also go by Son. He hoped Cookie wanted to be a third. He desperately wanted that. However, that was just the roll of the die, and who could tell what result might turn up?

Chapter 21

JOANIE slowed her Miata, gently tapping her brake as she approached the signal, turning the corner onto Vine just before the light turned red. As she did, she adjusted the volume on the radio, the buildings causing her signal to fade, before finally tapping it off. It was all talk, anyway. She searched for her CD, but it had fallen under the seat, and she couldn't reach it from where she sat.

She glanced up at the sky overhead, seeing the blue of a nearly cloudless day through the crumbling reaches of the buildings. This part of town was old, and it had seen its better days long before she was born. She remembered several of the boarded-up buildings having windows in them at some point in the past, but she remembered just as many looking this decrepit the first time she'd seen them. Several of the drunks decorating the fronts of the buildings were new, though. Those were a rotating ornamental element. They rotated to the city jail—or the morgue—and new drunks came in to take their places.

The sun was excruciatingly hot here in the city, and she wished she'd put the top up already. Out in the better parts of town, she'd been able to keep the car moving, and the wind had flooded around her. Occasionally, if she had a good view, and no cars were around, she had even run the red lights. Anything to keep the air moving. However, without a breeze, and now that the car was crawling along, it was stifling.

Looking far down the street, she paid attention to the pattern of lights, timing her speed so that she could make it all the way to Fourth without stopping. The signal lights had been timed that way for as long as she'd known. Miss one, though, and she might have to sit through every one. She didn't want to sit in the sun through twenty or more lights, not in this heat, and not in Southside. Southside was a place few individuals wanted to be, and even fewer people considered safe. She wouldn't even stop to put up the top on her car in this part of town.

She drove carefully.

If Charlie was waiting on her, she could do her deal and be gone. Piece of cake. She tried to remember just what he looked like. Distracted, she slammed her brakes as an old tank of a Buick with rusty fenders and a peeling vinyl roof made a right turn on red just in front of her. She cursed it again as it slowed down. That car would make her miss the next light. Now, she knew the heat wouldn't last *until* she got off Vine. It would be *if* she got off Vine. Twenty lights would be an eternity.

Reaching Fifth and being forced to sweat as she waited at yet another light, she breathed a sigh of relief. There was Charlie at the very next corner. The last time she'd seen him was the last time he'd bought some of his little white pills from her, or more specifically, the last time he'd actually had money to buy some of her little white pills. He'd tried once since then, but he'd had no bills. She chuckled sourly. She didn't think of that time as seeing him. She called it smelling him. It had been pungent, too.

She laughed at what he had on. It was the same pair of orange coveralls he had been wearing three weeks ago. If she remembered correctly, he'd stolen them from one of the city's utility workers, snagging them right out of the back of a truck. It was another good reason to stay out of Southside, especially in a convertible.

She thought about all that, abruptly unsure of this sale. Today he'd managed to rustle up some quarters to call her, but she wondered now about the fifty. He would've had to get the money from someone, perhaps a loan from a drunken friend, or maybe sleight of hand at the five-and-dime. As usual, she knew she'd have to make sure she saw the green before she handed over the white.

She laughed at that, the idea that she had to see the green before she would hand over the white. There was no green anywhere in this part of the city, cash or grass. Then, she laughed again. That last word had a double meaning. Grass. All the grass she owned was in her trunk, or in her apartment, and none of it was on the street.

The light overhead flickered as these always did before a shift in colors. It was changing, and she had to move.

248

She let up the brake, and her car windshield caught the sun reflecting off a broken window, causing her to squint. Then, Charlie was there, and she braked and pulled to the curb.

"Charlie!" She called his name hard and loud. He wasn't paying attention, and she called it again, as she reached beside her for a small, plastic bag. Charlie's stuff was wrapped in a tissue—she didn't want anyone who might be suspicious to see the actual pills—and secured in the bag. She wanted a good grip on it when he got to the car, because if he grabbed it and ran, she knew that chasing him also meant leaving her car unattended. It wasn't worth fifty to do that.

"Joanie?" Charlie tried to stand. Grabbing the rail on the steps at his side, he paused, coughing repeatedly before making it to his feet.

She grimaced. His face was oozing from a sore just under his eye, and it was clear he hadn't shaved in a week or more. Then, she groaned at how he'd smelled last time. It was sure to be worse, now. She prepared herself.

As he stumbled to her car, grabbing the top of the door, she grasped the bag in her hand. "Money, Charlie?" She held the bag at her side and flashed it carefully. "Do you have money?" His eyes were glassy, and he didn't seem to understand. She sighed. She much preferred the Kincaids of the city, but the Charlies were her bread and butter. Without them, there was no steady income. Not for her, anyway. Some day she would be big time enough. Just not yet.

"You have it, Joanie?" His words were slurred, and he

seemed unsure just what she had brought him.

"What are you needing, Charlie? Conversation?" She wanted gone, but she also wanted her money. She would try to be patient with him. He was here, and he had agreed to her price. Fifty.

"No conversation. Pills. Please, Joanie. Please." His eyes had started to water, and he dripped saliva when he spoke.

"Money, Charlie. We agreed on fifty. Otherwise, this little bag goes bye-bye." She watched some of his saliva drip onto her seat. She would have to clean that up later.

"Not bye-bye, Joanie. Please." His pleading was soft, but his desperation was clear and undeniable. "Please, Joanie."

"Fifty, Charlie." She paused, looking up at him expectantly. Sometimes the really bad ones like Charlie would have the money when they called, and it would wind up in a pocket. Then, by the time she arrived, they'd have forgotten where they put it. Give him enough time, and he might remember. If he didn't, then she would drive off.

"Don't have fifty, Joanie." He looked hungrily at the bag in her hand. "Please."

"Sorry, Charlie." She had endured enough, and she dropped the bag in the seat to shift the transmission into gear. "Bag goes bye-bye."

Turning her head to make sure the street was clear, she only fleetingly saw Charlie lunge just as she hit the gas. His hand reached into the seat, and he grasped the bag just as his arm was thrown wide by the acceleration of the moving car. She heard him cry out as he fell to the street. Glancing down, she saw the plastic bag was gone. She immediately slammed on the brakes and threw the transmission into park.

Half standing to look back at Charlie lying against the curb, she yelled at him, "What are you doing, Charlie? You're crazy!"

He was, too. He had the bag in his hands, and as she watched, he ripped it open, spilling its contents into the street. He lunged at one pill with a cry of distress as it rolled into an open gutter, and with trembling hands, grabbed at the others, forcing them into his mouth as quickly as he could.

Joanie threw herself back into her seat. She should have known Charlie would be too good to be true, and now she was short fifty, as well as those pills he'd just wasted. She slapped her hands against the wheel and slammed the transmission into drive, hitting the gas and sending the rear end of the car fishtailing. Then, in inspiration, she slammed the brakes and twisted the wheel around, sliding the small car 180 degrees. Old Troop had money. He had more money than God. By God, he was God! She laughed at that. She would just go back and tell him he'd been fifty dollars short. By the time she got there, he'd be so high, he'd just give her the money with no questions asked.

Brilliant, Joanie. Brilliant.

WHAT WASN'T so brilliant was Joanie's desperation. She didn't care any longer about the lights and how well she timed them. She drove by old Charlie and reached her hand out to flash him a vulgar sign. He raised his head but only glanced her direction, not giving her any recognition at all.

She was lucky there were no cars coming, because she ran the first few red lights as if they weren't even there. However, luck times twenty was hard to come by in Southside. It could be had to a degree, only. What hurt was when the luck ran out, and it always did. The question was, just when?

Chapter 22

"DAD, YOU die!" Casey yelled his threat as he ran from the basement for safety. He had finally gotten his father here, and his enthusiasm had him wired.

"Cody," Trooper panted, calling the wrong twin's name. "Give me some breathing space." He held up one hand as he stood in the yard gasping for breath. The dappled light from the trees caught his hair, but the gold from the morning service was gone. His hair was just good old Trooper's, belonging to the father the boys needed to see during the middle of the week.

Casey stopped, standing erect in his red board shorts with the yellow flower. He had flown from the pool to catch his father, and the water still poured down his body, gluing the red material to his legs like a second skin. The flower wrapped his leg like a tattooed sunburst. He felt dismay well up inside.

"Dad," he called out. "Can't you tell? It's me, Casey."

"Oh?" Trooper laughed. "Really? Sweet Casey? I don't think so. I am absolutely certain you're wilder-than-wild Cody." He pulled his wet shirt away from his body. He had been out of the pool longer than his son, but his clothes held the water better. "My Casey loves me. He wouldn't chase me just to throw me in again."

"Oh?" Casey was beginning to see the joke. He stood, panting, catching his breath. He tried his own form of banter. "Well, your wild Cody is in there with Emily on one of the floats. Go play with him if you want."

His father held out one arm. "I will, Casey. Head back with me." He walked up to his son, and just as he got to him, instead of putting his arm around the boy's shoulder, he feinted and wrapped his arm around the teen's waist, pressing his shoulder into the boy's stomach, and pushing him backward toward the house.

Caught off guard, Casey stumbled all the way through the doorway and inside the basement. He was quick enough, though, to grab his father beneath the arms before he tumbled backward into the water. Trooper flailed his arms and legs, but the momentum was his own, and it carried him right into the water on top of his son.

When they popped up, Casey saw his brother still floating on his mat, and he glanced to the girl at his side. His brother looked to him and raised his arm in a salute of approval. "Go, Casey! Kill the man. He deserves to drown."

Emily laughed and slapped him on the stomach.

Casey saw his brother as a sitting duck, though, and as

254

Cody turned to say something to the girl at his side, Casey motioned to his father. Without a word, they both disappeared under the water. With no noise and very little surface movement, they poised just under the float. Signaling each other under water, they placed their feet on the floor of the pool, bent their knees, and pushed upwards with all their might. They flung the mat upward into the air.

What happened next entertained everyone standing around the outside of the pool. Casey and Trooper held to the mat the entire time, but not to the people onboard. Instead, Cody and Emily were launched far into the air, their arms and legs pin wheeling, as Casey and his father brought the mat back with them down into the water. The two airborne travelers landed about ten feet away, sending spray over several of those on the side. When they surfaced, Emily sputtered, pushing the hair back from her face, and Cody glared, turning his head to find his brother, looking for revenge. Ignoring their dismay, those on the sidelines began calling out their scores.

"Ten!" That was from Cookie. She was the first to respond. She looked around and laughed, holding up all ten fingers. Casey hooted, one arm in the air, and slapped the water with his open palm.

Other scores were yelled out, also, including several from the boys, whose scores were much lower. The girls yelled out their support to Emily, as they helped her from the pool.

Sharon laughed, kneeling by the water to offer a hand to her husband.

Cody swam directly to his brother, catching him before he was halfway up the steps. Grabbing him around the waist, he pulled him backward, and falling together, a convulsing rush of water spread across the surface of the pool. Once they were in the middle, he held his twin tightly, chest to back, as they dog paddled to stay afloat.

"I had her, Casey." He whispered his words brusquely into his brother's ear. "I was right there with her on that float, side by side, you idiot. You messed that up, you moron!" He put his hands on his brother's shoulders, and in one sudden thrust, he forced him underwater.

Casey came up laughing. It was all a hoot to him. He hadn't been the one on the float. He pushed away, swimming hard, searching for his father.

In that burst of movement, he caught something from outside of the basement. Wiping water from his eyes, he squinted, immediately picking out his oldest brother. There was also a big man he didn't recognize. Swimming up to Cody and grabbing him tightly around the neck, he taunted, "Second best brother. That's you, now. Number one just showed up."

"Forget you, Casey." His brother chortled, slapping water in his face. "I get him, first. After all, he was mine before he was yours."

"Not if you're dead." He grabbed his brother on the forehead and forced him backward under the water. When Cody took off for the bottom of the pool, Casey grabbed at him, only catching one leg of his board shorts. He yanked and hooted when they slid partially down. From then on, the two were at war, oblivious to the family reunion on the surface.

"JEFFREY!" Trooper waved one arm as he shouted to his son. He motioned him inside. "Welcome, and you brought a friend! The whole family's here!" He reached a big hand to push his wet hair from his forehead. He was buzzed with adrenalin, alive from his chest all the way to the tips of his fingers. With zest he called to those standing around, "Look at who's coming to join the party."

"Dad!" Jeffrey raised one arm in return.

Trooper shook out his wet clothes as best as he could, and he loped across the grass to offer his hand to his son. Only hours before, he had felt abandoned by his wife and children, and now it seemed he had found a part of his life back. His eldest needed to be here to share in it with him. "Cookie didn't tell us you had come out, too."

Jeffrey grabbed him in a sudden, rough embrace, and wrapped his arms around him, pulling him to his chest.

Trooper was surprised. He was soaked, and Jeffrey was dressed in a nice, if somewhat unfamiliar, shirt. However, as his son didn't seem to care, he wrapped his long arms around him and returned his hug in earnest. As his son continued to hold him, he realized this wasn't just a hug. His body was wracked with sobs.

"Jeffrey?" The last time he remembered a response this strong had been after his last youth camp when the boy had snuck out one of the family cars and wound up with a friend in a ditch, half drunk. He repeated, "Jeffrey?" After a moment, he tried to put some space between them, but Jeffrey wasn't ready to let go.

"I'm sorry, Dad." Jeffrey sniffled as his sobs slowly settled. He pulled his father even tighter before releasing his hold.

"You're soaked, Jeffrey, and I've done it to you. Look at you." Trooper chuckled. "At least we don't have to worry about you getting my shoulder any wetter."

"Trooper!"

They turned at the voice from inside the basement. It was Sharon. When they looked, the twins were still in the pool chasing each other, with one of them holding a pair of red swim trunks over his head, whooping with victory. Cookie raised her hand in a wave and smiled.

Sharon called to him, "Don't keep our boy out there all afternoon. Remember that Cookie's here." She put her arm around her future daughter-in-law, and she waved, also.

Jeffrey turned to look his father in the face. His eyes were a mess, though, and before speaking, he glanced at the heavy man at his side. Trooper watched him silently plead for *something*, and he could see the relief in his son's face when the man nodded.

Jeffrey turned back to his father. "I'm sorry for all that, Dad. It's been a rough day." He coughed and looked down at his clothes. "I don't guess I need to worry about changing into a swim suit. If so, it at least looks like one of the twins has one I can borrow."

Trooper glanced back to see the red suit still waving in the air. "Yeah. They'd better be careful with those girls in there. You've been that age, Jeffrey. You know." He glanced back at his son just in time to catch a grimace. He didn't understand it, but Jeffrey's friend seemed to, and he

258

reached to give Jeffrey a quick pat on the shoulder.

"Probably they both need their suits on. Right, Dad?"

Trooper laughed. "It's all in fun, but I guess you're right." He turned and called, "Casey? Cody? I want that suit on whoever's body it came off of. Pronto."

The girls off to the side giggled, and the boy holding the suit immediately gave it up, tossing it to his brother. He leaped to his twin's side, though, and wrapped his arms around his chest, attempting to pull him out of the water before he could put the shorts on.

"Sharon?" Trooper called to her. "He's your son. Stop him."

However, they were already half out, even as one brother fought to stay underwater. His modesty was saved by his mother, who stepped up behind them and pushed down on their shoulders, refusing to let either one back out any farther.

"Not until your brother has his suit on. You have company watching." The reprimand carried across the yard, and Trooper smiled at her words.

"Mom. It's a joke. No one cares. Besides, Dad's here. He can tell us no, if he wants us to stop."

"I think he just did. Besides, while I've seen all those parts on your brother, those girls haven't. It's none of their business, either. Now, let your brother dress."

Trooper chuckled, turning to his eldest. "See? That's why I'm wet like this. It's your brothers' fault."

"Still, Dad." Jeffrey reached to wipe at his nose, taking a tissue from Bucky when it was offered.

"It's all in fun." Trooper chuckled, looking back to the

259

house where his sons, both dressed, had climbed out of the pool and were chasing each other through the crowd of teenagers. Finally, several of the other boys tackled one of them, giving the second twin time to leap back into the water. Twisting violently, the first brother threw the boys off and dove headfirst into the pool. It hadn't done him much good to put his suit back on, it seemed, because after he hit the water, one of his friends stood up and whooped, dancing a victory dance. His war flag was a pair of red board shorts with a giant yellow flower on one leg.

Trooper grinned, bumping his son's side with his elbow. "Teenagers are hopeless. It's not that far away for you, Son. You remember. Just look at them. Already, one of them is sans suit again." He laughed, pointing, as he put his arm over his son's shoulder. "Also, Jeffrey, never think you have to apologize for giving your father a hug."

Jeffrey took another ragged breath. "My dad. For giving my dad a hug."

Trooper laughed. "Same thing, Son." He pulled Jeffrey tightly to his side before releasing him again.

Bucky cleared his throat. "Um, sir. Not to your son." He stepped up to Trooper. "After today, Jeffery knows there's a world of difference between just being a father and being a dad."

"And you are?" Trooper held his hand out to Bucky with a smile. He might not know this man, but he was a prominent minister used to charming others. The last few years, it had mostly been from an unreasonably high church platform and over television broadcasts, but he had not forgotten the skill.

"Dad, not yet." Jeffrey reached to push his father's arm away. "I want to introduce him to everyone at the same time."

"Sure, Son. Any way you want to handle your introductions is fine." Trooper kept his hand out anyway, waiting as Jeffrey headed on to the house. He kept a smile on his face as he spoke, "Any friend of my son is a friend of mine. I'm glad to meet you, mystery man."

Bucky laughed, throwing his own hand into Trooper's. "Just call me Benji. I'm an old friend of your son's from youth camp, oh, about thirteen years ago. He was in my dorm once and slept in the bunk underneath me."

"Thirteen years ago. That must have been around the time he last went." They started toward the house, and Trooper wondered if this man might answer an old question. "You wouldn't have any idea of the reason he stopped going, would you? About that time, what was he, fifteen? He came home one year and never went back. We encouraged him, but he wouldn't budge."

"Sorry, sir. I did short sheet his bed all week, but alas, I can't claim that fine distinction."

"Ah. Well, there's our boy, and he's found his girl. She's the first serious girlfriend he's ever had. We're waiting on them to set a date."

"So I hear, sir."

Trooper watched Jeffrey give Cookie the same hug he had just received. All these spontaneous, very public demonstrations of affection seemed out of character for his son, but then, the whole day had been unusual. What was one more oddity?

261

AS ENCOURAGING as Bucky had been back in the guest house, Jeffrey still dreaded the fallout from his family. He glanced out to see the newspaper man with his father. He could guess how the Kincaids looked to him, so wholesome gathered around the pool on this Sunday afternoon. Everyone was all hugs, perfect, cheerful, and homey. If his revelation spoiled that, how cheerful would it all seem then? He might need that newspaper job after all. Bucky had just thought he was kidding.

"Jeffrey?" Sharon pulled at her son's arm to get his attention. "Where's my hug?"

He turned his head to study his mother's face. She loved him now. Would she love him when he told the family his news? He was just twenty-eight. He could see the accusations that would grow in her eyes, and it broke his heart. Wanting to feel her arms around him, not knowing if this woman who had been his most ardent sup-porter would ever want to hold him again, he grabbed her in his arms.

"I'm sorry, Mom. I know I'm supposed to be so perfect, but I'm not." He spoke into her hair as he kept his arms wrapped around her, running his hands over her back. It was one he had held many times, and this might be his last. He squeezed her again.

"Nonsense," Sharon whispered back. "Perfect is how a son is seen through the eyes of love. You'll always be perfect to me."

Hearing his mother's words, he felt an overwhelming urgency to break his news. The need to tell what he had done, and that he had a son, was irresistible. If he kept it bottled inside any longer, he'd explode. He released her, and his words poured out, "It's something I've done, Mom. I can't undo it, either. It's awful. Not all of it's awful, not anymore. It was when I did it, though."

Her eyes jumped to Cookie. "Jeffrey, you're getting married soon, anyway. We'll just move up the date. Is Cookie okay? She doesn't show at all."

"Cookie? It's not Cookie, Mom." He frowned, not understanding at first. Then, he stepped back and looked at her, surprised. He had not been intimate with his fiancée. That lesson had been learned long ago. "What do you think I'm telling you?"

When she discreetly patted her stomach, he smiled, sniffling and brushing his eyes with the back of one hand. He shook his head, her assumption and easy suggestion of a remedy easing some of the tension. His mother was only one of six, though. He had five more people to approach, and even so, his mother didn't know the real problem.

"Close, Mom, but you're twelve years off."

"Twelve years? What do you mean, twelve years?" She turned to her husband and motioned him to join them. "Trooper? I think you should be here to talk with Jeffrey and me."

"Wait, Mom. Dad said the whole family's here." He looked around. "Does that mean Lindsay? I don't see her." He wanted to get this over with at once. He didn't think he could endure facing down this disaster twice.

She nodded. "Upstairs with John. Why?" She put a hand on his face. "What's this about, Jeffrey? Are you in some sort of trouble?"

At that moment, Lindsay's voice yelled from the stairs, her words vibrating with emotional intensity.

"Mom! Dad! Get up here quick! I think Uncle John's dying!"

Chapter 23

TROOPER glanced at Sharon and Jeffrey, and it took a moment for Lindsay's words to register. It was a valid hesitation. No one would doubt that. This was a man who, over thirty years, had let other things in his life—money, public recognition, his ministry—crowd out what was really important to him. His family and his devotion to God had taken a backseat in his life, and on this one fateful day, he had seen himself as he really was. He hadn't liked what he had seen, either.

Now, his wife needed him; his son needed him. He had pushed those he loved aside far too long. To turn loose of that first reconnection with his family ripped at the fabric of his heart. For those few precious seconds, the world was silent, and nothing existed for Trooper except the eyes of the people directly in front of him.

Then, Lindsay's cry came again, and the noise of the

world crashed in upon him: the sounds of the twins' roughhousing in the pool; a chair knocked over and suddenly clattering to the deck; a teen girl crying out the words, "Oh, my God! Someone's dying?" Trooper's longing for his wife released its hold on his muscles, and he vaulted for the steps, reaching to touch Sharon's extended fingers as he passed.

In that moment, Jeffrey's hand found his father's shoulder, his own trauma paling in the urgency of the moment, and he leaped to be at his side. Together, they took the steps three at a time. In the stark stairwell, its utility designed as a barrier between the pool and the house, their footsteps reverberated with urgency. Jeffrey was the first to grab his sister, wrapping his arms around her and pulling her to his side.

Trooper's response was more practical. "Where, Lindsay?" He put his hand on her back, and when she looked up at him, her eyes were red. He repeated, "Where's John, Lindsay?"

"Your office, Dad." She used Jeffrey's shirt to wipe her tears. "He keeps holding his head, and he's started convulsing. I tried to help, but he's only gotten worse."

"9-1-1, Lindsay. Have you called?" Jeffrey looked into her face as she shook her head.

"I knew Mom and Dad would know what to do." Her voice shook, and she threw her arms around her brother. Together, they made their way into the office.

Trooper knew that voice. When she was a little girl, and he'd still been able to fix anything, she had used it when she was scared. It was clear to him that she was frightened for John.

Just then, their hair wet and askew, and their red trunks glued to their skin, the water still running in rivulets down their legs, the twins reached the top of the stairs. Of the four children, Trooper knew John was most truly an uncle to them. They saw the tears on their sister's face, and their eyes found their dad's.

"Dad, Mom said it was Uncle John. Is he okay?" That was from one of the twins. Immediately, the other burst in, "I want see Uncle John, Dad."

"Hang on, boys. It'll be all right."

One of the twins draped an arm over his brother's identical shoulder, gripping his big hand around a wiry neck he knew as well as his own. Trooper glanced between his sons, only then able to tell which one was which. It was Cody who would try to protect Casey.

"What if he dies?" That was from Casey.

Identical eyes caught identical eyes, and Trooper saw they were red.

"Then, I'm still here for you." That was from Cody. "You're my best friend, Case. You know that always." He looked at his father. "Right, Dad? Uncle John'll be all right?"

"Cody," he began, shaking off the building emotions, and shifting into action. "Call 9-1-1. I'll get Jeffrey to keep the other kids downstairs. You, Casey," and he pointed to his youngest son, "come with me to my office. Your Uncle John needs our help." He reached and grasped his son's bare shoulder, and he pulled him forward. "Don't be frightened. I haven't seen him yet, and I don't know what we'll find."

"Dad."

Casey's voice made Trooper pause and turn his way.

"I'm not frightened."

"It's your Uncle John, Casey."

"Dad, I know that. I'm not frightened, because you're here."

Trooper's heart surged in his chest, and he remembered sitting in his truck outside the gate, wanting to run away from this boy, willing to use his damaged vehicle as an excuse not to spend the day with him. How could he have been so stupid? When did his priorities get so mixed up that he had let something—anything—come between him and this boy who cared so much about him? He threw his arms around his son's damp shoulders and pulled him tight. They were a good fit together, father and son. It had just taken this disaster for him to see that.

"I love you, Casey." He squeezed his boy tighter, for the moment unwilling to let go of him. He had nearly missed the boy's final years of childhood—the most important ones—and in that moment, he wanted them all back again.

Casey patted his dad's back, his father's wet clothes hardly any drier than his own dripping trunks, and he cleared his throat. "Uncle John, Dad. He needs our help."

"Right, Son." In that moment, John had been put aside. Not intentionally, and not because Trooper didn't care. It was quite the opposite. Trooper was finding he cared very much, and caring takes time. Intent is not enough. At times, important things must be pushed aside, because a son has to know that his father's arms around him take precedence over everything else. Only by taking that time in the midst of an overwhelming emergency can the child really know beyond a shadow of a doubt that he holds the highest place in his father's heart.

Casey disengaged himself from his father's arms, and with one arm on Trooper's shoulder, pulled him into the office. Trooper was taken aback with the severity of his friend's condition. He looked at Lindsay and Jeffery, whispering that he'd take over for them, if they didn't mind watching over the teens down by the pool.

"Uncle John?" Casey leaned over the back of the sofa, and when John didn't respond, he looked up at his father for direction. "What's wrong with him, Dad?"

"I don't know, Son." He stepped around the sofa to kneel at his old friend's side. John lay with one hand over his forehead, but it was limp. His breathing was shallow and quick, and his skin was pasty. Trooper reached to grasp John's jaw in his hand, gently patting his face in hopes of a response. "John? Can you hear me, John?"

"Is he alive, Dad?" The boy sounded afraid. "Is Uncle John going to be all right?"

"Come over here, Son." He motioned to him, indicating he wanted him at his side.

"Sure, Dad."

"Down here, Casey, with me." He put his hand on his son's shoulder as he knelt at his side. "Son, I minister at the church and encourage the people to pray. I don't always do it the way I tell others, though. Now's a good time for one of those prayers. Agree with me, Son." He held out his hand.

"Can I pray first, Dad?" Tears had begun to run freely down Casey's face.

"John would like that. Go ahead." Trooper squeezed his hand and closed his eyes.

"God, thank you for giving me back my dad. I've missed him." He paused for a moment, squeezing Trooper's hand in return. "He's my best friend, and I don't want to lose him again."

Listening to his son's prayer, Trooper's tears began to trickle down his face. John was the one in need of prayer, but before taking time for a man he knew the boy loved, Casey was thanking God for him. He hadn't realized his son thought he had been lost to him. It seemed there were a lot of things he hadn't realized.

Casey continued, "God, Uncle John's sick. He's Dad's best friend, just like Dad's mine."

Trooper looked at Casey. His son's words opened his eyes still again. John was indeed his best friend and had been for forty years. Where had his children been during much of that time? This boy at his side should have been his best friend the last seventeen years. Cody, Jeffrey, and Lindsay, too. *Lindsay.* He had pushed her aside long ago, not understanding her, and finally refusing to try. What sort of parent had he been?

"Son," Trooper interrupted, "my turn." He squeezed the boy's hand, and his words took over. "My son is my best friend, God. My second best friend is at my side, and he needs something we can't give. My son has asked for your help for his uncle. God, if you're there . . . no, I don't

270

mean that, God. You are there. Today you gave me my family back, and I appreciate that. God, help my friend, John. We ask all this in your name." He looked up at Casey and released his hand.

Then, without warning, Casey grabbed his father and wrapped his arms around him. "I love you, Dad."

Trooper let his arms encircle his son once again, slowly at first, then with a vengeance that surprised even him. "And I love you, Son. I always have."

There was a rustling noise on the sofa, and they turned to John. He was attempting to speak.

"Uncle John?"

"Two Points?" John's words were a whisper. His eyes opened for a quick moment, then immediately closed, his lids tightening in obvious pain.

"John, it's me, and Casey's here, too. What is it? How can we help?"

"Cody's calling 9-1-1, Uncle John."

His father reached and placed a hand on his arm, and he squeezed it. Then he shook his head for the boy to be quiet.

"My Aunt Bessie, Two Points. Did you ever meet her?" John had barely started, and then he was silenced, as another spasm of pain wracked his body. His face contorted with its severity.

"Aunt Bessie? I think so, John. Years ago." Trooper was unsure of the point of his question. Noticing movement at the door, he glanced up to see his other three children looking in. Sharon was at their side. He motioned for them to keep their distance. Turning back to John, he

271

prompted him, "What is it about your aunt that you want me to know?"

"She died, Two Points."

"Sure, John. I knew that. Is there anything else?"

"That's me, Two Points. I've become my Aunt Bessie. It's my time, I think."

"Dad," Casey started. Trooper held his son's arm firmly, shaking his head once again. With no warning, John again convulsed violently at his side.

Trooper called across the room to Cody, "Did you call 9-1-1, Son?"

"They'll be here in twenty minutes, Dad. I already opened the gate."

"Good thinking, Cody. You did that well." Trooper shot him a thumbs up. He knew what he'd been missing by ignoring his own family. He would remedy that, and it had started today. He would not let them down again.

Now, though, was for John.

"Dad, Uncle John's trying to talk again."

He looked down to see his friend's hand moving, and he took it in his. "Yes, John?"

"Forgive me, Two Points." John's eyes were filled with tears, and as he squeezed them shut, water washed down his face.

"For what, John? There's nothing to forgive. Now, quiet. Help is on the way." Trooper finally recalled how John's Aunt Bessie had died, and he felt a new concern wash over him. It had been a massive brain hemorrhage that stemmed from an undiagnosed tumor. In that moment, he was frightened, too. He had gone to the hospital with his friend, and her end had been excruciating. It seemed John knew something he hadn't shared before.

"As boys, when we were camping, I . . . I . . ." John's voice faded, and his head began to shake. As the movement diminished, he tried once again to speak, but his voice was slurred, and his words could barely be understood.

"John, I loved those trips we took." Trooper was certain he was losing his friend, and all he knew to do was talk to him. "You pulled me out of my shell, and I knew you cared about me. You were the best friend a teenager could have, and I don't regret one night we spent out in that old tent of yours." He saw John smile, and he chuckled, letting his emotions from those times spill out in an uncontrolled flood. "I didn't get much sleep, though. You told more stories, keeping me awake until I couldn't hold my eyes open. I remember laughing, and I was always gone before the end of the last story. I never even remembered getting undressed, but my clothes were always off to the side, folded up when I woke the next day. The next morning, you'd be outside wandering around, always the early bird. I never knew why you got up so early on those trips. You really loved the outdoors, I guessed. As soon as you knew I was awake, you'd come back inside the tent, and as I put my clothes back on, you'd tell me the ending of that last story. I would always end up laughing all over again." He squeezed John's hand. "I loved you, John, for all those camping trips. I have no memories any better, not from those early years together with you."

He looked at his son. Then, when Casey squeezed his knee and grinned, he winked at him and smiled. Everyone knew of those camping trips.

John's hand tapped at Trooper's arm, and when father and son looked down, his mouth moved frantically, but only slurred sounds came out.

"Slow down, John. I'm listening." Trooper leaned closer. "Say it slowly."

John's words were still slurred, but this time he was able to make himself understood. "Loved you, too. Only loved you." Then, violent convulsions shook his body, and they refused to stop.

"Cody, 9-1-1? Go outside and check. Sharon and Lindsay, get me blankets." Trooper stood, and his self-control broke. "I think we're losing him." The faint sound of sirens caught his attention, and he turned to the front of the house. Through the windows, he could see flashing lights through the trees. "They're here. Thank God."

"Here, Dad." Lindsay ran in carrying several blankets. Tears were on her face when she looked at him, and she chewed her bottom lip for a few seconds before speaking. "I'm so sorry, Dad."

"Go to him, Lindsay. He loves you best, you know." Trooper touched her on the shoulder, and then he grabbed her in his arms. "I love you, too, Lindsay. I'm sorry I never tell you." He released her with tears on his cheeks. "There are too many things I don't say enough. Go to John. I think he's fading fast."

LINDSAY did, and she tried to warm her old friend with

274

one of the blankets. However, she looked at her father as he pulled her mother to him, wrapping his arms around her in his distress. Her mother caught Lindsay's eyes, and Lindsay gave her a teary smile. Then, she looked to John, his body still shaking with the convulsions no one could stop. She sat beside him and patted that face she loved so, the only person she had ever felt really understood her, and she smiled as she leaned to place a kiss on his face.

"Those were the magic words, John. Dad finally said them. You've saved me, and you don't even know it. However, you didn't love me best." Her words were whispered ones for John alone to hear, but more, for her to say. She needed to get this out, and John had always kept her secrets. "You've always loved Dad best, and he doesn't even know why. God love you, John. You've been the best friend my dad could have ever had. Godspeed."

With her thumb, she gently rubbed the strained skin just under one of his eyes, and she let her tears fall freely. As her thumb passed, the skin was left smooth and unmarred, and John suddenly looked far younger than his fifty-three years. Lindsay could see in his face the skinny teenager who must have fallen in love with her father, the budding young man who knew no other way to spend time with the tall, gangly basketball player who was the toast of the school, other than to lie beside him in the woods inside an old tent, and tell him funny stories far into the night.

John's eyes were opened by then, and he stared into the room. Lindsay knew he didn't see her. He would keep all of her secrets forever. He had never told them to a soul when he was alive, and he couldn't tell anyone now.

Chapter 24

BUCKY STOOD at the edge of the pool and looked out at the sun-washed lawn wending its way down to the shore. He felt at a bit of a loss in all this. He had been upstairs, and he'd seen some of what had transpired. He hadn't wanted to intrude, but he was a newspaperman, and not much of what went on escaped his attention. He had seen the lights that still flashed outside the house, the front door standing wide as the paramedics rushed inside, their suits covered with reflective tape, wearing their helmets on their heads. They had hurried into the office, pulling the blankets from the dying man's body, and stripping his shirt back. With dexterity, they had unwound equipment in suitcase-like containers and attached pads to his chest to jumpstart his heart, but his body had refused to respond. Finally, they stood at his side, and he lay covered with a blanket once again, although this time none of him showed.

Jeffrey had returned downstairs to help the teenagers who had come with his brothers, telling Bucky they had to call someone at their homes to come. He needed to see that they did, and did Bucky mind waiting around a while?

Of course he'd waited. It had given him time to think about how he'd come to find his nephew a father. Now, he was enmeshed in a family mired in grief.

Eventually, he followed Jeffrey down the steps.

It wasn't long before he saw the teenagers begin filtering away. Parents who had places on the lake arrived within minutes. Others in town took a bit longer. Those that lived on the other side of the city doubled up with some of their friends, walking around the side of the house in order to avoid going upstairs.

When the last teenager was gone, the last except for those grieving upstairs, Bucky located Jeffrey outside. He had pulled a chair from beside the pool and carried it out into the grass. He motioned to Bucky to do the same. They sat side-by-side, Jeffrey leaning forward, his elbows on his knees. He wrapped his hands around the back of his head and looked at the grass at his feet. Leaning down, he plucked one long blade and held it up.

"That's grass, Jeffrey." Bucky broke the silence.

"Yeah." He let out a long sigh.

"Nothing special about grass, I don't guess."

"You're right. It's just a blade of grass." Jeffrey held the end between two fingers and ran another finger down its edge. "What if I told Cookie that Jack really is my younger brother, and that he was adopted out as a child?

277

My parents were afraid to tell anyone, and it's still a big secret. She must never mention it to them." He looked at Bucky with hope in his eyes.

"Oh, you are thinking big. Better yet, I'll hire you right now. Then, when your parents kick you out, you're all set. There. Feel better? You are an official newspaperman with a real position and a salary."

"What position, Bucky?"

He shrugged. "I don't know, yet. I'll think of something, though. Just give me a few minutes." He reached over and plucked the blade of grass from Jeffrey's hand.

"Hey!" Jeffrey frowned at him.

He slipped it in his mouth to chew on it. He immediately spit it out, tumbling over backward in his chair.

Jeffrey stood and leaned over to offer him a hand up. "Are you all right?"

"Nasty!" He spit several times. "I don't guess you can actually chew grass." He wiped at his mouth, ignoring the proffered hand. Nothing could be more disgusting.

Jeffrey laughed, continuing to hold out his hand. "Let me help you up."

Bucky climbed to his feet and worked with the chair for a moment. "There's a hole here. That's why I went over. I didn't see it earlier." He looked at Jeffrey as if it were his fault. "Why do you have holes in your yard?"

"Gophers, Bucky. It's called the country." He reached and patted the man's girth, laughing. "Probably that helped, too. Well, I'm standing now. I suppose I should at least talk to Cookie. It's hard, though. Right now, I have

278

the most wonderful fiancée in the whole of the city. In half an hour, I might have no one."

Bucky grinned. "Jack Jack Jack Jack Jack." He ran the words together in a torrent, waiting to see if Jeffrey got the gist.

"What?" Jeffrey frowned in puzzlement.

"Your son. Remember? He's looking for you, and he knows. He wrote your name all over that flyer. You've got someone no matter what your fiancée says. Think about him."

"I have been." He looked up at the house to see Cookie walking from the basement. His eyes were red as he continued. "That's all I've thought about all day. For longer than that, actually. Nine years. I've thought about him for nine years."

"I'm sure he's saying the same thing about you." By then, though, Cookie was waving, and Bucky switched into his friendly thing. "Hey, little lady. I didn't get to introduce myself earlier. I've been hogging your honey, here, and I know you're missing him." He put out his hand as she drew close. "Name's Bucky." He glanced at Jeffrey and grinned. "Er, if you'd rather, Jeffrey knows me by Benji. We go way back. I gather you go by Cookie?"

She smiled, the gracious upper class girl. "I'm glad to meet you, Benji. You may, indeed, call me Cookie. How do you know Jeffrey?"

"Oh, Jeffrey and I used to sleep together." He grinned as he looked from one to the other. Cookie's expression showed she clearly didn't understand that at all, and Jeffrey only returned a wan smile.

"Slept together? Jeffrey? What does your friend mean?"

Bucky caught what she had done. She had dehumanized him as she spoke. She hadn't yet warmed up to his sense of humor.

"Um, Cookie—" Jeffrey took a deep breath. "It's not quite what it sounds like."

"Jeffrey seems to be tongue tied, Mr. Benji. His uncle has just died, and you stand here telling me you slept with my fiancé. You need to explain that to me. What do you mean? And I want it clearly said without that silly grin on your face."

Bucky couldn't remove the grin, though. "Jeffrey, you've got a good one, here." He reached and slapped him on the shoulder, leaving Jeffrey looking miserable.

"Mr. Benji! Are you planning to answer my question or not? Otherwise, Jeffrey and I will leave here without your answers, and you may make your crude comments to the empty air." Cookie glared at Bucky, then she turned her eyes to Jeffrey with a determined expression on her face.

"Cookie, may I still call you that?"

"You already have, Mr. Benji." She looked back at him, with ice in her expression.

"Stop that," he said. "Just Benji, or Bucky is even better. Please." He sighed as he abandoned his humorous approach, realizing he had to get serious. He could see Jeffrey was clearly unprepared to plow through the mess that was ahead of him this day.

"Thank you." Cookie smiled. "At least I hear the

280

beginnings of polite conversation."

"Do you love Jeffrey?" He needed her to declare it out loud. It would make it harder for her to back down when she heard the news.

She frowned. "Jeffrey, have you slept with this man?"

"Not like you think, Cookie."

She snapped, "What other way is there?" Tears came to her eyes. "Talk to me, Jeffrey."

"Youth camp, Cookie. I slept in the bunk under his. That's not what this is about, though. I started to talk to Mom about it, and then Lindsay called us upstairs."

"Something that happened twelve years ago?"

Jeffrey looked at her, and Bucky could see the surprise on his face. He was equally surprised. How could the man's fiancée know about this? Jeffrey was the only one he'd told.

"Was it, Jeffrey? Your mother talked to me back in the house while you were getting the children home. Your mother said she thought I was pregnant when you first mentioned whatever this is to her. Well, she didn't say exactly that, but I knew what she meant. I was horrified, to tell you the truth. You're not gay, are you?"

Bucky interrupted, "He's not gay, at least not with me, and with what we know, I doubt it seriously in any case."

"Will you shut up!" Cookie was clearly irritated now. "My conversation is with my fiancé. You are not part of this."

Jeffrey intervened. "He is part of it, Cookie. Trust me. And, no, I'm not gay."

"Do you love Jeffrey?" Bucky pressed her again for an

answer. He was nothing if not persistent, and he wasn't about to let up. He wouldn't have been able to reach Jeffrey on his personal phone if he wasn't. He was a newspaper man, after all.

"Yes, I love Jeffrey. Why do you need to know that?" Fur was about to fly, and it showed in the narrowing of her eyes.

"Even if he's done something you don't know about? Will you still love him?"

She marched to Jeffrey's side, standing with him against this onslaught to their relationship. "Sir, there is nothing Jeffrey can have done that will cause me not to love him. I can assure you of that." She wrapped her arm in his.

"Can your love weather something big, something serious?"

"Say what you mean, sir. You keep suggesting, but you never say what you mean." She pulled on Jeffrey's arm. "Let's go, Jeffrey. They need us back at the house."

"Wait, Cookie. I need to hear this. Can our love weather something very serious?"

"Anything, Jeffrey. There's nothing we can't weather."

"Memphis?" Bucky's question leaped into the air. He wasn't finished, yet, and he knew the word should mean something to her. It certainly had to Jeffrey earlier. Besides, Jeffrey was stalling again, and Bucky wanted to wrap this up, whether it went well or poorly.

"Memphis?" Cookie turned to Bucky. "What about Memphis?"

Jeffrey reached to turn her face to look at him. "I have

a son, Cookie. That's what Bucky came out here to tell me."

She looked into Jeffrey's eyes for a long time. She glanced at Bucky, and then back to Jeffrey. "The boy? The one at Uncle Jim's?" She blinked rapidly. "How?"

Bucky chuckled. "That's pretty obvious."

"Not now, Bucky." Jeffrey motioned him away, and then he whispered to Cookie, "I love you with all my heart, Cookie. You know that."

"I knew he looked like you. But, how . . . you're twenty-eight. You must have been fifteen."

"May I hug you, Cookie?" She nodded as if in a daze, and he pulled her to him. Once she was in his arms, he whispered, "I was fifteen and at youth camp. It was a mistake the final night. I'm sorry, Cookie. It wasn't meant to happen, and I thought it went away. I didn't even know there was a baby until I was nineteen, and even then, all I knew was that he had been adopted out at birth."

"Did you love her? The girl?"

"I was fifteen, Cookie. I barely knew her. It was the fourth night of youth camp, and I barely knew her. At fifteen, how would I know love if it jumped into my face?"

"Does she still love you?"

"She died four years ago," Bucky interrupted. "She was my sister."

"Oh, Benji. I am so sorry." Cookie whispered her words as she laid her head on Jeffrey's chest. "All that happened a very long time ago, didn't it, Jeffrey? What about the boy?" She looked up at Jeffrey and then to

Bucky. Her voice was suddenly curt, and her question laid her realization out for all to see. "You're his uncle. You want to take him? Is that what this is about?" She looked back to Jeffrey with pleading in her eyes. "He's yours, Jeffrey. You cannot let this man have your son. You should have seen him. He was so sad, as if he needed someone to come and rescue him."

Jeffrey wrapped her tightly in his arms and rocked her as tears streamed down his cheeks. "That was exactly what I'd hoped you'd say, Cookie. Oh, I do love you so very much."

However, she stepped back and slapped him on the chest. "So, that's what all this was about, whether I wanted that little boy? I told you at lunch today I wanted to bring him home with me. Everyone just laughed at me. Why didn't you just ask?"

Jeffrey just grabbed her up and swung her in a circle, forcing Bucky to jump out of the way.

Bucky didn't care. He was glad the boy would have a home, and it would be with his father. He wanted that, too. It was what Jeffrey should have had the opportunity to do a dozen years ago. It might be late, but it was never too late, not when talking about a man's son.

Chapter 25

TWO FINGERPRINTS.

Sharon reached to the mirror, but she didn't touch it. There were two fingerprints. Her hand shook with the memory of one. John had lashed out at her, telling her she was losing her family. Now, he was gone. What else had he said?

I'm offering you your children back.

She knew what he meant. How many weeks had she lived here, mired in depression, just wishing for the days to end, often wearing the same thing on Friday that she had put on that Monday?

The second fingerprint. She placed her hand close, only to see what her heart hadn't wanted to believe. It was a fingerprint the size and shape of hers. Lindsay's. When John had shown her the bottles, she hadn't wanted to believe him, refusing to accept that her daughter would come here to plan her own end. Now, she was willing to face that fact. Why else would the second fingerprint match hers? The bottles of pills had come from this cabinet.

Placing her finger where her daughter's had left its mark, she pressed, and the mirror swung free. She stared at the collection of medicines ... pills, mostly, no, *drugs*. She took them, this one to stay awake, and that one for headaches. There was one container that she had gotten for that time after the twins were born. She had routinely had it refilled for years. Now, it had been months since she had taken one of those. Soon, she would no longer need that prescription at all. Her body would change, and that possibility would be gone forever.

She took all those, and yet there was one she had refused to consider.

God has given you your healing. It is in this bottle. Your family needs you.

She took a deep breath. John wasn't here to chide her anymore. He would never be here again. Yet, he had been a good friend. He had been willing to anger her, to alienate himself, and still, his only concern had been her family. She was lucky he had picked her husband as his friend all those years ago.

She reached to the top shelf, and she grasped the bottle in her hand. Turning, she walked into her bedroom and to the window. There were so many tears in the other room, and she needed to be away from it all. Just for a moment, she needed to step away to a place of calm. She pulled back the curtain to look outside.

286

She watched Jeffrey as he swung Cookie in a circle. The sun shone on them, and the grass was green. Just beyond were the waters of the Green Fork, and across the other side, the property her parents had owned for years— even before the lake was built—stretched off into the hills. The whole scene was out of a storybook. The children looked so happy, as if the world was their oyster, and nothing could get in their way. Perhaps they were, too. Jeffrey was like that, always driven with the need to be perfect, to show only his best side to the world, even to his mother. It had surprised her—and pleased her—when he'd broken down in front of her. It had been nice to see a slice of the little boy who used to fall on his bike and come to her with his scraped knees.

She had asked Cookie about Jeffrey's horrible news, and the young woman had seemed totally mystified, laughing when she had asked if the wedding needed to be planned soon. However, she had seen the shock behind her eyes. Possibly it was something small, the ring, perhaps. If Jeffrey needed money to cover its cost, it would be a small thing for him to ask. She knew it was beautiful, but beautiful cost money, and he still drove that old truck Trooper had given him three years earlier. Was that it? Possibly.

There was one other thing that bothered her. No one had explained that rotund man to her, and who knew what part he might play in Jeffrey's terrible news. The bill collector? She dropped the curtain and laughed aloud, then she looked at the bottle in her hand. On this day, she really did believe she had her family back. Lindsay? Did she have Lindsay back? Dear God, she hoped so. She had Jeffrey, and he certainly seemed happy enough out on the lawn. The twins, well, they were seventeen, and the problems in their world were easily solved with an extra dozen friends and the occasional removal of a brother's swimsuit. More importantly, she had Trooper back. Truly, she felt she had her husband back.

"John, thank you," she whispered to a man she knew could no longer hear her. He might hear her prayers, though. Surely, God could pass those along, for if anyone was in Heaven today, it had to be John. "John, you have brought us all together, again. Don't you think I don't know what you've done. I'll not lose them again, John."

Then, without hesitation, she removed the top of the container, and she shook out one of the pills. She looked at it for a moment, amazed at how small it was, and she realized it had almost destroyed her family. No. That was not true. She paused, glancing back at the window. She knew differently. The pill had done no such thing. *She* had almost destroyed her family. Raising the pill to her mouth, she placed it on her tongue, and with a quick motion, it was gone.

"Now, Lindsay, my beautiful daughter. You have to know that I know. I love you, and I will keep you around. I've ignored you entirely too long." With a determined step, Sharon marched back to the bathroom. Placing the bottle in the center of the counter, the exact place John had slammed it down earlier that day, she grabbed the orange-red purse in her hand, and she marched down the hall. She had a daughter to save, and she knew just how to do it. Her daughter needed love, and that was exactly what she was about to get.

SHARON stepped into the kitchen, and she held the purse under her arm. She paused, puzzled, at the sight of her two, red-suited sons, their muscular backs bare, sitting hunched over the kitchen table. Her daughter, her beautiful daughter, who had very nearly finished a four-year fashion degree in three, was sitting across from them. Across the table papers were spread in haphazard fashion.

Stepping quietly to stand behind the boys, she put her hand on one bare back. She rubbed it in a gentle circle, feeling the rise and fall of her fingers as they rippled across the muscles that were so similar to Trooper's. She knew those muscles, this back, and the one she wasn't touching as well. She knew them intimately. They had grown up under her hands, had changed from toddlers to boys to adolescents to almost men, and her hands had been there all the way in hugs and sometimes reprimands. They would be grown soon, and they would one day belong to some other woman. When it came, it would be time, and she would let them go. Not just yet, though. Not just yet.

She breathed a small prayer. Thank you, John.

The boy whose back she had touched looked up at her, and seeing her face, he smiled. She knew him this time, the crinkle around an eye as he first recognized his mother. Once his smile was there, the crinkle was gone, but it had been there. That had been how she'd recognized him all along, and she'd never known just what it was. Only one of her boys had that crinkle. She had been watching, had *paid attention*, and she had known.

"Casey, how are you doing?"

"Okay, Mom. Are you handling Uncle John all right? They didn't take him. The funeral home is on the way."

His smile faded for a moment, and when Sharon saw it flash back across his face, she watched carefully. Yes, it was there. The crinkle was there. Her Casey had a crinkle.

Cody turned to her, and his eyes were filled with excitement. "Mom, you have to see what Lindsay's planning to do. It's brilliant." He stood and turned the chair for her to sit, bright with enthusiasm. "Show her, Lindsay. She said Uncle John gave her the idea."

When Sharon moved to sit, Cody took the purse from her hand and set it off to the side, just to where it covered the edges of several of the papers. Sharon saw Lindsay's eyes catch it, and then her daughter smiled, turning away.

"So, Lindsay. What is this brilliant idea John left you?" She reached to one of the papers and turned it around a quarter turn.

"That's an idea for a new jacket for next fall." Casey slid it closer and grinned. "See? Those buttons will be real silver. You just can't tell yet." He looked up at his sister, adoration in his gaze. "Isn't that what you said, Lindsay? Silver on these?"

"Silver, Casey." Lindsay smiled and reached with her pencil, scribbling in a word next to one of the buttons. "See? It says it now. Silver. And that was your idea, Casey. Thank you very much, because I expect that coat to be a very big success."

"What is all this?" All these drawings—there must be

290

twenty—didn't seem to be the work of a girl who intended to end her life. "Lindsay?"

It was Cody who answered, though. He leaned far over the table, and as his long body stretched past Sharon, she inhaled his smell. It was the smell of pool and boy. Man, rather. Pool and man. She liked the smell, but then she had always liked the smell of her men, all four of them.

"Lindsay just sat here and drew these up. She's fast, too. This one is the hat she wore this morning."

Sharon looked at it, and it was exactly the same. She had to admit that her daughter was good.

"Lindsay wants to wear one of these each week for the broadcast." Casey made his proclamation as if it was his own idea, and he was very proud of it. Sharon suspected he was proud of his sister.

"This was John's idea?" Sharon frowned, puzzled. "He wanted you to create your own fashions and wear them to church?"

Lindsay laughed, and it was the laugh of an excited young woman, one who finds life enjoyable, one who plans to do lots of things in her years on this earth.

"Yes, Mom. The hat I wore this morning, the one you hated?" That made Sharon laugh. "It received seventeen thousand hits on the church website. Seventeen thousand hits, each willing to pay money to get one just like it. John suggested it as a marketing tool for emerging designers— for donations, of course—and I realized, that's me. I'm an emerging designer, if ever there was one." Lindsay turned several of the sheets of paper Sharon's direction. "I've got the twins giving me ideas. I think we make a pretty good team. What do you think?"

Sharon's eyes watered, and she pointed to the purse. "Cody, hand me that." When he did, she sat it in the middle of the table. "Where does this fit in, Lindsay?"

"Mom, what is it?" Casey reached for it, and she pushed his hand away.

"Lindsay? I have to know." Sharon sniffled and tried to blink her tears away, but she was unsuccessful. When she reached to wipe them with her hand, Casey stood and grabbed a napkin, handing it to his mother. "Thank you, Casey. Lindsay?"

Lindsay smiled, and it was bright. Reaching for the purse, she stood and walked to the trash. Very dramatically, she lifted the lid and dropped the purse inside.

"You don't mind, do you?" She laughed as she returned to the table.

"No." Sharon smiled. "I never liked that purse, anyway."

"Was anything in it?" Casey glanced at the trashcan.

"Only bad dreams," Sharon said, as she patted his hand. "They're all gone now." She turned to Lindsay. "Tell me more of your designs. I want to know everything."

It was Cody who answered, though. He had several favorites, and of course, each of them, according to him, Lindsay had drawn from his inspiration.

TROOPER sat in the chair Lindsay had occupied earlier, looking at the prone form of his friend. He was amazed at how easily he had been taken. Just hours before, John had driven him in his car, working the machine skillfully, and working Trooper's emotions just as well. Now, his body was nothing but a shell.

"Dad, they're here." Casey stepped into his father's office, and he touched Trooper on the shoulder. "Mom's outside with the men. She said to let you know. They'll be in after a couple of minutes. Okay, Dad?"

He looked up and lifted his hand in a quick motion as he smiled. "Sure, Son. I'll wait here." He was pleased when Casey sat on the arm of the chair beside him.

"I'll stay with you, Dad." He grabbed his father's hand and squeezed it. Releasing the clasp, he stood. Walking to the bookshelf, he pulled one volume down.

"What book is that, Son?"

"An old storybook, Dad. You used to read it to us when Cody and I were little. It's about a toy that was alive until its owner got too grown up to pay it any attention. Then, it just became a lifeless toy all over again."

"Let me see it." Trooper reached for it, turning it over in his hand and studying the front. It had a tree and a small boy on it. The boy was daydreaming. "I remember this book. When I was out of town, and John would stay with you kids, I always told him this was the one book you boys would lie still for. It was, too. I cannot believe we still have this."

"I saved it from when we moved. It was in the garage sale items, and I rescued it." He took it back from Trooper and opened the cover. "Do you think that's what happened to Uncle John?"

"What do you mean? Like the toy?"

"Well, Uncle John seemed to always know the right things to say. I mean, maybe he grew up too much for his body, and like the toy in the story, he just didn't need it anymore."

Trooper smiled. That wasn't too far off Christian theology as it was taught in the church. Add Christ's salvation message, and it would all be there, after a fashion.

"I think you're pretty smart, Casey. Uncle John would be proud of you." A knock came at the door. "Go see, Son. That's them, I'm sure."

There were two men with a gurney. Sharon followed them in. A death certificate was required, and then John was gone. The sofa suddenly seemed very empty.

"Sharon, come sit with me. Casey, let your mother and I have some privacy." He waved his son away. When Sharon moved toward the sofa, he patted his knee. "Here, Sharon." She settled herself there and didn't resist when he pulled her against him.

"I've missed this, Trooper. I've always loved you, even when I've stayed away. You must know that." She placed her hand on his chest, and she let it rest there, moving with the rise and fall brought on by his breathing.

"I've stayed away, too, Sharon. I've just done it in the guise of the church. It was wrong, too. I should have been here with you and the kids."

"Here?" She chuckled. "You love that house in Stone Creek."

"I love you. I should have been wherever you and the kids were. Do you forgive me?"

"Always, Trooper. Can we fix things? We can't go

back to what we were doing. If we do, then we'll just be back where we were."

"I've been thinking about that. Jeffrey's wanted to take a bigger part in the ministry. He's good. We both know that. We need to tone things down, anyway. The church is overburdened."

"You would step down, Trooper?" She didn't say it kindly, either. "I don't want you to make a decision like this in the light of John's death."

"No." He chuckled, understanding her completely. "I don't think so. Just let Jeffrey have a greater hand. I want more time with you and the twins. Lindsay, too. I want to know my daughter before she's off and on her own." He took her hand and put it to his mouth, letting his lips rest against it for a moment before pulling it away. "We could even sell one of the houses. They're far too much for us. This one could be a retreat for the church. Conferences. Weekend camps. Or we could live here and sell the one in Stone Creek. I just want to spend time with my family." He paused, looking through the windows to the sunny world outside. It was still afternoon, and yet so much had changed. "I've been reborn today, Sharon. Believe that. I'm a new man, and God's done it. Can you follow me there?"

"I love you too much not to." She smiled. "Isn't it in Ruth that she says, Whither thou goest? That's us, Trooper."

"Can we haul our kids along?" He chuckled. He'd been given his family back today, and he wanted all of them.

295

"Every one, Trooper. Let's haul every one along."

Then, unexpectedly, Cody slammed through the door, and right behind him, Casey followed, crashing into his brother and almost knocking him down. Both were breathless, and the look of excitement on their faces was immeasurable.

"What, boys?" Trooper smiled, and he whispered to Sharon, "Maybe we can take just one weekend a month off from the kids." She slapped him on the chest, but she was smiling, too.

"Dad, Mom." That had to be Cody. He always jumped in first.

"We're uncles." That was Casey. He was more specific. They both had broad grins on their faces.

"Please explain that to me, boys." Trooper's instructtion was simple and to the point. Uncles?

"Jack's got a son."

Sharon sat up in panic. "He's not twelve, is he?"

"Mom!" Cody turned in a complete circle, as he made a face of despair. "You know everything. How do you do that?"

Now, Trooper was sitting up. He looked at Sharon. "Jeffrey has a son? And he's twelve? How did this happen?"

"Okay, Trooper. If you haven't figured that out, there's likely to be a lot more of those under your feet." She pointed to the twins across the room. "You're a big boy. Think about it." She stood and reached for his hand to help him stand. "However, I do believe our not quite perfect son has a few questions to answer."

"I guess so." He stood also. However, he was in a very forgiving mood. Much had been forgiven him on this day, and he could hardy do less for others. How did the Good Book say it? Forgive someone seven times seventy. Jeffrey could have a whole lot of children, and still, Trooper knew, no one could out forgive God.

Chapter 26

THE POWER plant in the big Mercedes GL550 was built for the Autobahn. It had been constructed with precision by precision people, and every nuance of its driving experience was reputed to be the very ultimate possible. It was, too, with its sumptuous trim and deep leather seats. The driver never had to be concerned about the outside temperature or the road conditions. This ultimate machine did it all, testing the temperature of the exterior air and adjusting that in the cabin accordingly, feeling the road conditions and raising or lowering the suspension, and even dimming the reflections in the outside mirrors to ease the strain on the driver's eyes. The machine was truly a work of art. Oh, and it had one more way in that it was the best there was. It had been evaluated for crashworthiness by the United States government, and it had been given a five-star rating, particularly in front-end crash results.

Combined with its extensive airbag system, the sleek automobile virtually guaranteed that any occupant riding inside, whether in the driver's seat or anywhere else, would survive any but the most devastating of accidents.

Keith was lucky to be driving a Mercedes. He was also very angry. For over thirty years, he had been deeply in love with Sharon. Yet, in all that time, he had never once laid a hand on her. It had enraged him to see her suffering needlessly over the past several months, stuck out there all alone, living at that enormous monstrosity that had been assembled out on the lake. Trooper didn't deserve her, but she wasn't Keith's, either, and he knew it. John's accusations had infuriated him.

Passing Trooper's black Navigator on the road had done nothing but fuel his anger. He had pushed his Mercedes hard after that, taking corners too fast, barely giving the nod to roadside warning signs. With unformed plans at first, he knew simply that he had been accused unjustly, and he wanted to drive and drive fast.

Then, approaching the city, a destination had formed in his mind, one that in his blinding rage seemed oddly reasonable. He had the gate codes to the Kincaid mansion. He performed all the landscaping maintenance there, or his company did. He would go there. Sharon might come. She might see Trooper at the lake place and know Keith would find somewhere to wait for her, somewhere familiar to her, somewhere he could explain away John's misunderstanding. If Trooper showed up instead, Keith could vent his anger at John's accusations, proclaiming his innocence. He was, indeed, innocent, after all. He was Trooper's

299

friend, and at that moment, he believed he was, even if he had hated the man just an hour before. Trooper would believe him, though. Trooper was forgiving, and he would accept that Keith's intentions had always been honorable.

The most direct way to the Stone Creek mansion was directly through the city, and Keith took the first exit that led him downtown. Of course, it also cut across the edge of the deplorable Southside, but Keith had no concerns there. Southside was a wasteland that was to be approached and left behind, and the people who lived there were just the same.

The streets seemed eerily bare as he entered the concrete canyons. As he flew past, he took note that the lights were all green, and there were no other cars on the road. With a smirk of satisfaction, he depressed the accelerator harder.

By the fourth red light, he was flying. Southside would soon be only a blip in his day. None of that was on his mind, though. He could only see red, and it was not the red of the changing lights. Nor was it the red of passing cars. It was the red of rage, and it blinded him to all else. That was why he didn't see the seventh light as it changed from green to yellow to red. His eyes saw only the striking mansion perched above Stone Creek, the massive home where he might meet Sharon—or Trooper—and salve his fury with either lust or forgiveness.

Keith also didn't see a small, red convertible fly through the intersection just ahead of him, its driver just as angry as he was. His Mercedes did, though, and in that microsecond of time it had available, its autobraking mechanism tried valiantly to slow his approach. It was a useless gesture, though. Fate, or the Hand of God, as those of a religious bent would suggest, had already written this part of Keith's story, and it had to play itself out as it would.

The enormous, gold Mercedes GL550 impacted the small red convertible just where Charlie had leaned so recently on the door. Within the GL550's front bumper, small, very high-tech sensors noticed the pressure, and as the deceleration gradient increased in an ever-sharper curve, it triggered messages that traveled to the interior of the sumptuous passenger cabin. The SUV's electronic brain checked each of the seats inside to see which were occupied and unoccupied, and finally satisfied, simul-taneously triggered each of the airbags that were required to ensure the safety of the lone occupant traveling within its protective environment.

However, the airbag deployment didn't change what was happening outside the passenger cabin. The Mercedes was large, and it was heavy. It was also tall, and when it impacted Joanie's red Miata, it floated right over the small car's undercarriage, pushing the passenger door into the interior, and ripping the empty seat from its mounts in the floor. Even the small car's console offered little protect-tion. The big Mercedes was nearly three tons of momen-tum, and it was built to protect its occupants, not to save lives on the outside. So, while the front crumple zone of the SUV did give, crushing the front end of the Mercedes to an unrecognizable wad of tangled metal, the cage that wrapped around Keith and his exploding airbags stayed perfectly intact, barreling forward as if the Miata were not even there.

When the Mercedes came to rest on the far side of the intersection, it was no longer clear just what model of car had been in its way. The front of the small car, still attached to the undercarriage, together with the back wheels, had continued to travel another half block before coming to rest against a vacated storefront. The back end, still full of Joanie's grass, rested in the intersection. It had torn from its moorings, spun several times, and then fallen to the concrete street, its last wild dance complete.

The doors and the rest of the passenger compartment were wedged firmly underneath the front of the gold Mercedes. If not for the car's striking red paint, a casual observer might think the two vehicles were one. They might also think no one was injured. Red was the color of blood, and red on red . . . who could tell?

Keith sat in his seat and looked around, stunned. He had been driving with his hand stretched across the steering wheel, and when the airbag in the steering column had slammed into him, it had wrenched his arm into his chest. The explosive forces had kept him alive, but his arm was clearly broken. He glanced down at it, aware it was crooked, but he didn't feel it, not yet.

Except for the airbags, the cabin's interior seemed undamaged. His coffee, of course, had showered the dash, but the seats were still as sumptuous, and the windows were all intact. Even the steam cleaning stripes from yesterday's detailing could still be seen in the carpet on the floor. He didn't think to look for his cell phone, but then it had lodged up under the dash, probably lost forever. Outside the window, though, things were very different. The vehicle's crumpled hood obscured his vision, and smoke billowed into the air.

Pulling the door handle, Keith was relieved to find the catch released effortlessly, and the door swung open smoothly. He hadn't even seen another car, and he looked around to locate what he'd hit. His first view was of the back clip of the red Mazda resting in the intersection alongside his Mercedes. Holding his broken arm and looking around, he saw the front end on the other side, far down the block. His stomach sickening with the realization that the passenger compartment was nowhere to be seen, he stepped to the front of his gold SUV. He saw her, then. However, her eyes were wide, and there was no life in her. Her arm still rested on the door at her side, and her face, on one side, at least, was still young and pretty.

Keith looked around for help, and seeing no one, he called as loudly as he could. No one answered, though. He sat on the street and leaned back against the red door of the small convertible, aware of the dead girl just at his back. He had killed her, and no one knew. No one. No one had stepped outside to see.

He knew why. This was Southside. People didn't live in Southside, not real people, anyway. The only ones within blocks were the ever-changing decorations provided by the drunks and drug addicts. No one cared. Not even the police. They didn't even know. How would they? When no one cares, no one calls.

In spite of the lack of local interest in the horrific crash that had left a girl dead, faintly, a voice could be heard in the gold Mercedes, asking if everything was all right, that a report of a collision had been received. The authorities were being notified, and someone would arrive soon.

Keith sat and waited, but Joanie's body would start to cool long before a trauma team would arrive.

THE GREAT sports arena that comprised International Faith Center was silent, and the air conditioning was stilled. In the near darkness that flooded the enormous space, the live plants surrounding the platform basked under lights that were not visible during the church's Sunday services. When the great arena was unoccupied, automatic timers regularly whirred in their hidden locations, and small motors opened doors in the sides of the ten-foot-tall platform. With the movement of other motors, fluorescent lights, ones specifically formulated for the tropical growth that perfumed the room's air, grew long arms and extended their life-giving bulbs to glow in the darkness. At least once a day, one of the staff horticulturalists would come by to check on each of the plants growing there. For the broadcasts, they must be perfect. Culling and replanting from the ministry's private greenhouses were part of their jobs.

Far overhead, small lights indicated the presence of intrusion sensors and fire prevention systems. At each door, even those that were used only on Sunday mornings, red exit signs glowed. Even though this was a ministry, and in many ways stood apart from the rules and strictures given other secular businesses, some elements of the law tied even the ministry's hands.

Then, unseen to anyone, the main lights centered within the great ceiling girders far overhead clicked on with an audible sound. They glowed with a reddish color. It would be another five minutes before they provided any appreciable light, but even still, all along the platform, the small motors whirred, the long arms withdrew into their hidden spaces, and the small, specially formulated fluorescent lights flickered into darkness.

The great building was not ready, though, and preparations continued. Deep within the floor, far away in rooms the church members never saw, great fans whirred into life. Air began to move through ductwork so massive that two men could walk abreast, and their shoulders would never touch the walls. Men did walk those ducts regularly, too. They were dusted and sanitized each week. Nothing, no expense, no effort, was too good for the House of the Lord.

All along the front of the platform, the flowers began to sway, the movement of the air pulling in their fragrances and expelling them back again onto the platform just above. The great expanse of burgundy carpet gave the vast space a richness that few buildings could match. International Faith Center was truly a place even God would love to call home, for it was as enormous as Solomon's Temple, as luxurious as the Fontainebleau Hotel, and as iconic as the Taj Mahal.

Slowly, one of the lower doors swung open, and an elderly woman stepped through. Her hair was white, and her steps were slow, but in her arms she carried The Bible. Her copy was large and thick, and it was stuffed with pieces of paper, bookmarks, and notes at every page. It even had at the very center a church pamphlet, one that folded and then folded again. On the glossy front was an overhead picture of International Faith Center, but that wasn't why she kept the pamphlet in her Bible. No, inside were the pictures of the Reverend's family.

For three years she had arrived early for each service. Three years ago, her faith had been under attack, and she had already decided to leave the church. Then, one weekday, she had found a plastic bag on her door, and the pamphlet had been inside. God had sent it to her, she knew. When she traced her fingers along the images of the family inside, she had felt His call to prayer. That's why she kept the pamphlet in her Bible. She carried it there because it had come to her door at just a time when she had felt her faith in the Most Reverend Kincaid failing alarmingly.

Now, she was always the first to arrive in the auditorium. She arrived early, and standing in the cavernous foyer, she listened for the dull click that told of the lights turning on. Then, a five full minutes later, she would enter slowly and find the seat she always occupied. However, she would never sit, even though her old knees sometimes begged her to. No, she always placed her Bible in the seat and knelt before it, an embroidered hand-kerchief in her hand, with her old knees resting against the soft burgundy carpet that flowed across the floor. Later, minutes, sometimes, and longer at other times, more people would enter. They would laugh at a joke that had followed them inside, or they would be involved in a child's reprimand, but the old woman never noticed. Occasionally, someone would place a hand on her shoulder for a moment, but for that hour before every service, the old woman did what God had told her to do. She had no choice. She had been spoken to by the Lord.

Pray, Mabelle. I am testing my most loyal son with the fires of tribulation. Without your prayers, he will stumble, and his family will be lost. Pray for him, and do not stop.

Finally, organ music began to swell, and the animation of people's voices filled the air. Mabelle pulled herself up from the floor and dabbed her eyes, for the evening service was about to start. Picking up her Bible and sitting with it in her lap, she fingered the slips of paper that protruded from almost every page. There were thirty years' worth of slips, one for every message Reverend Kincaid had shared. Mabelle had been there at his very first meeting, and she had been faithful to his ministry all along. She had seen his troubles, and the Lord had instructed her to pray him through. She knew that if he could hold on just a little while longer, God would provide his redemption. Tonight might even be the night. God's timing was mysterious, but to Mabelle, this night felt like one in which the Word of the Lord might become real.

"Welcome this evening, ladies and gentlemen." It was an unfamiliar voice that rang out much too brashly over the massive speaker system. There was a chuckle, then the voice returned, quieter. "That was a bit loud. Forgive me."

This was not the Sunday morning broadcast, with tens

of thousands in attendance. Tonight just the main, over-head lights were on. Sunday evening services were never as full as those on Sunday mornings, and the balconies remained dark. It was just as well. In the evening service, the true core of believers attended, and the service took on a livelier air. Hands would be raised, and feet would stamp with feeling. Amens would be heard, and occasionally a Spoken Message from the Lord would ring out from a member of the congregation.

Sunday evenings were special.

However, Mabelle was puzzled. She didn't see the Most Reverend Kincaid, or his son, the handsome Jeffrey, on the platform. True, Jeffrey wasn't always there on Sunday evenings, but on the rare occasion the Reverend was gone, his son was always in attendance.

"I apologize for this slight change in our regular manner of presentation." The unfamiliar speaker chuckled again. "I'm new to this, and I keep making mistakes. Please forgive me beforehand. I appreciate your kind understanding. However, our much-loved pastor will be unable to attend with us this evening. There has been a death in the family."

Sounds of dismay could be heard all over the concourse floor.

"God," Mabelle whispered. "You promised. Your Word says you keep your promises forever and amen. I'm reminding you, God. You promised." She held her breath, and she hoped for the best.

"My dearest church friends, many of you know our own John Winston. He has been here on the ministry staff for nearly twenty-five years. He grew up with Reverend Kincaid and was his closest friend for forty years. The Kincaid children have always known him affectionately as Uncle John." Chuckles could be heard throughout the crowd of listening people. Many of them remembered the youngest Kincaid twins calling out those two words right here in this auditorium. Those in the congregation knew Uncle John, and they knew how much the Reverend loved his friend.

"Our Christian brother, John Winston, went to be with the Lord today. He was where he wanted to be, with the family he loved most, enjoying this wonderful day out at the lake. We shouldn't feel sorry for our Brother John. Rather, we should rejoice that he was surrounded by people he loved and who loved him in return. Right now, John Winston is in the Father's presence, and there is no better place to be. Amen?"

Multiple shouts rang from the crowd, and several people stood to raise their hands into the air. Tears on their cheeks sparkled in the lights that shined down from the distant ceiling overhead, but smiles were on their faces. One man started to clap spontaneously. A woman at his side picked it up, and soon, the sound rang from almost every hand in the place.

"Thank you, Father!" The speaker no longer felt ill at ease. Instead, the Power of the Lord flowed among the people, and he raised his hands, jumping up and down on the platform in his emotional euphoria. "Thank you, Jesus! You are the Most High God!" After several moments, the prayers of praise slowed, and the speaker looked out over the people to share once again.

"Our wonderful pastor has chosen to spend the evening at his lake house with his wife, Sharon, at his side. Also at his side are his children, Jeffrey, Lindsay, and the twins, Cody and Casey." There were numerous chuckles at the mention of the twins' given names. In addition to being known around the church, they had spent time at the homes of various members of the congregation. The pastor's time with his family wasn't likely to be exactly restful. "Also, Jeffrey's fiancée, Cookie, has joined the family to share in their time of mourning. Please hold them up in your prayers."

He stepped back, and the floodlights all along the bottom of the balcony brightened. At the back of the platform, the choir, standing on stepped risers wearing green and burgundy robes, lifted smoothly from the floor, the hydraulics underneath their feet floating them upward as they raised their voices to the Lord.

"Thank you, Lord," Mabelle whispered. The Reverend's family was together again. She knew her prayers had finally been answered. With a sigh of relief, she reached and rubbed one of her old knees. "My knees thank you, also, Lord."

"IT WAS A very long time ago, Dad. I was only fifteen, and it was a very big mistake. However, Cookie supports me, and I want your forgiveness and support, also." Jeffrey stood with his fiancée at his side, and Cookie had her arm around his waist. This was not easy for him.

"What of the boy's family?" Trooper glanced at

Sharon and then back at his son. "You've told us his parents, I mean his adoptive parents, were killed. He must have other family, though. Legally, they would have rights to the boy. Forgiveness, of course, Jeffrey. You have that, unquestionably. To take on the responsibility? Are you sure? You are not the only one involved, and I don't just mean Cookie. Surely you must realize that."

"Mr. Kincaid, please let me speak, if you don't mind." Bucky stepped forward.

Sharon spoke up. "How to you fit into this?" She looked at her son and back at the rotund man who had appeared into their lives so unexpectedly. "Benji? Or is it Bucky? I wish to know how you fit in before you speak. I'm still not convinced our son has not been lied to."

"I'm sorry," Bucky said. "So much has happened that I forget I haven't introduced myself to everyone. I will gladly answer to either Benji or Bucky. Jeffrey knew me by Benji from youth camp many years ago. Most people know me by Bucky. Bucky Simms."

Trooper interrupted, "Bucky Simms of the Chronicle?" He frowned at that.

"Wait, Dad." Jeffrey knew the sour chord Bucky's name rang at the ministry. "He's here as a friend. This isn't about the ministry at all. Please let him speak. He can tell it all better than I can." He glanced at Cookie and tried to smile, but he could barely get it out.

"Mr. Simms. Bucky, if you wish. For me." Sharon looked at her husband and then took his hand before turning back to Bucky. "I'm Jeffrey's mother, and I want to know what's happening, before I claim a grandson not

311

too much younger than my own boys. You have to understand how shocking this sounds to me."

"I am the boy's uncle—"

"Adoptive or birth?" Trooper's question shot out, and Sharon put her finger to his lips.

"Jack. The boy, my nephew, goes by Jack. It's not his real name. He got it from your son, from one of those pamphlets your church passes out." He held up his hand when he saw Trooper start to speak. "He somehow found out your son's nickname. Who knows how? The point is that he knows, or at least suspects, Jeffrey is his father. My sister was his mother."

"Was?"

Jeffrey let himself smile at his mother's remark. It was the question he would have asked.

"Was, Mrs. Kincaid. Was, because she died four years ago. The boy is with his elderly godparents who have no room for him. The authorities tried to place him with his birth parents but were unable locate the natural father. I did. Your son."

"You've forced Jeffrey to do this?" Steel erupted in Sharon's voice. "I know your reputation as well as my husband does, and I don't want to drag this through the newspapers. A mistake at fifteen shouldn't haunt a boy forever."

"No. I was willing to take my nephew and let your son walk away. He wants the boy." Bucky looked at them for a moment. "I don't attend much anymore. Hardly, in fact, but I remember the scriptures talking about how faith is rewarded to the thousandth generation. Fathers are

312

important to sons."

"No one doubts that." Trooper glanced around the room at his own children.

"Easy Eddie. Have you ever heard of him?" Bucky kept his eyes on Trooper.

Casey laughed. "He sounds like a drug dealer."

"Close. You're Casey, right?"

The boy grinned at being correctly identified, and for the second time, Jeffrey smiled. Bucky was turning out to be okay, after all. For the moment, everything was all right.

"Easy Eddie was one of Al Capone's men. His lawyer, to be exact. He had power and money. He also had a son, and he realized he couldn't give his son one thing."

"What?" Casey, again. However, Cody hit him on the shoulder, putting his finger to his lips to shut him up.

Bucky smiled at their antics as he continued. "Easy Eddie realized he couldn't give his son a good name, not involved in the Mob. So, he turned informant, told all he knew, and his revelations broke Al Capone."

"His son got his father back, right?" Casey looked at his father, and his eyes twinkled.

"Easy Eddie was killed just before Al Capone was released from prison. A mob hit, I'm told. It seems true, too, since he was in his car driving around the city when he was shot. During World War II, his son, Butch O'Hare, became a Navy pilot on the U.S.S. Lexington. On one sortie, he took off from his ship with his squadron only to discover the Lexington was under attack. He was the only one of the squadron close enough to the enemy to intercept them in time."

"I've never heard this, have you, Trooper?" Sharon held his arm. The steel in her voice had softened. "But what does the Mafia have to do with Jeffrey?"

"The Mob," Bucky corrected, "but that's unimportant. It gets better, Mrs. Kincaid. Battling alone because his wingman's guns were jammed, and with no one else to help him, Butch O'Hare fights the enemy planes. Using every bit of his ammunition, he destroys five of the planes before his fellow pilots can join him. He received a Congressional Medal of Honor, and to quote the government, it was for one of, if not the single most daring action by one airplane in naval history."

"That's nice, but as I've already asked, how does this apply here?"

"You don't recognize him yet, do you?" Bucky laughed softly. "Chicago's O'Hare Airport? The City of Chicago named it after Easy Eddie's son. They wanted to honor the son of a mobster. Why? When the father does what is right, God rewards the children to the thousandth generation. If that's true, what happens if the father doesn't do what is right?"

Trooper laughed uneasily. He pulled his wife close. "Well, Sharon?"

"I've met him." Cookie looked at Jeffrey, and when he smiled at her, she turned to Sharon. "In Memphis this past week. I didn't know, of course, but I fell in love with the boy. I sat beside him at my uncle's midweek service, and I even spoke to him. I thought he must be Jeffrey's brother, and I even said that to your son when we were at my parents' for lunch."

"Another brother?" Lindsay was watching all this. She repeated, "Another brother? Cookie, we've got enough brothers in this family." She jerked her head toward the twins.

Cody reached to her and threw an arm around her neck, running his long fingers roughly through his sister's hair. "Hey! I resemble that," he growled out.

"Enough, children." Trooper looked at Cookie. "You would raise this twelve-year-old? There might be resentment issues. I'm sure with his parents gone, that will cause other problems. A new marriage is hard. One with a half-grown son is harder."

"We spoke of that outside, Jeffrey and I. We could wait for a year to get married, if necessary. You know, to give Jeffrey's son time to adjust. I know it will be hard, but we both really want this." She laughed and looked up at Jeffrey for a moment. "I wanted him this morning, even before I knew he was Jeffrey's son. My mother forbade me to think about it."

"Mom, Dad." The twins could contain themselves no longer. Their words came interchangeably, as they ran over each other with their voices. "Please say yes. He can call us Uncle Cody and Uncle Casey. How cool would that be?"

Sharon smiled as she walked up and gave Jeffrey a kiss. "I love you, Jeffrey. You can call me Grandmother from now on." She smiled, as she released him to give Cookie a kiss, also.

Immediately, Cookie grabbed Jeffrey in a hug. "Your

mother said yes!"

He held her tight and whispered into her ear, "I'm glad she did, but it wouldn't have mattered what Mom said. He's my son, and he's coming home with me."

"Oh, Jeffrey. I love you so much."

Then, in front of God and everybody, she kissed him right on the lips, and Jeffrey didn't mind at all.

Epilogue

THE SIGN outside the big church had been changed. It still read International Faith Center, but it now had an additional name underneath. Co-Pastor Jeffrey Kincaid. In addition, the new co-pastor had started a second Sunday morning service to accommodate the church's ever-increasing crowds. What charmed those attending these special services each Sunday was the mini-Jeffrey who shared the platform with the co-pastor. It was Jack, to be specific.

This evening, though, thirteen-year-old Jack was not on the platform where he should be. He had performed most of his required duties, leaving only one undone, and then he had snuck out a side door, joining his two uncles for something much more exciting. Together, the three young men, all dressed in formal, white tuxedos, were walking along one of the service catwalks at the apex of

317

the old sports arena's ceiling. The catwalk's solid floor shielded them somewhat from being seen from below, and behind them they dragged the final three bags of special balloons they had spent the day filling with compressed air, adding just a bit of sand so each one would fall quickly and land just where the boys intended. To drop the bags from one location and still have them go exactly where the boys wanted the balloons to fall, Cody had planned an elaborate system of ropes to tie the bags to, and they had spent the day before setting it all up. Now, with grins on their faces, they attached the bags to the waiting ropes, positioning each one carefully, and untying the tops, all twenty-one of them. Barely able to contain their excitement, they prepared them to go over the side.

Looking down, the three boys could view the entire concourse. It had been cleared of seats, and a broad strip of white carpet flowed from the far end, leading directly up to the platform. There, white steps had been constructed, rising to a great, flower-covered arch.

All around the sides and into the highest levels of each balcony, the church was packed.

The three boys were poised for the fun to begin.

AS THE BRIDE stepped down the aisle to the swelling sound of live organ music, all across the auditorium, people dressed in their very best stood to watch. Yet, even as Cookie thrilled in the moment, she was aware of something that was missing. There were seventeen bridesmaids, but only fifteen groomsmen. Jeffrey's son was missing, too. He was to be holding the ring. Her eyes glanced around, searching for the three white tuxedoes that should be there but weren't.

However, her veil was long and elaborate. The dress was Lindsay's creation, and it had been designed with Cookie in mind. It must look perfect for everyone to see. She could hardly crane her neck to search for the missing tuxedos.

She sighed, resigned. In front of ten thousand people, she intended to swallow the discrepancies and get on with the show. After all, it was Jeffrey she was marrying, and he was at the top of the steps. He was the one who mattered, and if he didn't have her ring, then Cookie's maid of honor at least carried his. She didn't think Lindsay would forget something as important as that.

Trooper moved forward as she ascended the steps, his own white tuxedo cut expertly to fit his lanky frame. He winked at his son, and then he reached for her hand. Before starting the ceremony, he helped her to lift her veil, draping it to fall at her back, and turned her to face the crowd.

"Isn't she beautiful? My soon-to-be daughter-in-law, Miss Cookie Hamilton." He paused, as scattered clapping passed through the audience. The two big screens at his back, up until then showing a background of beautiful white lilies, belatedly flickered to show the wedding party. There was Cookie's face, bigger than life, the image revealing her beauty to all those in even the highest rows. After a moment, the clapping started up again with force. There were occasional hoots and one very loud whistle that seemed to come from high up in the center of the auditorium. She grinned with embarrassment.

Trooper continued, "I would like to introduce her to you again in just a few moments. She will have a different name then, I'm afraid."

Jeffrey's grin was as wide as his father's.

No one besides Cookie had noticed the missing boys. It was when Trooper asked if anyone had any objections that everyone found out where they were. Out of the superstructure overhead, twenty-one hundred balloons were dumped into the air. Each one was white to match the wedding's theme, and they fell quickly, the ropes carrying the bags to their intended destinations, with the balloons scattering among the wedding celebrants. On the outside of the balloons, each one was the same. There was a picture of Jeffrey at thirteen, really his son Jack, of course, and in it he smiled with the charm that came so easily to the Kincaid siblings. Below it, in letters designed to mimic his youthful handwriting, his message was clear.

"My name is Jack, and Jeffrey is my dad. I want Cookie for my mother. Please don't say no."

Cookie looked up as the balloons fell, but the ceiling was very high, and the lights kept her from seeing much of anything, especially the three white-suited people far overhead. She thought the balloons were a nice surprise, and she looked at her fiancé with a smile.

"Thank you, Jeffrey."

However, he shrugged, and he looked around for his son. A youthful voice yelled from far overhead, as one final, red balloon drifted down.

"Here, Dad. This one's for you."

Cookie watched it fall, and then Jeffrey ran down to the concourse to catch it before it landed on the floor. Before he turned back to the steps, one of his brothers' friends ran to him to hand him one of the white balloons. He looked at it and smiled as he ran back up the steps to hand it to her.

The red balloon seemed rather heavy, though, and when she shook it, it rattled. With a shrug, she handed it back to him. Looking at her with a perplexed expression, he squeezed it until it popped. There, in the tattered latex remains, was the wedding ring Jack was supposed to provide.

Jeffrey looked up and laughed, finally finding the three rambunctious, white-suited forms, and he yelled, "Thank you, Son!"

Cookie knew it wasn't exactly upper class behavior during a wedding, but she also knew these circumstances required something special, so she yelled out her own sentiments.

"I love you, Jack." And she did. She truly did.

UP ON THE catwalk, as soon as the red balloon was dropped, a completely different sort of ceremony was put in play.

"Jack," Cody whispered. "Do you want to *really* be part of the family?" His eyes had a mischievous glint that should have told the boy to run. Cody motioned to his twin standing on Jack's opposite side.

"Sure. What do I do?"

Casey was right behind him, and he whispered in his

ear, "Just stand there." Without further warning, he threw his big, basketball player's hands under his nephew's arms and pulled him to his chest. "Now, Cody."

"What?" The boy's eyes went wide.

Cody laughed. "Initiation time." He grabbed the boy's feet and started to remove his shoes.

"Initiation time? What does that mean?"

"Well," Casey said into his ear. "This would be better if we were in the pool, but Jack and Cookie aren't getting married at the lake house."

"So," Cody chimed in with a grin, the shoes and socks already off to the side. "We have to do it here." He reached to undo the boy's pants.

"Stop! I'll yell to everyone! I will!"

"And mess up your dad's wedding? I don't think so. Now, we're almost finished." With those words, he yanked Jack's pants from his body, leaving the boy with his bright blue boxers exposed. Cody stood with the white tuxedo pants held high in the air.

"Throw them over!" Casey laughed, even as he held Jack under the arms. "Go ahead, Cody. Make 'em fly."

Cody held them out over the edge. "Just like one last balloon. What do you think? Casey? Jack?"

"Don't! Please!" The boy struggled against Casey's long arms, his bare legs and feet thrashing the air. Just then, they heard Jeffrey and Cookie yell up from below.

"Thank you, son!" That was Jeffrey.

A few moments later, another voice called, "I love you, Jack." A woman, Cookie, obviously.

Cody grabbed the boy's bare ankles and made like he

intended to pick him up and throw him over, but instead, he snickered. "Yell back, Jack. Yell as loudly as you can that they're welcome, and we might give you your clothes back."

"Yeah," Casey said with a malevolent snicker of his own. "Just be glad this catwalk has a solid floor. They can't see anything, yet. Yet. Did you get that? Say it, Jack." He stood and pulled the boy to his feet, leaning to the side and forcing him partway over. "Say it, or you're over the edge."

Jack took a deep breath and yelled at the top of his lungs, covering all the bases, "You're welcome! I love you, too!"

"Good boy." Cody smiled. He looked at his brother. "Should we give him his pants back?"

"Not in a million years. I think we should take the boxers, too."

"No!" Jack involuntarily yelled the word, but by then the organ had started up, and no one could hear. Casey clamped a hand over the boy's mouth and grinned.

"Do it, Cody, then throw them to me."

He did, and Jack jumped up to find Casey on one side of him with his underwear, and Cody on the other side with his white pants. Then, with laughter, the two twins ran off laughing in opposite directions, one holding the underwear high in the air, and the other holding the pants to his tuxedo.

It was at the end of the catwalk that relief finally came. It seemed that the initiation rite had been planned all along. There, just beside the door, was a paper sack with

Jack's name on it. Inside was a black pair of boxers with white letters printed on the front. They spelled out his name, *Jack Kincaid*, and smaller, underneath, *It's official. You're one of us.* Underneath the boxers were his white tuxedo pants.

As he finished dressing, the door opened, and two faces peered in, holding the blue boxers like a flag. Casey was winded. He had run from one side of the building to the other. Still, he spoke first.

"Truce, little nephew?"

"Truce." Jack grinned.

However, as they walked back into the main part of the building, Cody put his long arm around Jack's neck, and his big hand covered the boy's chest. He leaned to whisper to him, "You realize that's just the start. Wait until the next weekend retreat, when we get into the pool out at the lake house."

Casey leaned in, also. "That's when the fun really begins."

"Because all the girls will be there."

For no good reason, that's also when Jack twisted free and took off running down the hall as fast as he could go.

"Dad! Help! Cody and Casey are crazy!"

As he ran down the hallway away from them, the two brothers looked at each other and laughed, as they spoke in unison, "Hey! That resembles us."

THE RECEPTION was beautiful, with a white cake five layers tall. Even the punch was the creamiest white anyone could imagine. Just as Jeffrey and Cookie held up slices of cake to give each other a bite, a boy's yelling voice caused them to stop and look around. Jack came running in, his face frantic, only stopping when he got to their side, where he stood with his hands on his knees, panting in exhaustion. The guests seated around the room chuckled at the boy. They remembered the Kincaid twins at that age, and this didn't surprise them at all.

"What, Jack?" Jeffrey held his hand to his mouth to lick off a bit of icing.

"Stop that, Jeffrey." Cookie grinned. She reached for a napkin to wipe the icing away.

He looked at her and winked before turning back to his son. "Now, Jack, what's wrong?"

"It's Uncle Cody and Uncle Casey." The boy paused to catch his breath. "They're crazy."

Jeffrey laughed. "I've known that for eighteen years. I'm sure they're looking for you about now. Go find them and have a good time."

Jack gave his dad a crazed look, but when Jeffrey waved him away, he dutifully took off in a weary jog, only pausing to tiredly open a door, letting its pneumatic closers swing it slowly shut once he was through.

As the couple ate their cake, Cookie whispered to her new husband, "Jack gets along with the twins well, doesn't he?"

"Just like we all did growing up." He pictured Cody jumping on his bed with a can of Silly String. "I'm sure they're making great memories."

Across the room, Jack burst through the door once again, and immediately after him, Cody and Casey flew inside, also. In Cody's hand was a can of Silly String, and he had it poised right at Jack's head. Feinting forward to surround him, Casey grabbed Jack's shoulders, and Cody let the Silly String fly. Then, twisting free, Jack was gone once again, dashing into a convenient hallway with the two older boys on his heels.

Jeffrey grinned at Cookie. "As I said, they're making great memories."

She smiled back. "I'm glad I get to be a part. I love you, Jeffrey."

"And I love you."

He reached to give her a kiss, and he didn't even look up when he heard his son yell, "Dad! My uncles are crazy!" He was too busy enjoying the company of the woman he loved.